J.R.R. TOLKIEN

THE LORD OF THE RINGS

comprising:

BOOK ONE
THE RING SETS OUT

BOOK TWO
THE RING GOES SOUTH

BOOK THREE
THE TREASON OF ISENGARD

BOOK FOUR
THE RING GOES EAST

BOOK FIVE
THE WAR OF THE RING

BOOK SIX
THE END OF THE THIRD AGE

and

APPENDICES

THE TREASON
OF ISENGARD

BEING THE THIRD BOOK OF
THE LORD OF THE RINGS

BY

J.R.R. TOLKIEN

Collins

An imprint of HarperCollins*Publishers*

First published in Great Britain by
George Allen & Unwin 1954
Second edition 1966
This new reset edition published by
HarperCollins*Publishers* 1994
First published in seven volumes 1999
This seven-volume edition 2001

1 3 5 7 9 10 8 6 4 2

Collins is an imprint of HarperCollins*Publishers* Ltd,
77–85 Fulham Palace Road, Hammersmith, London W6 8JB

The HarperCollins website address is
www.**fire**and**water**.com

 ® is a registered trademark of
The J.R.R. Tolkien Estate Limited

www.tolkien.co.uk

ISBN 0 00 763560 5

Printed and bound in Great Britain by
Omnia Books Limited, Glasgow

CONTENTS

Three Rings for the Elven-kings under the sky,
  Seven for the Dwarf-lords in their halls of stone,
Nine for Mortal Men doomed to die,
  One for the Dark Lord on his dark throne
In the Land of Mordor where the Shadows lie.
  One Ring to rule them all, One Ring to find them,
  One Ring to bring them all and in the darkness bind them
In the Land of Mordor where the Shadows lie.

CHAPTER I

THE DEPARTURE OF BOROMIR

Aragorn sped on up the hill. Every now and again he bent to the ground. Hobbits go light, and their footprints are not easy even for a Ranger to read, but not far from the top a spring crossed the path, and in the wet earth he saw what he was seeking.

'I read the signs aright,' he said to himself. 'Frodo ran to the hill-top. I wonder what he saw there? But he returned by the same way, and went down the hill again.'

Aragorn hesitated. He desired to go to the high seat himself, hoping to see there something that would guide him in his perplexities; but time was pressing. Suddenly he leaped forward, and ran to the summit, across the great flag-stones, and up the steps. Then sitting in the high seat he looked out. But the sun seemed darkened, and the world dim and remote. He turned from the North back again to North, and saw nothing save the distant hills, unless it were that far away he could see again a great bird like an eagle high in the air, descending slowly in wide circles down towards the earth.

Even as he gazed his quick ears caught sounds in the woodlands below, on the west side of the River. He stiffened. There were cries, and among them, to his horror, he could distinguish the harsh voices of Orcs. Then suddenly with a deep-throated call a great horn blew, and the blasts of it smote the hills and echoed in the hollows, rising in a mighty shout above the roaring of the falls.

'The horn of Boromir!' he cried. 'He is in need!' He sprang down the steps and away, leaping down the path. 'Alas! An ill fate is on me this day, and all that I do goes amiss. Where is Sam?'

As he ran the cries came louder, but fainter now and

desperately the horn was blowing. Fierce and shrill rose the yells of the Orcs, and suddenly the horn-calls ceased. Aragorn raced down the last slope, but before he could reach the hill's foot, the sounds died away; and as he turned to the left and ran towards them they retreated, until at last he could hear them no more. Drawing his bright sword and crying *Elendil! Elendil!* he crashed through the trees.

A mile, maybe, from Parth Galen in a little glade not far from the lake he found Boromir. He was sitting with his back to a great tree, as if he was resting. But Aragorn saw that he was pierced with many black-feathered arrows; his sword was still in his hand, but it was broken near the hilt; his horn cloven in two was at his side. Many Orcs lay slain, piled all about him and at his feet.

Aragorn knelt beside him. Boromir opened his eyes and strove to speak. At last slow words came. 'I tried to take the Ring from Frodo,' he said. 'I am sorry. I have paid.' His glance strayed to his fallen enemies; twenty at least lay there. 'They have gone: the Halflings: the Orcs have taken them. I think they are not dead. Orcs bound them.' He paused and his eyes closed wearily. After a moment he spoke again.

'Farewell, Aragorn! Go to Minas Tirith and save my people! I have failed.'

'No!' said Aragorn, taking his hand and kissing his brow. 'You have conquered. Few have gained such a victory. Be at peace! Minas Tirith shall not fall!'

Boromir smiled.

'Which way did they go? Was Frodo there?' said Aragorn.

But Boromir did not speak again.

'Alas!' said Aragorn. 'Thus passes the heir of Denethor, Lord of the Tower of Guard! This is a bitter end. Now the Company is all in ruin. It is I that have failed. Vain was Gandalf's trust in me. What shall I do now? Boromir has laid it on me to go to Minas Tirith, and my heart desires it; but where are the Ring and the Bearer? How shall I find them and save the Quest from disaster?'

He knelt for a while, bent with weeping, still clasping Boromir's hand. So it was that Legolas and Gimli found him. They came from the western slopes of the hill, silently, creeping through the trees as if they were hunting. Gimli had his axe in hand, and Legolas his long knife: all his arrows were spent. When they came into the glade they halted in amazement; and then they stood a moment with heads bowed in grief, for it seemed to them plain what had happened.

'Alas!' said Legolas, coming to Aragorn's side. 'We have hunted and slain many Orcs in the woods, but we should have been of more use here. We came when we heard the horn – but too late, it seems. I fear you have taken deadly hurt.'

'Boromir is dead,' said Aragorn. 'I am unscathed, for I was not here with him. He fell defending the hobbits, while I was away upon the hill.'

'The hobbits!' cried Gimli. 'Where are they then? Where is Frodo?'

'I do not know,' answered Aragorn wearily. 'Before he died Boromir told me that the Orcs had bound them; he did not think that they were dead. I sent him to follow Merry and Pippin; but I did not ask him if Frodo or Sam were with him: not until it was too late. All that I have done today has gone amiss. What is to be done now?'

'First we must tend the fallen,' said Legolas. 'We cannot leave him lying like carrion among these foul Orcs.'

'But we must be swift,' said Gimli. 'He would not wish us to linger. We must follow the Orcs, if there is hope that any of our Company are living prisoners.'

'But we do not know whether the Ring-bearer is with them or not,' said Aragorn. 'Are we to abandon him? Must we not seek him first? An evil choice is now before us!'

'Then let us do first what we must do,' said Legolas. 'We have not the time or the tools to bury our comrade fitly, or to raise a mound over him. A cairn we might build.'

'The labour would be hard and long: there are no stones

that we could use nearer than the water-side,' said Gimli.

'Then let us lay him in a boat with his weapons, and the weapons of his vanquished foes,' said Aragorn. 'We will send him to the Falls of Rauros and give him to Anduin. The River of Gondor will take care at least that no evil creature dishonours his bones.'

Quickly they searched the bodies of the Orcs, gathering their swords and cloven helms and shields into a heap.

'See!' cried Aragorn. 'Here we find tokens!' He picked out from the pile of grim weapons two knives, leaf-bladed, damasked in gold and red; and searching further he found also the sheaths, black, set with small red gems. 'No orc-tools these!' he said. 'They were borne by the hobbits. Doubtless the Orcs despoiled them, but feared to keep the knives, knowing them for what they are: work of Westernesse, wound about with spells for the bane of Mordor. Well, now, if they still live, our friends are weaponless. I will take these things, hoping against hope, to give them back.'

'And I,' said Legolas, 'will take all the arrows that I can find, for my quiver is empty.' He searched in the pile and on the ground about and found not a few that were undamaged and longer in the shaft than such arrows as the Orcs were accustomed to use. He looked at them closely.

And Aragorn looked on the slain, and he said: 'Here lie many that are not folk of Mordor. Some are from the North, from the Misty Mountains, if I know anything of Orcs and their kinds. And here are others strange to me. Their gear is not after the manner of Orcs at all!'

There were four goblin-soldiers of greater stature, swart, slant-eyed, with thick legs and large hands. They were armed with short broad-bladed swords, not with the curved scimitars usual with Orcs; and they had bows of yew, in length and shape like the bows of Men. Upon their shields they bore a strange device: a small white hand in the centre of a black field; on the front of their iron helms was set an S-rune, wrought of some white metal.

'I have not seen these tokens before,' said Aragorn. 'What do they mean?'

'S is for Sauron,' said Gimli. 'That is easy to read.'

'Nay!' said Legolas. 'Sauron does not use the Elf-runes.'

'Neither does he use his right name, nor permit it to be spelt or spoken,' said Aragorn. 'And he does not use white. The Orcs in the service of Barad-dûr use the sign of the Red Eye.' He stood for a moment in thought. 'S is for Saruman, I guess,' he said at length. 'There is evil afoot in Isengard, and the West is no longer safe. It is as Gandalf feared: by some means the traitor Saruman has had news of our journey. It is likely too that he knows of Gandalf's fall. Pursuers from Moria may have escaped the vigilance of Lórien, or they may have avoided that land and come to Isengard by other paths. Orcs travel fast. But Saruman has many ways of learning news. Do you remember the birds?'

'Well, we have no time to ponder riddles,' said Gimli. 'Let us bear Boromir away!'

'But after that we must guess the riddles, if we are to choose our course rightly,' answered Aragorn.

'Maybe there is no right choice,' said Gimli.

Taking his axe the Dwarf now cut several branches. These they lashed together with bowstrings, and spread their cloaks upon the frame. Upon this rough bier they carried the body of their companion to the shore, together with such trophies of his last battle as they chose to send forth with him. It was only a short way, yet they found it no easy task, for Boromir was a man both tall and strong.

At the water-side Aragorn remained, watching the bier, while Legolas and Gimli hastened back on foot to Parth Galen. It was a mile or more, and it was some time before they came back, paddling two boats swiftly along the shore.

'There is a strange tale to tell!' said Legolas. 'There are only two boats upon the bank. We could find no trace of the other.'

'Have Orcs been there?' asked Aragorn.

'We saw no signs of them,' answered Gimli. 'And Orcs would have taken or destroyed all the boats, and the baggage as well.'

'I will look at the ground when we come there,' said Aragorn.

Now they laid Boromir in the middle of the boat that was to bear him away. The grey hood and elven-cloak they folded and placed beneath his head. They combed his long dark hair and arrayed it upon his shoulders. The golden belt of Lórien gleamed about his waist. His helm they set beside him, and across his lap they laid the cloven horn and the hilts and shards of his sword; beneath his feet they put the swords of his enemies. Then fastening the prow to the stern of the other boat, they drew him out into the water. They rowed sadly along the shore, and turning into the swift-running channel they passed the green sward of Parth Galen. The steep sides of Tol Brandir were glowing: it was now mid-afternoon. As they went south the fume of Rauros rose and shimmered before them, a haze of gold. The rush and thunder of the falls shook the windless air.

Sorrowfully they cast loose the funeral boat: there Boromir lay, restful, peaceful, gliding upon the bosom of the flowing water. The stream took him while they held their own boat back with their paddles. He floated by them, and slowly his boat departed, waning to a dark spot against the golden light; and then suddenly it vanished. Rauros roared on unchanging. The River had taken Boromir son of Denethor, and he was not seen again in Minas Tirith, standing as he used to stand upon the White Tower in the morning. But in Gondor in after-days it long was said that the elven-boat rode the falls and the foaming pool, and bore him down through Osgiliath, and past the many mouths of Anduin, out into the Great Sea at night under the stars.

For a while the three companions remained silent, gazing after him. Then Aragorn spoke. 'They will look for him from the White Tower,' he said, 'but he will not return from mountain or from sea.' Then slowly he began to sing:

> Through Rohan over fen and field where the long grass
>   grows
> The West Wind comes walking, and about the walls it goes.
> 'What news from the West, O wandering wind, do you
>   bring to me tonight?
> Have you seen Boromir the Tall by moon or by starlight?'
> 'I saw him ride over seven streams, over waters wide and
>   grey;
> I saw him walk in empty lands, until he passed away
> Into the shadows of the North. I saw him then no more.
> The North Wind may have heard the horn of the son of
>   Denethor.'
> 'O Boromir! From the high walls westward I looked afar,
> But you came not from the empty lands where no men are.'

Then Legolas sang:

> From the mouths of the Sea the South Wind flies, from the
>   sandhills and the stones;
> The wailing of the gulls it bears, and at the gate it moans.
> 'What news from the South, O sighing wind, do you bring
>   to me at eve?
> Where now is Boromir the Fair? He tarries and I grieve.'
> 'Ask not of me where he doth dwell – so many bones there
>   lie
> On the white shores and the dark shores under the stormy
>   sky;
> So many have passed down Anduin to find the flowing Sea.
> Ask of the North Wind news of them the North Wind sends
>   to me!'
> 'O Boromir! Beyond the gate the seaward road runs south,
> But you came not with the wailing gulls from the grey
>   sea's mouth.'

Then Aragorn sang again:

> *From the Gate of Kings the North Wind rides, and past the*
> *   roaring falls;*
> *And clear and cold about the tower its loud horn calls.*
> *'What news from the North, O mighty wind, do you bring*
> *   to me today?*
> *What news of Boromir the Bold? For he is long away.'*
> *'Beneath Amon Hen I heard his cry. There many foes he*
> *   fought.*
> *His cloven shield, his broken sword, they to the water*
> *   brought.*
> *His head so proud, his face so fair, his limbs they laid to*
> *   rest;*
> *And Rauros, golden Rauros-falls, bore him upon its breast.'*
> *'O Boromir! The Tower of Guard shall ever northward gaze*
> *To Rauros, golden Rauros-falls, until the end of days.'*

So they ended. Then they turned their boat and drove it
with all the speed they could against the stream back to Parth
Galen.

'You left the East Wind to me,' said Gimli, 'but I will say
naught of it.'

'That is as it should be,' said Aragorn. 'In Minas Tirith
they endure the East Wind, but they do not ask it for tidings.
But now Boromir has taken his road, and we must make
haste to choose our own.'

He surveyed the green lawn, quickly but thoroughly, stooping often to the earth. 'No Orcs have been on this ground,'
he said. 'Otherwise nothing can be made out for certain. All
our footprints are here, crossing and re-crossing. I cannot
tell whether any of the hobbits have come back since the
search for Frodo began.' He returned to the bank, close to
where the rill from the spring trickled out into the River.
'There are some clear prints here,' he said. 'A hobbit waded
out into the water and back; but I cannot say how long ago.'

'How then do you read this riddle?' asked Gimli.

Aragorn did not answer at once, but went back to the camping-place and looked at the baggage. 'Two packs are missing,' he said, 'and one is certainly Sam's: it was rather large and heavy. This then is the answer: Frodo has gone by boat, and his servant has gone with him. Frodo must have returned while we were all away. I met Sam going up the hill and told him to follow me; but plainly he did not do so. He guessed his master's mind and came back here before Frodo had gone. He did not find it easy to leave Sam behind!'

'But why should he leave us behind, and without a word?' said Gimli. 'That was a strange deed!'

'And a brave deed,' said Aragorn. 'Sam was right, I think. Frodo did not wish to lead any friend to death with him in Mordor. But he knew that he must go himself. Something happened after he left us that overcame his fear and doubt.'

'Maybe hunting Orcs came on him and he fled,' said Legolas.

'He fled, certainly,' said Aragorn, 'but not, I think, from Orcs.' What he thought was the cause of Frodo's sudden resolve and flight Aragorn did not say. The last words of Boromir he long kept secret.

'Well, so much at least is now clear,' said Legolas: 'Frodo is no longer on this side of the River: only he can have taken the boat. And Sam is with him; only he would have taken his pack.'

'Our choice then,' said Gimli, 'is either to take the remaining boat and follow Frodo, or else to follow the Orcs on foot. There is little hope either way. We have already lost precious hours.'

'Let me think!' said Aragorn. 'And now may I make a right choice, and change the evil fate of this unhappy day!' He stood silent for a moment. 'I will follow the Orcs,' he said at last. 'I would have guided Frodo to Mordor and gone with him to the end; but if I seek him now in the wilderness, I must abandon the captives to torment and death. My heart speaks clearly at last: the fate of the Bearer is in my hands no longer. The Company has played its part. Yet we that remain cannot forsake our companions while we have strength left. Come! We will go now. Leave all that can be spared behind! We will press on by day and dark!'

They drew up the last boat and carried it to the trees. They laid beneath it such of their goods as they did not need and could not carry away. Then they left Parth Galen. The afternoon was fading as they came back to the glade where Boromir had fallen. There they picked up the trail of the Orcs. It needed little skill to find.

'No other folk make such a trampling,' said Legolas. 'It seems their delight to slash and beat down growing things that are not even in their way.'

'But they go with a great speed for all that,' said Aragorn, 'and they do not tire. And later we may have to search for our path in hard bare lands.'

'Well, after them!' said Gimli. 'Dwarves too can go swiftly, and they do not tire sooner than Orcs. But it will be a long chase: they have a long start.'

'Yes,' said Aragorn, 'we shall all need the endurance of Dwarves. But come! With hope or without hope we will follow the trail of our enemies. And woe to them, if we prove the swifter! We will make such a chase as shall be accounted a marvel among the Three Kindreds: Elves, Dwarves, and Men. Forth the Three Hunters!'

Like a deer he sprang away. Through the trees he sped. On and on he led them, tireless and swift, now that his mind was at last made up. The woods about the lake they left behind. Long slopes they climbed, dark, hard-edged against the sky already red with sunset. Dusk came. They passed away, grey shadows in a stony land.

CHAPTER II

THE RIDERS OF ROHAN

Dusk deepened. Mist lay behind them among the trees below, and brooded on the pale margins of the Anduin, but the sky was clear. Stars came out. The waxing moon was riding in the West, and the shadows of the rocks were black. They had come to the feet of stony hills, and their pace was slower, for the trail was no longer easy to follow. Here the highlands of the Emyn Muil ran from North to South in two long tumbled ridges. The western side of each ridge was steep and difficult, but the eastward slopes were gentler, furrowed with many gullies and narrow ravines. All night the three companions scrambled in this bony land, climbing to the crest of the first and tallest ridge, and down again into the darkness of a deep winding valley on the other side.

There in the still cool hour before dawn they rested for a brief space. The moon had long gone down before them, the stars glittered above them; the first light of day had not yet come over the dark hills behind. For the moment Aragorn was at a loss: the orc-trail had descended into the valley, but there it had vanished.

'Which way would they turn, do you think?' said Legolas. 'Northward to take a straighter road to Isengard, or Fangorn, if that is their aim as you guess? Or southward to strike the Entwash?'

'They will not make for the river, whatever mark they aim at,' said Aragorn. 'And unless there is much amiss in Rohan and the power of Saruman is greatly increased, they will take the shortest way that they can find over the fields of the Rohirrim. Let us search northwards!'

★   ★   ★

The dale ran like a stony trough between the ridged hills, and a trickling stream flowed among the boulders at the bottom. A cliff frowned upon their right; to their left rose grey slopes, dim and shadowy in the late night. They went on for a mile or more northwards. Aragorn was searching, bent towards the ground, among the folds and gullies leading up into the western ridge. Legolas was some way ahead. Suddenly the Elf gave a cry and the others came running towards him.

'We have already overtaken some of those that we are hunting,' he said. 'Look!' He pointed, and they saw that what they had at first taken to be boulders lying at the foot of the slope were huddled bodies. Five dead Orcs lay there. They had been hewn with many cruel strokes, and two had been beheaded. The ground was wet with their dark blood.

'Here is another riddle!' said Gimli. 'But it needs the light of day, and for that we cannot wait.'

'Yet however you read it, it seems not unhopeful,' said Legolas. 'Enemies of the Orcs are likely to be our friends. Do any folk dwell in these hills?'

'No,' said Aragorn. 'The Rohirrim seldom come here, and it is far from Minas Tirith. It might be that some company of Men were hunting here for reasons that we do not know. Yet I think not.'

'What do you think?' said Gimli.

'I think that the enemy brought his own enemy with him,' answered Aragorn. 'These are Northern Orcs from far away. Among the slain are none of the great Orcs with the strange badges. There was a quarrel, I guess: it is no uncommon thing with these foul folk. Maybe there was some dispute about the road.'

'Or about the captives,' said Gimli. 'Let us hope that they, too, did not meet their end here.'

Aragorn searched the ground in a wide circle, but no other traces of the fight could be found. They went on. Already the eastward sky was turning pale; the stars were fading, and a grey light was slowly growing. A little further north they came to a fold in which a tiny stream, falling and winding, had cut a stony path down into the valley. In it some bushes grew, and there were patches of grass upon its sides.

'At last!' said Aragorn. 'Here are the tracks that we seek! Up this water-channel: this is the way that the Orcs went after their debate.'

Swiftly now the pursuers turned and followed the new path. As if fresh from a night's rest they sprang from stone to stone. At last they reached the crest of the grey hill, and a sudden breeze blew in their hair and stirred their cloaks: the chill wind of dawn.

Turning back they saw across the River the far hills kindled. Day leaped into the sky. The red rim of the sun rose over the shoulders of the dark land. Before them in the West the world lay still, formless and grey; but even as they looked, the shadows of night melted, the colours of the waking earth returned: green flowed over the wide meads of Rohan; the white mists shimmered in the water-vales; and far off to the left, thirty leagues or more, blue and purple stood the White Mountains, rising into peaks of jet, tipped with glimmering snows, flushed with the rose of morning.

'Gondor! Gondor!' cried Aragorn. 'Would that I looked on you again in happier hour! Not yet does my road lie southward to your bright streams.

Gondor! Gondor, between the Mountains and the Sea!
West Wind blew there; the light upon the Silver Tree
Fell like bright rain in gardens of the Kings of old.
O proud walls! White towers! O wingéd crown and throne
*   of gold!*
O Gondor, Gondor! Shall Men behold the Silver Tree,
Or West Wind blow again between the Mountains and the
*   Sea?*

Now let us go!' he said, drawing his eyes away from the South, and looking out west and north to the way that he must tread.

*   *   *

The ridge upon which the companions stood went down steeply before their feet. Below it twenty fathoms or more, there was a wide and rugged shelf which ended suddenly in the brink of a sheer cliff: the East Wall of Rohan. So ended the Emyn Muil, and the green plains of the Rohirrim stretched away before them to the edge of sight.

'Look!' cried Legolas, pointing up into the pale sky above them. 'There is the eagle again! He is very high. He seems to be flying now away, from this land back to the North. He is going with great speed. Look!'

'No, not even my eyes can see him, my good Legolas,' said Aragorn. 'He must be far aloft indeed. I wonder what is his errand, if he is the same bird that I have seen before. But look! I can see something nearer at hand and more urgent; there is something moving over the plain!'

'Many things,' said Legolas. 'It is a great company on foot; but I cannot say more, nor see what kind of folk they may be. They are many leagues away: twelve, I guess; but the flatness of the plain is hard to measure.'

'I think, nonetheless, that we no longer need any trail to tell us which way to go,' said Gimli. 'Let us find a path down to the fields as quick as may be.'

'I doubt if you will find a path quicker than the one that the Orcs chose,' said Aragorn.

They followed their enemies now by the clear light of day. It seemed that the Orcs had pressed on with all possible speed. Every now and again the pursuers found things that had been dropped or cast away: food-bags, the rinds and crusts of hard grey bread, a torn black cloak, a heavy iron-nailed shoe broken on the stones. The trail led them north along the top of the escarpment, and at length they came to a deep cleft carved in the rock by a stream that splashed noisily down. In the narrow ravine a rough path descended like a steep stair into the plain.

At the bottom they came with a strange suddenness on the grass of Rohan. It swelled like a green sea up to the very foot of the Emyn Muil. The falling stream vanished into a deep growth of cresses and water-plants, and they could hear it tinkling away in green tunnels, down long gentle slopes towards the fens of Entwash Vale far away. They seemed to have left winter clinging to the hills behind. Here the air was softer and warmer, and faintly scented, as if spring was already stirring and the sap was flowing again in herb and leaf. Legolas took a deep breath, like one that drinks a great draught after long thirst in barren places.

'Ah! the green smell!' he said. 'It is better than much sleep. Let us run!'

'Light feet may run swiftly here,' said Aragorn. 'More swiftly, maybe, than iron-shod Orcs. Now we have a chance to lessen their lead!'

They went in single file, running like hounds on a strong scent, and an eager light was in their eyes. Nearly due west the broad swath of the marching Orcs tramped its ugly slot; the sweet grass of Rohan had been bruised and blackened as they passed. Presently Aragorn gave a cry and turned aside.

'Stay!' he shouted. 'Do not follow me yet!' He ran quickly to the right, away from the main trail; for he had seen footprints that went that way, branching off from the others, the marks of small unshod feet. These, however, did not go far before they were crossed by orc-prints, also coming out from the main trail behind and in front, and then they curved sharply back again and were lost in the trampling. At the furthest point Aragorn stooped and picked up something from the grass; then he ran back.

'Yes,' he said, 'they are quite plain: a hobbit's footprints. Pippin's, I think. He is smaller than the other. And look at this!' He held up a thing that glittered in the sunlight. It looked like the new-opened leaf of a beech-tree, fair and strange in that treeless plain.

'The brooch of an elven-cloak!' cried Legolas and Gimli together.

'Not idly do the leaves of Lórien fall,' said Aragorn. 'This did not drop by chance: it was cast away as a token to any that might follow. I think Pippin ran away from the trail for that purpose.'

'Then he at least was alive,' said Gimli. 'And he had the use of his wits, and of his legs too. That is heartening. We do not pursue in vain.'

'Let us hope that he did not pay too dearly for his boldness,' said Legolas. 'Come! Let us go on! The thought of those merry young folk driven like cattle burns my heart.'

The sun climbed to the noon and then rode slowly down the sky. Light clouds came up out of the sea in the distant South and were blown away upon the breeze. The sun sank. Shadows rose behind and reached out long arms from the East. Still the hunters held on. One day now had passed since Boromir fell, and the Orcs were yet far ahead. No longer could any sight of them be seen in the level plains.

As nightshade was closing about them Aragorn halted. Only twice in the day's march had they rested for a brief while, and twelve leagues now lay between them and the eastern wall where they had stood at dawn.

'We have come at last to a hard choice,' he said. 'Shall we rest by night, or shall we go on while our will and strength hold?'

'Unless our enemies rest also, they will leave us far behind, if we stay to sleep,' said Legolas.

'Surely even Orcs must pause on the march?' said Gimli.

'Seldom will Orcs journey in the open under the sun, yet these have done so,' said Legolas. 'Certainly they will not rest by night.'

'But if we walk by night, we cannot follow their trail,' said Gimli.

'The trail is straight, and turns neither right nor left, as far as my eyes can see,' said Legolas.

'Maybe, I could lead you at guess in the darkness and hold to the line,' said Aragorn; 'but if we strayed, or they turned aside, then when light came there might be long delay before the trail was found again.'

'And there is this also,' said Gimli: 'only by day can we see if any tracks lead away. If a prisoner should escape, or if one should be carried off, eastward, say, to the Great River, towards Mordor, we might pass the signs and never know it.'

'That is true,' said Aragorn. 'But if I read the signs back yonder rightly, the Orcs of the White Hand prevailed, and the whole company is now bound for Isengard. Their present course bears me out.'

'Yet it would be rash to be sure of their counsels,' said Gimli. 'And what of escape? In the dark we should have passed the signs that led you to the brooch.'

'The Orcs will be doubly on their guard since then, and the prisoners even wearier,' said Legolas. 'There will be no escape again, if we do not contrive it. How that is to be done cannot be guessed, but first we must overtake them.'

'And yet even I, Dwarf of many journeys, and not the least hardy of my folk, cannot run all the way to Isengard without any pause,' said Gimli. 'My heart burns me too, and I would have started sooner; but now I must rest a little to run the better. And if we rest, then the blind night is the time to do so.'

'I said that it was a hard choice,' said Aragorn. 'How shall we end this debate?'

'You are our guide,' said Gimli, 'and you are skilled in the chase. You shall choose.'

'My heart bids me go on,' said Legolas. 'But we must hold together. I will follow your counsel.'

'You give the choice to an ill chooser,' said Aragorn. 'Since we passed through the Argonath my choices have gone amiss.' He fell silent, gazing north and west into the gathering night for a long while.

'We will not walk in the dark,' he said at length. 'The peril of missing the trail or signs of other coming and going seems to me the greater. If the Moon gave enough light, we would use it, but alas! he sets early and is yet young and pale.'

'And tonight he is shrouded anyway,' Gimli murmured. 'Would that the Lady had given us a light, such a gift as she gave to Frodo!'

'It will be more needed where it is bestowed,' said Aragorn. 'With him lies the true Quest. Ours is but a small matter in the great deeds of this time. A vain pursuit from its beginning, maybe, which no choice of mine can mar or mend. Well, I have chosen. So let us use the time as best we may!'

He cast himself on the ground and fell at once into sleep, for he had not slept since their night under the shadow of Tol Brandir. Before dawn was in the sky he woke and rose. Gimli was still deep in slumber, but Legolas was standing, gazing northwards into the darkness, thoughtful and silent as a young tree in a windless night.

'They are far far away,' he said sadly, turning to Aragorn. 'I know in my heart that they have not rested this night. Only an eagle could overtake them now.'

'Nonetheless we will still follow as we may,' said Aragorn. Stooping he roused the Dwarf. 'Come! We must go,' he said. 'The scent is growing cold.'

'But it is still dark,' said Gimli. 'Even Legolas on a hill-top could not see them till the Sun is up.'

'I fear they have passed beyond my sight from hill or plain, under moon or sun,' said Legolas.

'Where sight fails the earth may bring us rumour,' said Aragorn. 'The land must groan under their hated feet.' He stretched himself upon the ground with his ear pressed against the turf. He lay there motionless, for so long a time that Gimli wondered if he had swooned or fallen asleep again. Dawn came glimmering, and slowly a grey light grew about them. At last he rose, and now his friends could see his face: it was pale and drawn, and his look was troubled.

'The rumour of the earth is dim and confused,' he said. 'Nothing walks upon it for many miles about us. Faint and far are the feet of our enemies. But loud are the hoofs of the horses. It comes to my mind that I heard them, even as I lay on the ground in sleep, and they troubled my dreams: horses galloping, passing in the West. But now they are drawing ever further from us, riding northward. I wonder what is happening in this land!'

'Let us go!' said Legolas.

So the third day of their pursuit began. During all its long hours of cloud and fitful sun they hardly paused, now striding, now running, as if no weariness could quench the fire that burned them. They seldom spoke. Over the wide solitude they passed and their elven-cloaks faded against the background of the grey-green fields; even in the cool sunlight of mid-day few but elvish eyes would have marked them, until they were close at hand. Often in their hearts they thanked the Lady of Lórien for the gift of *lembas*, for they could eat of it and find new strength even as they ran.

All day the track of their enemies led straight on, going north-west without a break or turn. As once again the day wore to its end they came to long treeless slopes, where the land rose, swelling up towards a line of low humpbacked downs ahead. The orc-trail grew fainter as it bent north towards them, for the ground became harder and the grass shorter. Far away to the left the river Entwash wound, a silver thread in a green floor. No moving thing could be seen. Often Aragorn wondered that they saw no sign of beast or man. The dwellings of the Rohirrim were for the most part many leagues away to the South, under the wooded eaves of the White Mountains, now hidden in mist and cloud; yet the Horse-lords had formerly kept many herds and studs in the Eastemnet, this easterly region of their realm, and there the herdsmen had wandered much, living in camp and tent, even in winter-time. But now all the land was empty, and there was a silence that did not seem to be the quiet of peace.

At dusk they halted again. Now twice twelve leagues they had passed over the plains of Rohan and the wall of the Emyn Muil was lost in the shadows of the East. The young moon was glimmering in a misty sky, but it gave small light, and the stars were veiled.

'Now do I most grudge a time of rest or any halt in our chase,' said Legolas. 'The Orcs have run before us, as if the very whips of Sauron were behind them. I fear they have already reached the forest and the dark hills, and even now are passing into the shadows of the trees.'

Gimli ground his teeth. 'This is a bitter end to our hope and to all our toil!' he said.

'To hope, maybe, but not to toil,' said Aragorn. 'We shall not turn back here. Yet I am weary.' He gazed back along the way that they had come towards the night gathering in the East. 'There is something strange at work in this land. I distrust the silence. I distrust even the pale Moon. The stars are faint; and I am weary as I have seldom been before, weary as no Ranger should be with a clear trail to follow. There is some will that lends speed to our foes and sets an unseen barrier before us: a weariness that is in the heart more than in the limb.'

'Truly!' said Legolas. 'That I have known since first we came down from the Emyn Muil. For the will is not behind us but before us.' He pointed away over the land of Rohan into the darkling West under the sickle moon.

'Saruman!' muttered Aragorn. 'But he shall not turn us back! Halt we must once more; for, see! even the Moon is falling into gathering cloud. But north lies our road between down and fen when day returns.'

As before Legolas was first afoot, if indeed he had ever slept. 'Awake! Awake!' he cried. 'It is a red dawn. Strange things await us by the eaves of the forest. Good or evil, I do not know; but we are called. Awake!'

The others sprang up, and almost at once they set off again. Slowly the downs drew near. It was still an hour before noon when they reached them: green slopes rising to bare ridges that ran in a line straight towards the North. At their feet the ground was dry and the turf short, but a long strip of sunken land, some ten miles wide, lay between them and the river wandering deep in dim thickets of reed and rush. Just to the West of the southernmost slope there was a great ring, where the turf had been torn and beaten by many trampling feet. From it the orc-trail ran out again, turning north along the dry skirts of the hills. Aragorn halted and examined the tracks closely.

'They rested here a while,' he said, 'but even the outward trail is already old. I fear that your heart spoke truly, Legolas: it is thrice twelve hours, I guess, since the Orcs stood where we now stand. If they held to their pace, then at sundown yesterday they would reach the borders of Fangorn.'

'I can see nothing away north or west but grass dwindling into mist,' said Gimli. 'Could we see the forest, if we climbed the hills?'

'It is still far away,' said Aragorn. 'If I remember rightly, these downs run eight leagues or more to the north, and then north-west to the issuing of the Entwash there lies still a wide land, another fifteen leagues it may be.'

'Well, let us go on,' said Gimli. 'My legs must forget the miles. They would be more willing, if my heart were less heavy.'

The sun was sinking when at last they drew near to the end of the line of downs. For many hours they had marched without rest. They were going slowly now, and Gimli's back was bent. Stone-hard are the Dwarves in labour or journey, but this endless chase began to tell on him, as all hope failed in his heart. Aragorn walked behind him, grim and silent, stooping now and again to scan some print or mark upon the ground. Only Legolas still stepped as lightly as ever, his feet hardly seeming to press the grass, leaving no footprints as he passed; but in the waybread of the Elves he found all the sustenance that he needed, and he could sleep, if sleep it could be called by Men, resting his mind in the strange paths of elvish dreams, even as he walked open-eyed in the light of this world.

'Let us go up on to this green hill!' he said. Wearily they
followed him, climbing the long slope, until they came out
upon the top. It was a round hill smooth and bare, standing
by itself, the most northerly of the downs. The sun sank and
the shadows of evening fell like a curtain. They were alone
in a grey formless world without mark or measure. Only far
away north-west there was a deeper darkness against the
dying light: the Mountains of Mist and the forest at their
feet.

'Nothing can we see to guide us here,' said Gimli. 'Well,
now we must halt again and wear the night away. It is growing
cold!'

'The wind is north from the snows,' said Aragorn.

'And ere morning it will be in the East,' said Legolas. 'But
rest, if you must. Yet do not cast all hope away. Tomorrow
is unknown. Rede oft is found at the rising of the Sun.'

'Three suns already have risen on our chase and brought
no counsel,' said Gimli.

The night grew ever colder. Aragorn and Gimli slept fit-
fully, and whenever they awoke they saw Legolas standing
beside them, or walking to and fro, singing softly to himself
in his own tongue, and as he sang the white stars opened in
the hard black vault above. So the night passed. Together
they watched the dawn grow slowly in the sky, now bare and
cloudless, until at last the sunrise came. It was pale and clear.
The wind was in the East and all the mists had rolled away;
wide lands lay bleak about them in the bitter light.

Ahead and eastward they saw the windy uplands of the
Wold of Rohan that they had already glimpsed many days
ago from the Great River. North-westward stalked the dark
forest of Fangorn; still ten leagues away stood its shadowy
eaves, and its further slopes faded into the distant blue.
Beyond there glimmered far away, as if floating on a grey
cloud, the white head of tall Methedras, the last peak of the
Misty Mountains. Out of the forest the Entwash flowed to
meet them, its stream now swift and narrow, and its banks

deep-cloven. The orc-trail turned from the downs towards it.

Following with his keen eyes the trail to the river, and then the river back towards the forest, Aragorn saw a shadow on the distant green, a dark swift-moving blur. He cast himself upon the ground and listened again intently. But Legolas stood beside him, shading his bright elven-eyes with his long slender hand, and he saw not a shadow, nor a blur, but the small figures of horsemen, many horsemen, and the glint of morning on the tips of their spears was like the twinkle of minute stars beyond the edge of mortal sight. Far behind them a dark smoke rose in thin curling threads.

There was a silence in the empty fields, and Gimli could hear the air moving in the grass.

'Riders!' cried Aragorn, springing to his feet. 'Many riders on swift steeds are coming towards us!'

'Yes,' said Legolas, 'there are one hundred and five. Yellow is their hair, and bright are their spears. Their leader is very tall.'

Aragorn smiled. 'Keen are the eyes of the Elves,' he said.

'Nay! The riders are little more than five leagues distant,' said Legolas.

'Five leagues or one,' said Gimli, 'we cannot escape them in this bare land. Shall we wait for them here or go on our way?'

'We will wait,' said Aragorn. 'I am weary, and our hunt has failed. Or at least others were before us; for these horsemen are riding back down the orc-trail. We may get news from them.'

'Or spears,' said Gimli.

'There are three empty saddles, but I see no hobbits,' said Legolas.

'I did not say that we should hear good news,' said Aragorn. 'But evil or good we will await it here.'

The three companions now left the hill-top, where they might be an easy mark against the pale sky, and they walked slowly down the northward slope. A little above the hill's foot they halted, and wrapping their cloaks about them, they sat huddled together upon the faded grass. The time passed slowly and heavily. The wind was thin and searching. Gimli was uneasy.

'What do you know of these horsemen, Aragorn?' he said. 'Do we sit here waiting for sudden death?'

'I have been among them,' answered Aragorn. 'They are proud and wilful, but they are true-hearted, generous in thought and deed; bold but not cruel; wise but unlearned, writing no books but singing many songs, after the manner of the children of Men before the Dark Years. But I do not know what has happened here of late, nor in what mind the Rohirrim may now be between the traitor Saruman and the threat of Sauron. They have long been the friends of the people of Gondor, though they are not akin to them. It was in forgotten years long ago that Eorl the Young brought them out of the North, and their kinship is rather with the Bardings of Dale, and with the Beornings of the Wood, among whom may still be seen many men tall and fair, as are the Riders of Rohan. At least they will not love the Orcs.'

'But Gandalf spoke of a rumour that they pay tribute to Mordor,' said Gimli.

'I believe it no more than did Boromir,' answered Aragorn.

'You will soon learn the truth,' said Legolas. 'Already they approach.'

At length even Gimli could hear the distant beat of galloping hoofs. The horsemen, following the trail, had turned from the river, and were drawing near the downs. They were riding like the wind.

Now the cries of clear strong voices came ringing over the fields. Suddenly they swept up with a noise like thunder, and the foremost horseman swerved, passing by the foot of the hill, and leading the host back southward along the western skirts of the downs. After him they rode: a long line of mail-clad men, swift, shining, fell and fair to look upon.

Their horses were of great stature, strong and clean-limbed; their grey coats glistened, their long tails flowed in the wind, their manes were braided on their proud necks. The Men that rode them matched them well: tall and long-limbed; their hair, flaxen-pale, flowed under their light helms, and streamed in long braids behind them; their faces were stern and keen. In their hands were tall spears of ash, painted shields were slung at their backs, long swords were at their belts, their burnished shirts of mail hung down upon their knees.

In pairs they galloped by, and though every now and then one rose in his stirrups and gazed ahead and to either side, they appeared not to perceive the three strangers sitting silently and watching them. The host had almost passed when suddenly Aragorn stood up, and called in a loud voice:

'What news from the North, Riders of Rohan?'

With astonishing speed and skill they checked their steeds, wheeled, and came charging round. Soon the three companions found themselves in a ring of horsemen moving in a running circle, up the hill-slope behind them and down, round and round them, and drawing ever inwards. Aragorn stood silent, and the other two sat without moving, wondering what way things would turn.

Without a word or cry, suddenly, the Riders halted. A thicket of spears were pointed towards the strangers; and some of the horsemen had bows in hand, and their arrows were already fitted to the string. Then one rode forward, a tall man, taller than all the rest; from his helm as a crest a white horsetail flowed. He advanced until the point of his spear was within a foot of Aragorn's breast. Aragorn did not stir.

'Who are you, and what are you doing in this land?' said the Rider, using the Common Speech of the West, in manner and tone like to the speech of Boromir, Man of Gondor.

'I am called Strider,' answered Aragorn. 'I came out of the North. I am hunting Orcs.'

The Rider leaped from his horse. Giving his spear to

another who rode up and dismounted at his side, he drew his sword and stood face to face with Aragorn, surveying him keenly, and not without wonder. At length he spoke again.

'At first I thought that you yourselves were Orcs,' he said; 'but now I see that it is not so. Indeed you know little of Orcs, if you go hunting them in this fashion. They were swift and well-armed, and they were many. You would have changed from hunters to prey, if ever you had overtaken them. But there is something strange about you, Strider.' He bent his clear bright eyes again upon the Ranger. 'That is no name for a Man that you give. And strange too is your raiment. Have you sprung out of the grass? How did you escape our sight? Are you elvish folk?'

'No,' said Aragorn. 'One only of us is an Elf, Legolas from the Woodland Realm in distant Mirkwood. But we have passed through Lothlórien, and the gifts and favour of the Lady go with us.'

The Rider looked at them with renewed wonder, but his eyes hardened. 'Then there is a Lady in the Golden Wood, as old tales tell!' he said. 'Few escape her nets, they say. These are strange days! But if you have her favour, then you also are net-weavers and sorcerers, maybe.' He turned a cold glance suddenly upon Legolas and Gimli. 'Why do you not speak, silent ones?' he demanded.

Gimli rose and planted his feet firmly apart: his hand gripped the handle of his axe, and his dark eyes flashed. 'Give me your name, horse-master, and I will give you mine, and more besides,' he said.

'As for that,' said the Rider, staring down at the Dwarf, 'the stranger should declare himself first. Yet I am named Éomer son of Éomund, and am called the Third Marshal of Riddermark.'

'Then Éomer son of Éomund, Third Marshal of Riddermark, let Gimli the Dwarf Glóin's son warn you against foolish words. You speak evil of that which is fair beyond the reach of your thought, and only little wit can excuse you.'

Éomer's eyes blazed, and the Men of Rohan murmured angrily, and closed in, advancing their spears. 'I would cut off your head, beard and all, Master Dwarf, if it stood but a little higher from the ground,' said Éomer.

'He stands not alone,' said Legolas, bending his bow and fitting an arrow with hands that moved quicker than sight. 'You would die before your stroke fell.'

Éomer raised his sword, and things might have gone ill, but Aragorn sprang between them, and raised his hand. 'Your pardon, Éomer!' he cried. 'When you know more you will understand why you have angered my companions. We intend no evil to Rohan, nor to any of its folk, neither to man nor to horse. Will you not hear our tale before you strike?'

'I will,' said Éomer lowering his blade. 'But wanderers in the Riddermark would be wise to be less haughty in these days of doubt. First tell me your right name.'

'First tell me whom you serve,' said Aragorn. 'Are you friend or foe of Sauron, the Dark Lord of Mordor?'

'I serve only the Lord of the Mark, Théoden King son of Thengel,' answered Éomer. 'We do not serve the Power of the Black Land far away, but neither are we yet at open war with him; and if you are fleeing from him, then you had best leave this land. There is trouble now on all our borders, and we are threatened; but we desire only to be free, and to live as we have lived, keeping our own, and serving no foreign lord, good or evil. We welcomed guests kindly in the better days, but in these times the unbidden stranger finds us swift and hard. Come! Who are you? Whom do *you* serve? At whose command do you hunt Orcs in our land?'

'I serve no man,' said Aragorn; 'but the servants of Sauron I pursue into whatever land they may go. There are few among mortal Men who know more of Orcs; and I do not hunt them in this fashion out of choice. The Orcs whom we pursued took captive two of my friends. In such need a man that has no horse will go on foot, and he will not ask for leave to follow the trail. Nor will he count the heads of the enemy save with a sword. I am not weaponless.'

Aragorn threw back his cloak. The elven-sheath glittered as he grasped it, and the bright blade of Andúril shone like a sudden flame as he swept it out. 'Elendil!' he cried. 'I am Aragorn son of Arathorn, and am called Elessar, the Elfstone, Dúnadan, the heir of Isildur Elendil's son of Gondor. Here is the Sword that was Broken and is forged again! Will you aid me or thwart me? Choose swiftly!'

Gimli and Legolas looked at their companion in amazement, for they had not seen him in this mood before. He seemed to have grown in stature while Éomer had shrunk; and in his living face they caught a brief vision of the power and majesty of the kings of stone. For a moment it seemed to the eyes of Legolas that a white flame flickered on the brows of Aragorn like a shining crown.

Éomer stepped back and a look of awe was in his face. He cast down his proud eyes. 'These are indeed strange days,' he muttered. 'Dreams and legends spring to life out of the grass.

'Tell me, lord,' he said, 'what brings you here? And what was the meaning of the dark words? Long has Boromir son of Denethor been gone seeking an answer, and the horse that we lent him came back riderless. What doom do you bring out of the North?'

'The doom of choice,' said Aragorn. 'You may say this to Théoden son of Thengel: open war lies before him, with Sauron or against him. None may live now as they have lived, and few shall keep what they call their own. But of these great matters we will speak later. If chance allows, I will come myself to the king. Now I am in great need, and I ask for help, or at least for tidings. You heard that we are pursuing an orc-host that carried off our friends. What can you tell us?'

'That you need not pursue them further,' said Éomer. 'The Orcs are destroyed.'

'And our friends?'

'We found none but Orcs.'

'But that is strange indeed,' said Aragorn. 'Did you search the slain? Were there no bodies other than those of orc-kind?

They would be small, only children to your eyes, unshod but clad in grey.'

'There were no dwarves nor children,' said Éomer. 'We counted all the slain and despoiled them, and then we piled the carcases and burned them, as is our custom. The ashes are smoking still.'

'We do not speak of dwarves or children,' said Gimli. 'Our friends were hobbits.'

'Hobbits?' said Éomer. 'And what may they be? It is a strange name.'

'A strange name for a strange folk,' said Gimli. 'But these were very dear to us. It seems that you have heard in Rohan of the words that troubled Minas Tirith. They spoke of the Halfling. These hobbits are Halflings.'

'Halflings!' laughed the Rider that stood beside Éomer. 'Halflings! But they are only a little people in old songs and children's tales out of the North. Do we walk in legends or on the green earth in the daylight?'

'A man may do both,' said Aragorn. 'For not we but those who come after will make the legends of our time. The green earth, say you? That is a mighty matter of legend, though you tread it under the light of day!'

'Time is pressing,' said the Rider, not heeding Aragorn. 'We must hasten south, lord. Let us leave these wild folk to their fancies. Or let us bind them and take them to the king.'

'Peace, Éothain!' said Éomer in his own tongue. 'Leave me a while. Tell the *éored* to assemble on the path, and make ready to ride to the Entwade.'

Muttering Éothain retired, and spoke to the others. Soon they drew off and left Éomer alone with the three companions.

'All that you say is strange, Aragorn,' he said. 'Yet you speak the truth, that is plain: the Men of the Mark do not lie, and therefore they are not easily deceived. But you have not told all. Will you not now speak more fully of your errand, so that I may judge what to do?'

'I set out from Imladris, as it is named in the rhyme, many weeks ago,' answered Aragorn. 'With me went Boromir of Minas Tirith. My errand was to go to that city with the son of Denethor, to aid his folk in their war against Sauron. But the Company that I journeyed with had other business. Of that I cannot speak now. Gandalf the Grey was our leader.'

'Gandalf!' Éomer exclaimed. 'Gandalf Greyhame is known in the Mark; but his name, I warn you, is no longer a password to the king's favour. He has been a guest in the land many times in the memory of men, coming as he will, after a season, or after many years. He is ever the herald of strange events: a bringer of evil, some now say.

'Indeed since his last coming in the summer all things have gone amiss. At that time our trouble with Saruman began. Until then we counted Saruman our friend, but Gandalf came then and warned us that sudden war was preparing in Isengard. He said that he himself had been a prisoner in Orthanc and had hardly escaped, and he begged for help. But Théoden would not listen to him, and he went away. Speak not the name of Gandalf loudly in Théoden's ears! He is wroth. For Gandalf took the horse that is called Shadowfax, the most precious of all the king's steeds, chief of the *Mearas*, which only the Lord of the Mark may ride. For the sire of their race was the great horse of Eorl that knew the speech of Men. Seven nights ago Shadowfax returned; but the king's anger is not less, for now the horse is wild and will let no man handle him.'

'Then Shadowfax has found his way alone from the far North,' said Aragorn; 'for it was there that he and Gandalf parted. But alas! Gandalf will ride no longer. He fell into darkness in the Mines of Moria and comes not again.'

'That is heavy tidings,' said Éomer. 'At least to me, and to many; though not to all, as you may find, if you come to the king.'

'It is tidings more grievous than any in this land can under-stand, though it may touch them sorely ere the year is much older,' said Aragorn. 'But when the great fall, the less must lead. My part it has been to guide our Company on the long road from Moria. Through Lórien we came – of which it were well that you should learn the truth ere you speak of it again – and thence down the leagues of the Great River to the falls of Rauros. There Boromir was slain by the same Orcs whom you destroyed.'

'Your news is all of woe!' cried Éomer in dismay. 'Great harm is this death to Minas Tirith, and to us all. That was a worthy man! All spoke his praise. He came seldom to the Mark, for he was ever in the wars on the East-borders; but I have seen him. More like to the swift sons of Eorl than to the grave Men of Gondor he seemed to me, and likely to prove a great captain of his people when his time came. But we have had no word of this grief out of Gondor. When did he fall?'

'It is now the fourth day since he was slain,' answered Aragorn; 'and since the evening of that day we have journeyed from the shadow of Tol Brandir.'

'On foot?' cried Éomer.

'Yes, even as you see us.'

Wide wonder came into Éomer's eyes. 'Strider is too poor a name, son of Arathorn,' he said. 'Wingfoot I name you. This deed of the three friends should be sung in many a hall. Forty leagues and five you have measured ere the fourth day is ended! Hardy is the race of Elendil!

'But now, lord, what would you have me do! I must return in haste to Théoden. I spoke warily before my men. It is true that we are not yet at open war with the Black Land, and there are some, close to the king's ear, that speak craven counsels; but war is coming. We shall not forsake our old alliance with Gondor, and while they fight we shall aid them: so say I and all who hold with me. The East-mark is my charge, the ward of the Third Marshal, and I have removed all our herds and herdfolk, withdrawing them beyond Entwash, and leaving none here but guards and swift scouts.'

'Then you do not pay tribute to Sauron?' said Gimli.

'We do not and we never have,' said Éomer with a flash

of his eyes; 'though it comes to my ears that that lie has been told. Some years ago the Lord of the Black Land wished to purchase horses of us at great price, but we refused him, for he puts beasts to evil use. Then he sent plundering Orcs, and they carry off what they can, choosing always the black horses: few of these are now left. For that reason our feud with the Orcs is bitter.

'But at this time our chief concern is with Saruman. He has claimed lordship over all this land, and there has been war between us for many months. He has taken Orcs into his service, and Wolf-riders, and evil Men, and he has closed the Gap against us, so that we are likely to be beset both east and west.

'It is ill dealing with such a foe: he is a wizard both cunning and dwimmer-crafty, having many guises. He walks here and there, they say, as an old man hooded and cloaked, very like to Gandalf, as many now recall. His spies slip through every net, and his birds of ill omen are abroad in the sky. I do not know how it will all end, and my heart misgives me; for it seems to me that his friends do not all dwell in Isengard. But if you come to the king's house, you shall see for yourself. Will you not come? Do I hope in vain that you have been sent to me for a help in doubt and need?'

'I will come when I may,' said Aragorn.

'Come now!' said Éomer. 'The Heir of Elendil would be a strength indeed to the Sons of Eorl in this evil tide. There is battle even now upon the Westemnet, and I fear that it may go ill for us.

'Indeed in this riding north I went without the king's leave, for in my absence his house is left with little guard. But scouts warned me of the orc-host coming down out of the East Wall three nights ago, and among them they reported that some bore the white badges of Saruman. So suspecting what I most fear, a league between Orthanc and the Dark Tower, I led forth my *éored*, men of my own household; and we overtook the Orcs at nightfall two days ago, near to the borders of the Entwood. There we surrounded them, and gave battle yesterday at dawn. Fifteen of my men I lost, and twelve horses alas! For the Orcs were greater in number than we counted on. Others joined them, coming out of the East across the Great River: their trail is plain to see a little north of this spot. And others, too, came out of the forest. Great Orcs, who also bore the White Hand of Isengard: that kind is stronger and more fell than all others.

'Nonetheless we put an end to them. But we have been too long away. We are needed south and west. Will you not come? There are spare horses as you see. There is work for the Sword to do. Yes, and we could find a use for Gimli's axe and the bow of Legolas, if they will pardon my rash words concerning the Lady of the Wood. I spoke only as do all men in my land, and I would gladly learn better.'

'I thank you for your fair words,' said Aragorn, 'and my heart desires to come with you; but I cannot desert my friends while hope remains.'

'Hope does not remain,' said Éomer. 'You will not find your friends on the North-borders.'

'Yet my friends are not behind. We found a clear token not far from the East Wall that one at least of them was still alive there. But between the wall and the downs we have found no other trace of them, and no trail has turned aside, this way or that, unless my skill has wholly left me.'

'Then what do you think has become of them?'

'I do not know. They may have been slain and burned among the Orcs; but that you will say cannot be, and I do not fear it. I can only think that they were carried off into the forest before the battle, even before you encircled your foes, maybe. Can you swear that none escaped your net in such a way?'

'I would swear that no Orc escaped after we sighted them,' said Éomer. 'We reached the forest-eaves before them, and if after that any living thing broke through our ring, then it was no Orc and had some elvish power.'

'Our friends were attired even as we are,' said Aragorn; 'and you passed us by under the full light of day.'

'I had forgotten that,' said Éomer. 'It is hard to be sure of anything among so many marvels. The world is all grown strange. Elf and Dwarf in company walk in our daily fields; and folk speak with the Lady of the Wood and yet live; and the Sword comes back to war that was broken in the long ages ere the fathers of our fathers rode into the Mark! How shall a man judge what to do in such times?'

'As he ever has judged,' said Aragorn. 'Good and ill have not changed since yesteryear; nor are they one thing among Elves and Dwarves and another among Men. It is a man's part to discern them, as much in the Golden Wood as in his own house.'

'True indeed,' said Éomer. 'But I do not doubt you, nor the deed which my heart would do. Yet I am not free to do all as I would. It is against our law to let strangers wander at will in our land, until the king himself shall give them leave, and more strict is the command in these days of peril. I have begged you to come back willingly with me, and you will not. Loth am I to begin a battle of one hundred against three.'

'I do not think your law was made for such a chance,' said Aragorn. 'Nor indeed am I a stranger; for I have been in this land before, more than once, and ridden with the host of the Rohirrim, though under other name and in other guise. You I have not seen before, for you are young, but I have spoken with Éomund your father, and with Théoden son of Thengel. Never in former days would any high lord of this land have constrained a man to abandon such a quest as mine. My duty at least is clear, to go on. Come now, son of Éomund, the choice must be made at last. Aid us, or at the worst let us go free. Or seek to carry out your law. If you do so there will be fewer to return to your war or to your king.'

Éomer was silent for a moment, then he spoke. 'We both have need of haste,' he said. 'My company chafes to be away, and every hour lessens your hope. This is my choice. You may go; and what is more, I will lend you horses. This only I ask: when your quest is achieved, or is proved vain, return with the horses over the Entwade to Meduseld, the high house in Edoras where Théoden now sits. Thus you shall prove to him that I have not misjudged. In this I place myself, and maybe my very life, in the keeping of your good faith. Do not fail.'

'I will not,' said Aragorn.

There was great wonder, and many dark and doubtful glances, among his men, when Éomer gave orders that the spare horses were to be lent to the strangers; but only Éothain dared to speak openly.

'It may be well enough for this lord of the race of Gondor, as he claims,' he said, 'but who has heard of a horse of the Mark being given to a Dwarf?'

'No one,' said Gimli. 'And do not trouble: no one will ever hear of it. I would sooner walk than sit on the back of any beast so great, free or begrudged.'

'But you must ride now, or you will hinder us,' said Aragorn.

'Come, you shall sit behind me, friend Gimli,' said Legolas. 'Then all will be well, and you need neither borrow a horse nor be troubled by one.'

A great dark-grey horse was brought to Aragorn, and he mounted it. 'Hasufel is his name,' said Éomer. 'May he bear you well and to better fortune than Gárulf, his late master!'

A smaller and lighter horse, but restive and fiery, was brought to Legolas. Arod was his name. But Legolas asked them to take off saddle and rein. 'I need them not,' he said, and leaped lightly up, and to their wonder Arod was tame and willing beneath him, moving here and there with but a spoken word: such was the elvish way with all good beasts. Gimli was lifted up behind his friend, and he clung to him, not much more at ease than Sam Gamgee in a boat.

'Farewell, and may you find what you seek!' cried Éomer. 'Return with what speed you may, and let our swords hereafter shine together!'

'I will come,' said Aragorn.

'And I will come, too,' said Gimli. 'The matter of the Lady

Galadriel lies still between us. I have yet to teach you gentle speech.'

'We shall see,' said Éomer. 'So many strange things have chanced that to learn the praise of a fair lady under the loving strokes of a Dwarf's axe will seem no great wonder. Farewell!'

With that they parted. Very swift were the horses of Rohan. When after a little Gimli looked back, the company of Éomer were already small and far away. Aragorn did not look back: he was watching the trail as they sped on their way, bending low with his head beside the neck of Hasufel. Before long they came to the borders of the Entwash, and there they met the other trail of which Éomer had spoken, coming down from the East out of the Wold.

Aragorn dismounted and surveyed the ground, then leaping back into the saddle, he rode away for some distance eastward, keeping to one side and taking care not to override the footprints. Then he again dismounted and examined the ground, going backwards and forwards on foot.

'There is little to discover,' he said when he returned. 'The main trail is all confused with the passage of the horsemen as they came back; their outward course must have lain nearer the river. But this eastward trail is fresh and clear. There is no sign there of any feet going the other way, back towards Anduin. Now we must ride slower, and make sure that no trace or footstep branches off on either side. The Orcs must have been aware from this point that they were pursued; they may have made some attempt to get their captives away before they were overtaken.'

As they rode forward the day was overcast. Low grey clouds came over the Wold. A mist shrouded the sun. Ever nearer the tree-clad slopes of Fangorn loomed, slowly darkling as the sun went west. They saw no sign of any trail to right or left, but here and there they passed single Orcs, fallen in their tracks as they ran, with grey-feathered arrows sticking in back or throat.

At last as the afternoon was waning they came to the eaves of the forest, and in an open glade among the first trees they found the place of the great burning: the ashes were still hot and smoking. Beside it was a great pile of helms and mail, cloven shields, and broken swords, bows and darts and other gear of war. Upon a stake in the middle was set a great goblin head; upon its shattered helm the white badge could still be seen. Further away, not far from the river, where it came streaming out from the edge of the wood, there was a mound. It was newly raised: the raw earth was covered with fresh-cut turves: about it were planted fifteen spears.

Aragorn and his companions searched far and wide about the field of battle, but the light faded, and evening soon drew down, dim and misty. By nightfall they had discovered no trace of Merry and Pippin.

'We can do no more,' said Gimli sadly. 'We have been set many riddles since we came to Tol Brandir, but this is the hardest to unravel. I would guess that the burned bones of the hobbits are now mingled with the Orcs'. It will be hard news for Frodo, if he lives to hear it; and hard too for the old hobbit who waits in Rivendell. Elrond was against their coming.'

'But Gandalf was not,' said Legolas.

'But Gandalf chose to come himself, and he was the first to be lost,' answered Gimli. 'His foresight failed him.'

'The counsel of Gandalf was not founded on foreknow-ledge of safety, for himself or for others,' said Aragorn. 'There are some things that it is better to begin than to refuse, even though the end may be dark. But I shall not depart from this place yet. In any case we must here await the morning-light.'

A little way beyond the battle-field they made their camp under a spreading tree: it looked like a chestnut, and yet it still bore many broad brown leaves of a former year, like dry hands with long splayed fingers; they rattled mournfully in the night-breeze.

Gimli shivered. They had brought only one blanket apiece.

'Let us light a fire,' he said. 'I care no longer for the danger. Let the Orcs come as thick as summer-moths round a candle!'

'If those unhappy hobbits are astray in the woods, it might draw them hither,' said Legolas.

'And it might draw other things, neither Orc nor Hobbit,' said Aragorn. 'We are near to the mountain-marches of the traitor Saruman. Also we are on the very edge of Fangorn, and it is perilous to touch the trees of that wood, it is said.'

'But the Rohirrim made a great burning here yesterday,' said Gimli, 'and they felled trees for the fire, as can be seen. Yet they passed the night after safely here, when their labour was ended.'

'They were many,' said Aragorn, 'and they do not heed the wrath of Fangorn, for they come here seldom, and they do not go under the trees. But our paths are likely to lead us into the very forest itself. So have a care! Cut no living wood!'

'There is no need,' said Gimli. 'The Riders have left chip and bough enough, and there is dead wood lying in plenty.' He went off to gather fuel, and busied himself with building and kindling a fire; but Aragorn sat silent with his back to the great tree, deep in thought; and Legolas stood alone in the open, looking towards the profound shadow of the wood, leaning forward, as one who listens to voices calling from a distance.

When the Dwarf had a small bright blaze going, the three companions drew close to it and sat together, shrouding the light with their hooded forms. Legolas looked up at the boughs of the tree reaching out above them.

'Look!' he said. 'The tree is glad of the fire!'

It may have been that the dancing shadows tricked their eyes, but certainly to each of the companions the boughs appeared to be bending this way and that so as to come above the flames, while the upper branches were stooping down; the brown leaves now stood out stiff, and rubbed together like many cold cracked hands taking comfort in the warmth.

There was a silence, for suddenly the dark and unknown

forest, so near at hand, made itself felt as a great brooding presence, full of secret purpose. After a while Legolas spoke again.

'Celeborn warned us not to go far into Fangorn,' he said. 'Do you know why, Aragorn? What are the fables of the forest that Boromir had heard?'

'I have heard many tales in Gondor and elsewhere,' said Aragorn, 'but if it were not for the words of Celeborn I should deem them only fables that Men have made as true knowledge fades. I had thought of asking you what was the truth of the matter. And if an Elf of the wood does not know, how shall a Man answer?'

'You have journeyed further than I,' said Legolas. 'I have heard nothing of this in my own land, save only songs that tell how the Onodrim, that Men call Ents, dwelt there long ago; for Fangorn is old, old even as the Elves would reckon it.'

'Yes, it is old,' said Aragorn, 'as old as the forest by the Barrow-downs, and it is far greater. Elrond says that the two are akin, the last strongholds of the mighty woods of the Elder Days, in which the Firstborn roamed while Men still slept. Yet Fangorn holds some secret of its own. What it is I do not know.'

'And I do not wish to know,' said Gimli. 'Let nothing that dwells in Fangorn be troubled on my account!'

They now drew lots for the watches, and the lot for the first watch fell to Gimli. The others lay down. Almost at once sleep laid hold on them. 'Gimli!' said Aragorn drowsily. 'Remember, it is perilous to cut bough or twig from a living tree in Fangorn. But do not stray far in search of dead wood. Let the fire die rather! Call me at need!'

With that he fell asleep. Legolas already lay motionless, his fair hands folded upon his breast, his eyes unclosed, blending living night and deep dream, as is the way with Elves. Gimli sat hunched by the fire, running his thumb thoughtfully along the edge of his axe. The tree rustled. There was no other sound.

Suddenly Gimli looked up, and there just on the edge of the firelight stood an old bent man, leaning on a staff, and wrapped in a great cloak; his wide-brimmed hat was pulled down over his eyes. Gimli sprang up, too amazed for the moment to cry out, though at once the thought flashed into his mind that Saruman had caught them. Both Aragorn and Legolas, roused by his sudden movement, sat up and stared. The old man did not speak or make a sign.

'Well, father, what can we do for you?' said Aragorn, leaping to his feet. 'Come and be warm, if you are cold!' He strode forward, but the old man was gone. There was no trace of him to be found near at hand, and they did not dare to wander far. The moon had set and the night was very dark.

Suddenly Legolas gave a cry. 'The horses! The horses!'

The horses were gone. They had dragged their pickets and disappeared. For some time the three companions stood still and silent, troubled by this new stroke of ill fortune. They were under the eaves of Fangorn, and endless leagues lay between them and the Men of Rohan, their only friends in this wide and dangerous land. As they stood, it seemed to them that they heard, far off in the night, the sound of horses whinnying and neighing. Then all was quiet again, except for the cold rustle of the wind.

'Well, they are gone,' said Aragorn at last. 'We cannot find them or catch them; so that if they do not return of their own will, we must do without. We started on our feet, and we have those still.'

'Feet!' said Gimli. 'But we cannot eat them as well as walk on them.' He threw some fuel on the fire and slumped down beside it.

'Only a few hours ago you were unwilling to sit on a horse of Rohan,' laughed Legolas. 'You will make a rider yet.'

'It seems unlikely that I shall have the chance,' said Gimli.

'If you wish to know what I think,' he began again after a while, 'I think it was Saruman. Who else? Remember the words of Éomer: *he walks about like an old man hooded and cloaked.* Those were the words. He has gone off with our horses, or scared them away, and here we are. There is more trouble coming to us, mark my words!'

'I mark them,' said Aragorn. 'But I marked also that this old man had a hat not a hood. Still I do not doubt that you guess right, and that we are in peril here, by night or day. Yet in the meantime there is nothing that we can do but rest, while we may. I will watch for a while now, Gimli. I have more need of thought than of sleep.'

The night passed slowly. Legolas followed Aragorn, and Gimli followed Legolas, and their watches wore away. But nothing happened. The old man did not appear again, and the horses did not return.

CHAPTER III

THE URUK-HAI

Pippin lay in a dark and troubled dream: it seemed that he could hear his own small voice echoing in black tunnels, calling *Frodo, Frodo!* But instead of Frodo hundreds of hideous orc-faces grinned at him out of the shadows, hundreds of hideous arms grasped at him from every side. Where was Merry?

He woke. Cold air blew on his face. He was lying on his back. Evening was coming and the sky above was growing dim. He turned and found that the dream was little worse than the waking. His wrists, legs, and ankles were tied with cords. Beside him Merry lay, white-faced, with a dirty rag bound across his brows. All about them sat or stood a great company of Orcs.

Slowly in Pippin's aching head memory pieced itself together and became separated from dream-shadows. Of course: he and Merry had run off into the woods. What had come over them? Why had they dashed off like that, taking no notice of old Strider? They had run a long way shouting – he could not remember how far or how long; and then suddenly they had crashed right into a group of Orcs: they were standing listening, and they did not appear to see Merry and Pippin until they were almost in their arms. Then they yelled and dozens of other goblins had sprung out of the trees. Merry and he had drawn their swords, but the Orcs did not wish to fight, and had tried only to lay hold of them, even when Merry had cut off several of their arms and hands. Good old Merry!

Then Boromir had come leaping through the trees. He had made them fight. He slew many of them and the rest fled. But they had not gone far on the way back when they

were attacked again, by a hundred Orcs at least, some of
them very large, and they shot a rain of arrows: always at
Boromir. Boromir had blown his great horn till the woods
rang, and at first the Orcs had been dismayed and had drawn
back; but when no answer but the echoes came, they had
attacked more fiercely than ever. Pippin did not remember
much more. His last memory was of Boromir leaning against
a tree, plucking out an arrow; then darkness fell suddenly.

'I suppose I was knocked on the head,' he said to himself.
'I wonder if poor Merry is much hurt. What has happened
to Boromir? Why didn't the Orcs kill us? Where are we, and
where are we going?'

He could not answer the questions. He felt cold and sick.
'I wish Gandalf had never persuaded Elrond to let us come,'
he thought. 'What good have I been? Just a nuisance: a pas-
senger, a piece of luggage. And now I have been stolen and
I am just a piece of luggage for the Orcs. I hope Strider or
someone will come and claim us! But ought I to hope for
it? Won't that throw out all the plans? I wish I could get
free!'

He struggled a little, quite uselessly. One of the Orcs sitting
near laughed and said something to a companion in their
abominable tongue. 'Rest while you can, little fool!' he said
then to Pippin, in the Common Speech, which he made
almost as hideous as his own language. 'Rest while you can!
We'll find a use for your legs before long. You'll wish you
had got none before we get home.'

'If I had my way, you'd wish you were dead now,' said
the other. 'I'd make you squeak, you miserable rat.' He
stooped over Pippin, bringing his yellow fangs close to his
face. He had a black knife with a long jagged blade in his
hand. 'Lie quiet, or I'll tickle you with this,' he hissed. 'Don't
draw attention to yourself, or I may forget my orders. Curse
the Isengarders! *Uglúk u bagronk sha pushdug Saruman-glob
búbhosh skai*': he passed into a long angry speech in his own
tongue that slowly died away into muttering and snarling.

Terrified Pippin lay still, though the pain at his wrists and ankles was growing, and the stones beneath him were boring into his back. To take his mind off himself he listened intently to all that he could hear. There were many voices round about, and though orc-speech sounded at all times full of hate and anger, it seemed plain that something like a quarrel had begun, and was getting hotter.

To Pippin's surprise he found that much of the talk was intelligible; many of the Orcs were using ordinary language. Apparently the members of two or three quite different tribes were present, and they could not understand one another's orc-speech. There was an angry debate concerning what they were to do now: which way they were to take and what should be done with the prisoners.

'There's no time to kill them properly,' said one. 'No time for play on this trip.'

'That can't be helped,' said another. 'But why not kill them quick, kill them now? They're a cursed nuisance, and we're in a hurry. Evening's coming on, and we ought to get a move on.'

'Orders,' said a third voice in a deep growl. '*Kill all but* NOT *the Halflings; they are to be brought back* ALIVE *as quickly as possible.* That's my orders.'

'What are they wanted for?' asked several voices. 'Why alive? Do they give good sport?'

'No! I heard that one of them has got something, something that's wanted for the War, some elvish plot or other. Anyway they'll both be questioned.'

'Is that all you know? Why don't we search them and find out? We might find something that we could use ourselves.'

'That is a very interesting remark,' sneered a voice, softer than the others but more evil. 'I may have to report that. The prisoners are NOT to be searched or plundered: those are *my* orders.'

'And mine too,' said the deep voice. '*Alive and as captured; no spoiling.* That's my orders.'

'Not our orders!' said one of the earlier voices. 'We have

come all the way from the Mines to kill, and avenge our folk. I wish to kill, and then go back north.'

'Then you can wish again,' said the growling voice. 'I am Uglúk. I command. I return to Isengard by the shortest road.'

'Is Saruman the master or the Great Eye?' said the evil voice. 'We should go back at once to Lugbúrz.'

'If we could cross the Great River, we might,' said another voice. 'But there are not enough of us to venture down to the bridges.'

'I came across,' said the evil voice. 'A winged Nazgûl awaits us northward on the east-bank.'

'Maybe, maybe! Then you'll fly off with our prisoners, and get all the pay and praise in Lugbúrz, and leave us to foot it as best we can through the Horse-country. No, we must stick together. These lands are dangerous: full of foul rebels and brigands.'

'Aye, we must stick together,' growled Uglúk. 'I don't trust you little swine. You've no guts outside your own sties. But for us you'd all have run away. We are the fighting Uruk-hai! We slew the great warrior. We took the prisoners. We are the servants of Saruman the Wise, the White Hand: the Hand that gives us man's-flesh to eat. We came out of Isengard, and led you here, and we shall lead you back by the way we choose. I am Uglúk. I have spoken.'

'You have spoken more than enough, Uglúk,' sneered the evil voice. 'I wonder how they would like it in Lugbúrz. They might think that Uglúk's shoulders needed relieving of a swollen head. They might ask where his strange ideas came from. Did they come from Saruman, perhaps? Who does *he* think he is, setting up on his own with his filthy white badges? They might agree with me, with Grishnákh their trusted messenger; and I Grishnákh say this: Saruman is a fool, and a dirty treacherous fool. But the Great Eye is on him.'

'*Swine* is it? How do you folk like being called *swine* by the muck-rakers of a dirty little wizard? It's orc-flesh they eat, I'll warrant.'

Many loud yells in orc-speech answered him, and the

ringing clash of weapons being drawn. Cautiously Pippin rolled over, hoping to see what would happen. His guards had gone to join in the fray. In the twilight he saw a large black Orc, probably Uglúk, standing facing Grishnákh, a short crook-legged creature, very broad and with long arms that hung almost to the ground. Round them were many smaller goblins. Pippin supposed that these were the ones from the North. They had drawn their knives and swords, but hesitated to attack Uglúk.

Uglúk shouted, and a number of other Orcs of nearly his own size ran up. Then suddenly, without warning, Uglúk sprang forwards, and with two swift strokes swept the heads off two of his opponents. Grishnákh stepped aside and vanished into the shadows. The others gave way, and one stepped backwards and fell over Merry's prostrate form with a curse. Yet that probably saved his life, for Uglúk's followers leaped over him and cut down another with their broad-bladed swords. It was the yellow-fanged guard. His body fell right on top of Pippin, still clutching its long saw-edged knife.

'Put up your weapons!' shouted Uglúk. 'And let's have no more nonsense! We go straight west from here, and down the stair. From there straight to the downs, then along the river to the forest. And we march day and night. That clear?'

'Now,' thought Pippin, 'if only it takes that ugly fellow a little while to get his troop under control, I've got a chance.' A gleam of hope had come to him. The edge of the black knife had snicked his arm, and then slid down to his wrist. He felt the blood trickling on to his hand, but he also felt the cold touch of steel against his skin.

The Orcs were getting ready to march again, but some of the Northerners were still unwilling, and the Isengarders slew two more before the rest were cowed. There was much cursing and confusion. For the moment Pippin was unwatched. His legs were securely bound, but his arms were only tied about the wrists, and his hands were in front of him. He could move them both together, though the bonds were cruelly tight. He pushed the dead Orc to one side, then hardly daring to breathe, he drew the knot of the wrist-cord up and down against the blade of the knife. It was sharp and the dead hand held it fast. The cord was cut! Quickly Pippin took it in his fingers and knotted it again into a loose bracelet of two loops and slipped it over his hands. Then he lay very still.

'Pick up those prisoners!' shouted Uglúk. 'Don't play any tricks with them! If they are not alive when we get back, someone else will die too.'

An Orc seized Pippin like a sack, put its head between his tied hands, grabbed his arms and dragged them down, until Pippin's face was crushed against its neck; then it jolted off with him. Another treated Merry in the same way. The Orc's clawlike hand gripped Pippin's arms like iron; the nails bit into him. He shut his eyes and slipped back into evil dreams.

Suddenly he was thrown on to the stony floor again. It was early night, but the slim moon was already falling westward. They were on the edge of a cliff that seemed to look out over a sea of pale mist. There was a sound of water falling nearby.

'The scouts have come back at last,' said an Orc close at hand.

'Well, what did you discover?' growled the voice of Uglúk.

'Only a single horseman, and he made off westwards. All's clear now.'

'Now, I daresay. But how long? You fools! You should have shot him. He'll raise the alarm. The cursed horsebreeders will hear of us by morning. Now we'll have to leg it double quick.'

A shadow bent over Pippin. It was Uglúk. 'Sit up!' said the Orc. 'My lads are tired of lugging you about. We have got to climb down, and you must use your legs. Be helpful now. No crying out, no trying to escape. We have ways of paying for tricks that you won't like, though they won't spoil your usefulness for the Master.'

He cut the thongs round Pippin's legs and ankles, picked

him up by his hair and stood him on his feet. Pippin fell down, and Uglúk dragged him up by his hair again. Several Orcs laughed. Uglúk thrust a flask between his teeth and poured some burning liquid down his throat: he felt a hot fierce glow flow through him. The pain in his legs and ankles vanished. He could stand.

'Now for the other!' said Uglúk. Pippin saw him go to Merry, who was lying close by, and kick him. Merry groaned. Seizing him roughly Uglúk pulled him into a sitting position, and tore the bandage off his head. Then he smeared the wound with some dark stuff out of a small wooden box. Merry cried out and struggled wildly.

The Orcs clapped and hooted. 'Can't take his medicine,' they jeered. 'Doesn't know what's good for him. Ai! We shall have some fun later.'

But at the moment Uglúk was not engaged in sport. He needed speed and had to humour unwilling followers. He was healing Merry in orc-fashion; and his treatment worked swiftly. When he had forced a drink from his flask down the hobbit's throat, cut his leg-bonds, and dragged him to his feet, Merry stood up, looking pale but grim and defiant, and very much alive. The gash in his forehead gave him no more trouble, but he bore a brown scar to the end of his days.

'Hullo, Pippin!' he said. 'So you've come on this little expedition, too? Where do we get bed and breakfast?'

'Now then!' said Uglúk. 'None of that! Hold your tongues. No talk to one another. Any trouble will be reported at the other end, and He'll know how to pay you. You'll get bed and breakfast all right: more than you can stomach.'

The orc-band began to descend a narrow ravine leading down into the misty plain below. Merry and Pippin, separated by a dozen Orcs or more, climbed down with them. At the bottom they stepped on to grass, and the hearts of the hobbits rose.

'Now straight on!' shouted Uglúk. 'West and a little north. Follow Lugdush.'

'But what are we going to do at sunrise?' said some of the Northerners.

'Go on running,' said Uglúk. 'What do you think? Sit on the grass and wait for the Whiteskins to join the picnic?'

'But we can't run in the sunlight.'

'You'll run with me behind you,' said Uglúk. 'Run! Or you'll never see your beloved holes again. By the White Hand! What's the use of sending out mountain-maggots on a trip, only half trained. Run, curse you! Run while night lasts!'

Then the whole company began to run with the long loping strides of Orcs. They kept no order, thrusting, jostling, and cursing; yet their speed was very great. Each hobbit had a guard of three. Pippin was far back in the line. He wondered how long he would be able to go on at this pace: he had had no food since the morning. One of his guards had a whip. But at present the orc-liquor was still hot in him. His wits, too, were wide-awake.

Every now and again there came into his mind unbidden a vision of the keen face of Strider bending over a dark trail, and running, running behind. But what could even a Ranger see except a confused trail of orc-feet? His own little prints and Merry's were overwhelmed by the trampling of the iron-shod shoes before them and behind them and about them.

They had gone only a mile or so from the cliff when the land sloped down into a wide shallow depression, where the ground was soft and wet. Mist lay there, pale-glimmering in the last rays of the sickle moon. The dark shapes of the Orcs in front grew dim, and then were swallowed up.

'Ai! Steady now!' shouted Uglúk from the rear.

A sudden thought leaped into Pippin's mind, and he acted on it at once. He swerved aside to the right, and dived out of the reach of his clutching guard, headfirst into the mist; he landed sprawling on the grass.

'Halt!' yelled Uglúk.

There was for a moment turmoil and confusion. Pippin sprang up and ran. But the Orcs were after him. Some suddenly loomed up right in front of him.

'No hope of escape!' thought Pippin. 'But there is a hope that I have left some of my own marks unspoilt on the wet ground.' He groped with his two tied hands at his throat, and unclasped the brooch of his cloak. Just as long arms and hard claws seized him, he let it fall. 'There I suppose it will lie until the end of time,' he thought. 'I don't know why I did it. If the others have escaped, they've probably all gone with Frodo.'

A whip-thong curled round his legs, and he stifled a cry.

'Enough!' shouted Uglúk running up. 'He's still got to run a long way yet. Make 'em both run! Just use the whip as a reminder.'

'But that's not all,' he snarled, turning to Pippin. 'I shan't forget. Payment is only put off. Leg it!'

Neither Pippin nor Merry remembered much of the later part of the journey. Evil dreams and evil waking were blended into a long tunnel of misery, with hope growing ever fainter behind. They ran, and they ran, striving to keep up the pace set by the Orcs, licked every now and again with a cruel thong cunningly handled. If they halted or stumbled, they were seized and dragged for some distance.

The warmth of the orc-draught had gone. Pippin felt cold and sick again. Suddenly he fell face downward on the turf. Hard hands with rending nails gripped and lifted him. He was carried like a sack once more, and darkness grew about him: whether the darkness of another night, or a blindness of his eyes, he could not tell.

Dimly he became aware of voices clamouring: it seemed that many of the Orcs were demanding a halt. Uglúk was shouting. He felt himself flung to the ground, and he lay as he fell, till black dreams took him. But he did not long escape from pain; soon the iron grip of merciless hands was on him again. For a long time he was tossed and shaken, and then slowly the darkness gave way, and he came back to the waking world and found that it was morning. Orders were shouted and he was thrown roughly on the grass.

There he lay for a while, fighting with despair. His head swam, but from the heat in his body he guessed that he had been given another draught. An Orc stooped over him, and flung him some bread and a strip of raw dried flesh. He ate the stale grey bread hungrily, but not the meat. He was famished but not yet so famished as to eat flesh flung to him by an Orc, the flesh of he dared not guess what creature.

He sat up and looked about. Merry was not far away. They were by the banks of a swift narrow river. Ahead mountains loomed: a tall peak was catching the first rays of the sun. A dark smudge of forest lay on the lower slopes before them.

There was much shouting and debating among the Orcs; a quarrel seemed on the point of breaking out again between the Northerners and the Isengarders. Some were pointing back away south, and some were pointing eastward.

'Very well,' said Uglúk. 'Leave them to me then! No killing, as I've told you before; but if you want to throw away what we've come all the way to get, throw it away! I'll look after it. Let the fighting Uruk-hai do the work, as usual. If you're afraid of the Whiteskins, run! Run! There's the forest,' he shouted, pointing ahead. 'Get to it! It's your best hope. Off you go! And quick, before I knock a few more heads off, to put some sense into the others.'

There was some cursing and scuffling, and then most of the Northerners broke away and dashed off, over a hundred of them, running wildly along the river towards the mountains. The hobbits were left with the Isengarders: a grim dark band, four score at least of large, swart, slant-eyed Orcs with great bows and short broad-bladed swords. A few of the larger and bolder Northerners remained with them.

'Now we'll deal with Grishnákh,' said Uglúk; but some even of his own followers were looking uneasily southwards.

'I know,' growled Uglúk. 'The cursed horse-boys have got wind of us. But that's all your fault, Snaga. You and the other scouts ought to have your ears cut off. But we are the fighters. We'll feast on horseflesh yet, or something better.'

At that moment Pippin saw why some of the troop had

been pointing eastward. From that direction there now came hoarse cries, and there was Grishnákh again, and at his back a couple of score of others like him: long-armed crook-legged Orcs. They had a red eye painted on their shields. Uglúk stepped forward to meet them.

'So you've come back?' he said. 'Thought better of it, eh?'

'I've returned to see that Orders are carried out and the prisoners safe,' answered Grishnákh.

'Indeed!' said Uglúk. 'Waste of effort. I'll see that orders are carried out in my command. And what else did you come back for? You went in a hurry. Did you leave anything behind?'

'I left a fool,' snarled Grishnákh. 'But there were some stout fellows with him that are too good to lose. I knew you'd lead them into a mess. I've come to help them.'

'Splendid!' laughed Uglúk. 'But unless you've got some guts for fighting, you've taken the wrong way. Lugbúrz was your road. The Whiteskins are coming. What's happened to your precious Nazgûl? Has he had another mount shot under him? Now, if you'd brought him along, that might have been useful – if these Nazgûl are all they make out.'

'Nazgûl, Nazgûl,' said Grishnákh, shivering and licking his lips, as if the word had a foul taste that he savoured painfully. 'You speak of what is deep beyond the reach of your muddy dreams, Uglúk,' he said. 'Nazgûl! Ah! All that they make out! One day you'll wish that you had not said that. Ape!' he snarled fiercely. 'You ought to know that they're the apple of the Great Eye. But the winged Nazgûl: not yet, not yet. He won't let them show themselves across the Great River yet, not too soon. They're for the War – and other purposes.'

'You seem to know a lot,' said Uglúk. 'More than is good for you, I guess. Perhaps those in Lugbúrz might wonder how, and why. But in the meantime the Uruk-hai of Isengard can do the dirty work, as usual. Don't stand slavering there! Get your rabble together! The other swine are legging it to the forest. You'd better follow. You wouldn't get back to the

Great River alive. Right off the mark! Now! I'll be on your heels.'

The Isengarders seized Merry and Pippin again and slung them on their backs. Then the troop started off. Hour after hour they ran, pausing now and again only to sling the hobbits to fresh carriers. Either because they were quicker and hardier, or because of some plan of Grishnákh's, the Isengarders gradually passed through the Orcs of Mordor, and Grishnákh's folk closed in behind. Soon they were gaining also on the Northerners ahead. The forest began to draw nearer.

Pippin was bruised and torn, his aching head was grated by the filthy jowl and hairy ear of the Orc that held him. Immediately in front were bowed backs, and tough thick legs going up and down, up and down, unresting, as if they were made of wire and horn, beating out the nightmare seconds of an endless time.

In the afternoon Uglúk's troop overtook the Northerners. They were flagging in the rays of the bright sun, winter sun shining in a pale cool sky though it was; their heads were down and their tongues lolling out.

'Maggots!' jeered the Isengarders. 'You're cooked. The Whiteskins will catch you and eat you. They're coming!'

A cry from Grishnákh showed that this was not mere jest. Horsemen, riding very swiftly, had indeed been sighted: still far behind but gaining on the Orcs, gaining on them like a tide over the flats on folk straying in a quicksand.

The Isengarders began to run with a redoubled pace that astonished Pippin, a terrific spurt it seemed for the end of a race. Then he saw that the sun was sinking, falling behind the Misty Mountains; shadows reached over the land. The soldiers of Mordor lifted their heads and also began to put on speed. The forest was dark and close. Already they had passed a few outlying trees. The land was beginning to slope upwards, ever more steeply; but the Orcs did not halt. Both Uglúk and Grishnákh shouted, spurring them on to a last effort.

*   *   *

'They will make it yet. They will escape,' thought Pippin. And then he managed to twist his neck, so as to glance back with one eye over his shoulder. He saw that riders away eastward were already level with the Orcs, galloping over the plain. The sunset gilded their spears and helmets, and glinted in their pale flowing hair. They were hemming the Orcs in, preventing them from scattering, and driving them along the line of the river.

He wondered very much what kind of folk they were. He wished now that he had learned more in Rivendell, and looked more at maps and things; but in those days the plans for the journey seemed to be in more competent hands, and he had never reckoned with being cut off from Gandalf, or from Strider, and even from Frodo. All that he could remember about Rohan was that Gandalf's horse, Shadowfax, had come from that land. That sounded hopeful, as far as it went.

'But how will they know that we are not Orcs?' he thought. 'I don't suppose they've ever heard of hobbits down here. I suppose I ought to be glad that the beastly Orcs look like being destroyed, but I would rather be saved myself.' The chances were that he and Merry would be killed together with their captors, before ever the Men of Rohan were aware of them.

A few of the riders appeared to be bowmen, skilled at shooting from a running horse. Riding swiftly into range they shot arrows at the Orcs that straggled behind, and several of them fell; then the riders wheeled away out of the range of the answering bows of their enemies, who shot wildly, not daring to halt. This happened many times, and on one occasion arrows fell among the Isengarders. One of them, just in front of Pippin, stumbled and did not get up again.

Night came down without the Riders closing in for battle. Many Orcs had fallen, but fully two hundred remained. In the early darkness the Orcs came to a hillock. The eaves of the forest were very near, probably no more than three fur-longs away, but they could go no further. The horsemen had encircled them. A small band disobeyed Uglúk's command, and ran on towards the forest: only three returned.

'Well, here we are,' sneered Grishnákh. 'Fine leadership! I hope the great Uglúk will lead us out again.'

'Put those Halflings down!' ordered Uglúk, taking no notice of Grishnákh. 'You, Lugdush, get two others and stand guard over them! They're not to be killed, unless the filthy Whiteskins break through. Understand? As long as I'm alive, I want 'em. But they're not to cry out, and they're not to be rescued. Bind their legs!'

The last part of the order was carried out mercilessly. But Pippin found that for the first time he was close to Merry. The Orcs were making a great deal of noise, shouting and clashing their weapons, and the hobbits managed to whisper together for a while.

'I don't think much of this,' said Merry. 'I feel nearly done in. Don't think I could crawl away far, even if I was free.'

'*Lembas!*' whispered Pippin. '*Lembas*: I've got some. Have you? I don't think they've taken anything but our swords.'

'Yes, I had a packet in my pocket,' answered Merry, 'but it must be battered to crumbs. Anyway I can't put my mouth in my pocket!'

'You won't have to. I've———'; but just then a savage kick warned Pippin that the noise had died down, and the guards were watchful.

The night was cold and still. All round the knoll on which the Orcs were gathered little watch-fires sprang up, golden-red in the darkness, a complete ring of them. They were within a long bowshot, but the riders did not show themselves against the light, and the Orcs wasted many arrows shooting at the fires, until Uglúk stopped them. The riders made no sound. Later in the night when the moon came out of the mist, then occasionally they could be seen, shadowy shapes that glinted now and again in the white light, as they moved in ceaseless patrol.

'They'll wait for the Sun, curse them!' growled one of the

guards. 'Why don't we get together and charge through? What's old Uglúk think he's doing, I should like to know?'

'I daresay you would,' snarled Uglúk stepping up from behind. 'Meaning I don't think at all, eh? Curse you! You're as bad as the other rabble: the maggots and the apes of Lugbúrz. No good trying to charge with them. They'd just squeal and bolt, and there are more than enough of these filthy horse-boys to mop up our lot on the flat.

'There's only one thing those maggots can do: they can see like gimlets in the dark. But these Whiteskins have better night-eyes than most Men, from all I've heard; and don't forget their horses! They can see the night-breeze, or so it's said. Still there's one thing the fine fellows don't know: Mauhúr and his lads are in the forest, and they should turn up any time now.'

Uglúk's words were enough, apparently, to satisfy the Isengarders; but the other Orcs were both dispirited and rebellious. They posted a few watchers, but most of them lay on the ground, resting in the pleasant darkness. It did indeed become very dark again; for the moon passed westward into thick cloud, and Pippin could not see anything a few feet away. The fires brought no light to the hillock. The riders were not, however, content merely to wait for the dawn and let their enemies rest. A sudden outcry on the east side of the knoll showed that something was wrong. It seemed that some of the Men had ridden in close, slipped off their horses, crawled to the edge of the camp and killed several Orcs, and then had faded away again. Uglúk dashed off to stop a stampede.

Pippin and Merry sat up. Their guards, Isengarders, had gone with Uglúk. But if the hobbits had any thought of escape, it was soon dashed. A long hairy arm took each of them by the neck and drew them close together. Dimly they were aware of Grishnákh's great head and hideous face between them; his foul breath was on their cheeks. He began to paw them and feel them. Pippin shuddered as hard cold fingers groped down his back.

'Well, my little ones!' said Grishnákh in a soft whisper. 'Enjoying your nice rest? Or not? A little awkwardly placed perhaps: swords and whips on one side, and nasty spears on the other! Little people should not meddle in affairs that are too big for them.' His fingers continued to grope. There was a light like a pale but hot fire behind his eyes.

The thought came suddenly into Pippin's mind, as if caught direct from the urgent thought of his enemy: 'Grishnákh knows about the Ring! He's looking for it, while Uglúk is busy: he probably wants it for himself.' Cold fear was in Pippin's heart, yet at the same time he was wondering what use he could make of Grishnákh's desire.

'I don't think you will find it that way,' he whispered. 'It isn't easy to find.'

'*Find it?*' said Grishnákh: his fingers stopped crawling and gripped Pippin's shoulder. 'Find what? What are you talking about, little one?'

For a moment Pippin was silent. Then suddenly in the darkness he made a noise in his throat: *gollum, gollum.* 'Nothing, my precious,' he added.

The hobbits felt Grishnákh's fingers twitch. 'O ho!' hissed the goblin softly. 'That's what he means, is it? O ho! Very ve-ry dangerous, my little ones.'

'Perhaps,' said Merry, now alert and aware of Pippin's guess. 'Perhaps; and not only for us. Still you know your own business best. Do you want it, or not? And what would you give for it?'

'Do I want it? Do I want it?' said Grishnákh, as if puzzled; but his arms were trembling. 'What would I give for it? What do you mean?'

'We mean,' said Pippin, choosing his words carefully, 'that it's no good groping in the dark. We could save you time and trouble. But you must untie our legs first, or we'll do nothing, and say nothing.'

'My dear tender little fools,' hissed Grishnákh, 'everything you have, and everything you know, will be got out of you in due time: everything! You'll wish there was more that you could tell to satisfy the Questioner, indeed you will: quite soon. We shan't hurry the enquiry. Oh dear no! What do you think you've been kept alive for? My dear little fellows, please believe me when I say that it was not out of kindness: that's not even one of Uglúk's faults.'

'I find it quite easy to believe,' said Merry. 'But you haven't got your prey home yet. And it doesn't seem to be going your way, whatever happens. If we come to Isengard, it won't be the great Grishnákh that benefits: Saruman will take all that he can find. If you want anything for yourself, now's the time to do a deal.'

Grishnákh began to lose his temper. The name of Saruman seemed specially to enrage him. Time was passing and the disturbance was dying down. Uglúk or the Isengarders might return at any minute. 'Have you got it – either of you?' he snarled.

'*Gollum, gollum!*' said Pippin.

'Untie our legs!' said Merry.

They felt the Orc's arms trembling violently. 'Curse you, you filthy little vermin!' he hissed. 'Untie your legs? I'll untie every string in your bodies. Do you think I can't search you to the bones? Search you! I'll cut you both to quivering shreds. I don't need the help of your legs to get you away – and have you all to myself!'

Suddenly he seized them. The strength in his long arms and shoulders was terrifying. He tucked them one under each armpit, and crushed them fiercely to his sides; a great stifling hand was clapped over each of their mouths. Then he sprang forward, stooping low. Quickly and silently he went, until he came to the edge of the knoll. There, choosing a gap between the watchers, he passed like an evil shadow out into the night, down the slope and away westward towards the river that flowed out of the forest. In that direction there was a wide open space with only one fire.

After going a dozen yards he halted, peering and listening. Nothing could be seen or heard. He crept slowly on, bent almost double. Then he squatted and listened again. Then he stood up, as if to risk a sudden dash. At that very moment the dark form of a rider loomed up right in front of him. A horse snorted and reared. A man called out.

Grishnákh flung himself on the ground flat, dragging the hobbits under him; then he drew his sword. No doubt he meant to kill his captives, rather than allow them to escape or to be rescued; but it was his undoing. The sword rang faintly, and glinted a little in the light of the fire away to his left. An arrow came whistling out of the gloom: it was aimed with skill, or guided by fate, and it pierced his right hand. He dropped the sword and shrieked. There was a quick beat of hoofs, and even as Grishnákh leaped up and ran, he was ridden down and a spear passed through him. He gave a hideous shivering cry and lay still.

The hobbits remained flat on the ground, as Grishnákh had left them. Another horseman came riding swiftly to his comrade's aid. Whether because of some special keenness of sight, or because of some other sense, the horse lifted and sprang lightly over them; but its rider did not see them, lying covered in their elven-cloaks, too crushed for the moment, and too afraid to move.

At last Merry stirred and whispered softly: 'So far so good; but how are *we* to avoid being spitted?'

The answer came almost immediately. The cries of Grishnákh had roused the Orcs. From the yells and screeches that came from the knoll the hobbits guessed that their disappearance had been discovered: Uglúk was probably knocking off a few more heads. Then suddenly the answering cries of orc-voices came from the right, outside the circle of watch-fires, from the direction of the forest and the mountains. Mauhúr had apparently arrived and was attacking the besiegers. There was the sound of galloping horses. The Riders were drawing in their ring close round the knoll, risking the orc-arrows, so as to prevent any sortie, while a company rode off to deal with the newcomers. Suddenly Merry and Pippin realized that without moving they were now outside the circle: there was nothing between them and escape.

'Now,' said Merry, 'if only we had our legs and hands free, we might get away. But I can't touch the knots, and I can't bite them.'

'No need to try,' said Pippin. 'I was going to tell you: I've managed to free my hands. These loops are only left for show. You'd better have a bit of *lembas* first.'

He slipped the cords off his wrists, and fished out a packet. The cakes were broken, but good, still in their leaf-wrappings. The hobbits each ate two or three pieces. The taste brought back to them the memory of fair faces, and laughter, and wholesome food in quiet days now far away. For a while they ate thoughtfully, sitting in the dark, heedless of the cries and sounds of battle nearby. Pippin was the first to come back to the present.

'We must be off,' he said. 'Half a moment!' Grishnákh's sword was lying close at hand, but it was too heavy and clumsy for him to use; so he crawled forward, and finding the body of the goblin he drew from its sheath a long sharp knife. With this he quickly cut their bonds.

'Now for it!' he said. 'When we've warmed up a bit, perhaps we shall be able to stand again, and walk. But in any case we had better start by crawling.'

They crawled. The turf was deep and yielding, and that helped them; but it seemed a long slow business. They gave the watch-fire a wide berth, and wormed their way forward bit by bit, until they came to the edge of the river, gurgling away in the black shadows under its deep banks. Then they looked back.

The sounds had died away. Evidently Mauhúr and his 'lads' had been killed or driven off. The Riders had returned to their silent ominous vigil. It would not last very much longer. Already the night was old. In the East, which had remained unclouded, the sky was beginning to grow pale.

'We must get under cover,' said Pippin, 'or we shall be seen. It will not be any comfort to us, if these riders discover that we are not Orcs after we are dead.' He got up and stamped his feet. 'Those cords have cut me like wires; but my feet are getting warm again. I could stagger on now. What about you, Merry?'

Merry got up. 'Yes,' he said, 'I can manage it. *Lembas* does put heart into you ! A more wholesome sort of feeling, too, than the heat of that orc-draught. I wonder what it was made of. Better not to know, I expect. Let's get a drink of water to wash away the thought of it!'

'Not here, the banks are too steep,' said Pippin. 'Forward now!'

They turned and walked side by side slowly along the line of the river. Behind them the light grew in the East. As they walked they compared notes, talking lightly in hobbit-fashion of the things that had happened since their capture. No listener would have guessed from their words that they had suffered cruelly, and been in dire peril, going without hope towards torment and death; or that even now, as they knew well, they had little chance of ever finding friend or safety again.

'You seem to have been doing well, Master Took,' said Merry. 'You will get almost a chapter in old Bilbo's book, if ever I get a chance to report to him. Good work: especially guessing that hairy villain's little game, and playing up to him. But I wonder if anyone will ever pick up your trail and find that brooch. I should hate to lose mine, but I am afraid yours is gone for good.

'I shall have to brush up my toes, if I am to get level with you. Indeed Cousin Brandybuck is going in front now. This is where he comes in. I don't suppose you have much notion where we are; but I spent my time at Rivendell rather better. We are walking west along the Entwash. The butt-end of the Misty Mountains is in front, and Fangorn Forest.'

Even as he spoke the dark edge of the forest loomed up straight before them. Night seemed to have taken refuge under its great trees, creeping away from the coming Dawn.

'Lead on, Master Brandybuck!' said Pippin. 'Or lead back!

We have been warned against Fangorn. But one so knowing will not have forgotten that.'

'I have not,' answered Merry; 'but the forest seems better to me, all the same, than turning back into the middle of a battle.'

He led the way in under the huge branches of the trees. Old beyond guessing, they seemed. Great trailing beards of lichen hung from them, blowing and swaying in the breeze. Out of the shadows the hobbits peeped, gazing back down the slope: little furtive figures that in the dim light looked like elf-children in the deeps of time peering out of the Wild Wood in wonder at their first Dawn.

Far over the Great River, and the Brown Lands, leagues upon grey leagues away, the Dawn came, red as flame. Loud rang the hunting-horns to greet it. The Riders of Rohan sprang suddenly to life. Horn answered horn again.

Merry and Pippin heard, clear in the cold air, the neighing of war-horses, and the sudden singing of many men. The Sun's limb was lifted, an arc of fire, above the margin of the world. Then with a great cry the Riders charged from the East; the red light gleamed on mail and spear. The Orcs yelled and shot all the arrows that remained to them. The hobbits saw several horsemen fall; but their line held on up the hill and over it, and wheeled round and charged again. Most of the raiders that were left alive then broke and fled, this way and that, pursued one by one to the death. But one band, holding together in a black wedge, drove forward resolutely in the direction of the forest. Straight up the slope they charged towards the watchers. Now they were drawing near, and it seemed certain that they would escape: they had already hewn down three Riders that barred their way.

'We have watched too long,' said Merry. 'There's Uglúk! I don't want to meet him again.' The hobbits turned and fled deep into the shadows of the wood.

So it was that they did not see the last stand, when Uglúk was overtaken and brought to bay at the very edge of Fangorn. There he was slain at last by Éomer, the Third Marshal of the Mark, who dismounted and fought him sword to sword. And over the wide fields the keen-eyed Riders hunted down the few Orcs that had escaped and still had strength to fly.

Then when they had laid their fallen comrades in a mound and had sung their praises, the Riders made a great fire and scattered the ashes of their enemies. So ended the raid, and no news of it came ever back either to Mordor or to Isengard; but the smoke of the burning rose high to heaven and was seen by many watchful eyes.

CHAPTER IV

TREEBEARD

Meanwhile the hobbits went with as much speed as the dark and tangled forest allowed, following the line of the running stream, westward and up towards the slopes of the mountains, deeper and deeper into Fangorn. Slowly their fear of the Orcs died away, and their pace slackened. A queer stifling feeling came over them, as if the air were too thin or too scanty for breathing.

At last Merry halted. 'We can't go on like this,' he panted. 'I want some air.'

'Let's have a drink at any rate,' said Pippin. 'I'm parched.' He clambered on to a great tree-root that wound down into the stream, and stooping drew up some water in his cupped hands. It was clear and cold, and he took many draughts. Merry followed him. The water refreshed them and seemed to cheer their hearts; for a while they sat together on the brink of the stream, dabbling their sore feet and legs, and peering round at the trees that stood silently about them, rank upon rank, until they faded away into grey twilight in every direction.

'I suppose you haven't lost us already?' said Pippin, leaning back against a great tree-trunk. 'We can at least follow the course of this stream, the Entwash or whatever you call it, and get out again the way we came.'

'We could, if our legs would do it,' said Merry; 'and if we could breathe properly.'

'Yes, it is all very dim, and stuffy, in here,' said Pippin. 'It reminds me, somehow, of the old room in the Great Place of the Tooks away back in the Smials at Tuckborough: a huge place, where the furniture has never been moved or changed for generations. They say the Old Took lived in it

year after year, while he and the room got older and shabbier
together – and it has never been changed since he died, a
century ago. And Old Gerontius was my great-great-
grandfather: that puts it back a bit. But that is nothing to the
old feeling of this wood. Look at all those weeping, trailing,
beards and whiskers of lichen! And most of the trees seem
to be half covered with ragged dry leaves that have never
fallen. Untidy. I can't imagine what spring would look like
here, if it ever comes; still less a spring-cleaning.'

'But the Sun at any rate must peep in sometimes,' said
Merry. 'It does not look or feel at all like Bilbo's description
of Mirkwood. That was all dark and black, and the home of
dark black things. This is just dim, and frightfully tree-ish.
You can't imagine *animals* living here at all, or staying for
long.'

'No, nor hobbits,' said Pippin. 'And I don't like the thought
of trying to get through it either. Nothing to eat for a hundred
miles, I should guess. How are our supplies?'

'Low,' said Merry. 'We ran off with nothing but a couple
of spare packets of *lembas*, and left everything else behind.'
They looked at what remained of the elven-cakes: broken
fragments for about five meagre days, that was all. 'And not
a wrap or a blanket,' said Merry. 'We shall be cold tonight,
whichever way we go.'

'Well, we'd better decide on the way now,' said Pippin.
'The morning must be getting on.'

Just then they became aware of a yellow light that had
appeared, some way further on into the wood: shafts of sunlight seemed suddenly to have pierced the forest-roof.

'Hullo!' said Merry. 'The Sun must have run into a cloud
while we've been under these trees, and now she has run out
again; or else she has climbed high enough to look down
through some opening. It isn't far – let's go and investigate!'

They found it was further than they thought. The ground
was rising steeply still, and it was becoming increasingly
stony. The light grew broader as they went on, and soon

they saw that there was a rock-wall before them: the side of a hill, or the abrupt end of some long root thrust out by the distant mountains. No trees grew on it, and the sun was falling full on its stony face. The twigs of the trees at its foot were stretched out stiff and still, as if reaching out to the warmth. Where all had looked so shabby and grey before, the wood now gleamed with rich browns, and with the smooth black-greys of bark like polished leather. The boles of the trees glowed with a soft green like young grass: early spring or a fleeting vision of it was about them.

In the face of the stony wall there was something like a stair: natural perhaps, and made by the weathering and splitting of the rock, for it was rough and uneven. High up, almost level with the tops of forest-trees, there was a shelf under a cliff. Nothing grew there but a few grasses and weeds at its edge, and one old stump of a tree with only two bent branches left: it looked almost like the figure of some gnarled old man, standing there, blinking in the morning-light.

'Up we go!' said Merry joyfully. 'Now for a breath of air, and a sight of the land!'

They climbed and scrambled up the rock. If the stair had been made it was for bigger feet and longer legs than theirs. They were too eager to be surprised at the remarkable way in which the cuts and sores of their captivity had healed and their vigour had returned. They came at length to the edge of the shelf almost at the feet of the old stump; then they sprang up and turned round with their backs to the hill, breathing deep, and looking out eastward. They saw that they had only come some three or four miles into the forest: the heads of the trees marched down the slopes towards the plain. There, near the fringe of the forest, tall spires of curling black smoke went up, wavering and floating towards them.

'The wind's changing,' said Merry. 'It's turned east again. It feels cool up here.'

'Yes,' said Pippin; 'I'm afraid this is only a passing gleam, and it will all go grey again. What a pity! This shaggy old forest looked so different in the sunlight. I almost felt I liked the place.'

'Almost felt you liked the Forest! That's good! That's uncommonly kind of you,' said a strange voice. 'Turn round and let me have a look at your faces. I almost feel that I dislike you both, but do not let us be hasty. Turn around!' A large knob-knuckled hand was laid on each of their shoulders, and they were twisted round, gently but irresistibly; then two great arms lifted them up.

They found that they were looking at a most extraordinary face. It belonged to a large Man-like, almost Troll-like, figure, at least fourteen foot high, very sturdy, with a tall head, and hardly any neck. Whether it was clad in stuff like green and grey bark, or whether that was its hide, was difficult to say. At any rate the arms, at a short distance from the trunk, were not wrinkled, but covered with a brown smooth skin. The large feet had seven toes each. The lower part of the long face was covered with a sweeping grey beard, bushy, almost twiggy at the roots, thin and mossy at the ends. But at the moment the hobbits noted little but the eyes. These deep eyes were now surveying them, slow and solemn, but very penetrating. They were brown, shot with a green light. Often afterwards Pippin tried to describe his first impression of them.

'One felt as if there was an enormous well behind them, filled up with ages of memory and long, slow, steady thinking; but their surface was sparkling with the present; like sun shimmering on the outer leaves of a vast tree, or on the ripples of a very deep lake. I don't know, but it felt as if something that grew in the ground – asleep, you might say, or just feeling itself as something between root-tip and leaf-tip, between deep earth and sky had suddenly waked up, and was considering you with the same slow care that it had given to its own inside affairs for endless years.'

'*Hrum, Hoom*,' murmured the voice, a deep voice like a very deep woodwind instrument. 'Very odd indeed! Do not be hasty, that is my motto. But if I had seen you, before I heard your voices – I liked them: nice little voices; they reminded me of something I cannot remember – if I had seen you before I heard you, I should have just trodden on you, taking you for little Orcs, and found out my mistake afterwards. Very odd you are, indeed. Root and twig, very odd!'

Pippin, though still amazed, no longer felt afraid. Under those eyes he felt a curious suspense, but not fear. 'Please,' he said, 'who are you? And what are you?'

A queer look came into the old eyes, a kind of wariness; the deep wells were covered over. '*Hrum*, now,' answered the voice; 'well, I am an Ent, or that's what they call me. Yes, Ent is the word. *The* Ent, I am, you might say, in your manner of speaking. *Fangorn* is my name according to some, *Treebeard* others make it. *Treebeard* will do.'

'An *Ent*?' said Merry. 'What's that? But what do you call yourself? What's your real name?'

'Hoo now!' replied Treebeard. 'Hoo! Now that would be telling! Not so hasty. And *I* am doing the asking. You are in *my* country. What are *you*, I wonder? I cannot place you. You do not seem to come in the old lists that I learned when I was young. But that was a long, long time ago, and they may have made new lists. Let me see! Let me see! How did it go?

> *Learn now the lore of Living Creatures!*
> *First name the four, the free peoples:*
> *Eldest of all, the elf-children;*
> *Dwarf the delver, dark are his houses;*
> *Ent the earthborn, old as mountains;*
> *Man the mortal, master of horses:*

Hm, hm, hm.

> *Beaver the builder, buck the leaper,*
> *Bear bee-hunter, boar the fighter;*
> *Hound is hungry, hare is fearful . . .*

hm, hm.

> *Eagle in eyrie, ox in pasture,*
> *Hart horn-crownéd; hawk is swiftest,*
> *Swan the whitest, serpent coldest . . .*

Hoom, hm; hoom, hm, how did it go? Room tum, room tum, roomty toom tum. It was a long list. But anyway you do not seem to fit in anywhere!'

'We always seem to have got left out of the old lists, and the old stories,' said Merry. 'Yet we've been about for quite a long time. We're *hobbits*.'

'Why not make a new line?' said Pippin.

> *'Half-grown hobbits, the hole-dwellers.*

Put us in amongst the four, next to Man (the Big People) and you've got it.'

'Hm! Not bad, not bad,' said Treebeard. 'That would do. So you live in holes, eh? It sounds very right and proper. Who calls you *hobbits*, though? That does not sound elvish to me. Elves made all the old words: they began it.'

'Nobody else calls us hobbits; we call ourselves that,' said Pippin.

'Hoom, hmm! Come now! Not so hasty! You call *yourselves* hobbits? But you should not go telling just anybody. You'll be letting out your own right names if you're not careful.'

'We aren't careful about that,' said Merry. 'As a matter of fact I'm a Brandybuck, Meriadoc Brandybuck, though most people call me just Merry.'

'And I'm a Took, Peregrin Took, but I'm generally called Pippin, or even Pip.'

'Hm, but you *are* hasty folk, I see,' said Treebeard. 'I am honoured by your confidence; but you should not be too free all at once. There are Ents and Ents, you know; or there are Ents and things that look like Ents but ain't, as you might say. I'll call you Merry and Pippin, if you please – nice names.

For I am not going to tell you *my* name, not yet at any rate.'
A queer half-knowing, half-humorous look came with a green
flicker into his eyes. 'For one thing it would take a long while:
my name is growing all the time, and I've lived a very long,
long time; so *my* name is like a story. Real names tell you
the story of the things they belong to in my language, in the
Old Entish as you might say. It is a lovely language, but it
takes a very long time to say anything in it, because we do
not say anything in it, unless it is worth taking a long time
to say, and to listen to.

'But now,' and the eyes became very bright and 'present',
seeming to grow smaller and almost sharp, 'what is going
on? What are you doing in it all? I can see and hear (*and*
smell *and* feel) a great deal from this, from this, from this
a-lalla-lalla-rumba-kamanda-lind-or-burúmë. Excuse me: that
is a part of my name for it; I do not know what the word is
in the outside languages: you know, the thing we are on,
where I stand and look out on fine mornings, and think about
the Sun, and the grass beyond the wood, and the horses, and
the clouds, and the unfolding of the world. What is going
on? What is Gandalf up to? And these – *burárum*,' he made
a deep rumbling noise like a discord on a great organ – 'these
Orcs, and young Saruman down at Isengard? I like news.
But not too quick now.'

'There is quite a lot going on,' said Merry; 'and even if
we tried to be quick, it would take a long time to tell. But
you told us not to be hasty. Ought we to tell you anything
so soon? Would you think it rude, if we asked what you are
going to do with us, and which side you are on? And did
you know Gandalf?'

'Yes, I do know him: the only wizard that really cares about
trees,' said Treebeard. 'Do you know him?'

'Yes,' said Pippin sadly, 'we did. He was a great friend,
and he was our guide.'

'Then I can answer your other questions,' said Treebeard.
'I am not going to do anything *with* you: not if you mean by
that "do something *to* you" without your leave. We might

do some things together. I don't know about *sides*. I go my own way; but your way may go along with mine for a while. But you speak of Master Gandalf, as if he was in a story that had come to an end.'

'Yes, we do,' said Pippin sadly. 'The story seems to be going on, but I am afraid Gandalf has fallen out of it.'

'Hoo, come now!' said Treebeard. 'Hoom, hm, ah well.' He paused, looking long at the hobbits. 'Hoom, ah, well I do not know what to say. Come now!'

'If you would like to hear more,' said Merry, 'we will tell you. But it will take some time. Wouldn't you like to put us down? Couldn't we sit here together in the sun, while it lasts? You must be getting tired of holding us up.'

'Hm, *tired*? No, I am not tired. I do not easily get tired. And I do not sit down. I am not very, hm, bendable. But there, the Sun *is* going in. Let us leave this – did you say what you call it?'

'Hill?' suggested Pippin. 'Shelf? Step?' suggested Merry.

Treebeard repeated the words thoughtfully. '*Hill*. Yes, that was it. But it is a hasty word for a thing that has stood here ever since this part of the world was shaped. Never mind. Let us leave it, and go.'

'Where shall we go?' asked Merry.

'To my home, or one of my homes,' answered Treebeard. 'Is it far?'

'I do not know. You might call it far, perhaps. But what does that matter?'

'Well, you see, we have lost all our belongings,' said Merry. 'We have only a little food.'

'O! Hm! You need not trouble about that,' said Treebeard. 'I can give you a drink that will keep you green and growing for a long, long while. And if we decide to part company, I can set you down outside my country at any point you choose. Let us go!'

Holding the hobbits gently but firmly, one in the crook of each arm, Treebeard lifted up first one large foot and then the other, and moved them to the edge of the shelf. The rootlike toes grasped the rocks. Then carefully and solemnly, he stalked down from step to step, and reached the floor of the Forest.

At once he set off with long deliberate strides through the trees, deeper and deeper into the wood, never far from the stream, climbing steadily up towards the slopes of the mountains. Many of the trees seemed asleep, or as unaware of him as of any other creature that merely passed by; but some quivered, and some raised up their branches above his head as he approached. All the while, as he walked, he talked to himself in a long running stream of musical sounds.

The hobbits were silent for some time. They felt, oddly enough, safe and comfortable, and they had a great deal to think and wonder about. At last Pippin ventured to speak again.

'Please, Treebeard,' he said, 'could I ask you something? Why did Celeborn warn us against your forest? He told us not to risk getting entangled in it.'

'Hmm, did he now?' rumbled Treebeard. 'And I might have said much the same, if you had been going the other way. Do not risk getting entangled in the woods of *Laurelindórenan*! That is what the Elves used to call it, but now they make the name shorter: *Lothlórien* they call it. Perhaps they are right: maybe it is fading, not growing. Land of the Valley of Singing Gold, that was it, once upon a time. Now it is the Dreamflower. Ah well! But it is a queer place, and not for just any one to venture in. I am surprised that you ever got out, but much more surprised that you ever got in: that has not happened to strangers for many a year. It is a queer land.

'And so is this. Folk have come to grief here. Aye, they have, to grief. *Laurelindórenan lindelorendor malinornélion ornemalin*,' he hummed to himself. 'They are falling rather behind the world in there, I guess,' he said. 'Neither this country, nor anything else outside the Golden Wood, is what it was when Celeborn was young. Still:

Taurelilómëa-tumbalemorna Tumbaletaurëa Lómëanor,＊

that is what they used to say. Things have changed, but it is still true in places.'

'What do you mean?' said Pippin. 'What is true?'

'The trees and the Ents,' said Treebeard. 'I do not understand all that goes on myself, so I cannot explain it to you. Some of us are still true Ents, and lively enough in our fashion, but many are growing sleepy, going tree-ish, as you might say. Most of the trees are just trees, of course; but many are half awake. Some are quite wide awake, and a few are, well, ah, well getting *Entish*. That is going on all the time.

'When that happens to a tree, you find that some have *bad* hearts. Nothing to do with their wood: I do not mean that. Why, I knew some good old willows down the Entwash, gone long ago, alas! They were quite hollow, indeed they were falling all to pieces, but as quiet and sweet-spoken as a young leaf. And then there are some trees in the valleys under the mountains, sound as a bell, and bad right through. That sort of thing seems to spread. There used to be some very dangerous parts in this country. There are still some very black patches.'

'Like the Old Forest away to the north, do you mean?' asked Merry.

'Aye, aye, something like, but much worse. I do not doubt there is some shadow of the Great Darkness lying there still away north; and bad memories are handed down. But there are hollow dales in this land where the Darkness has never been lifted, and the trees are older than I am. Still, we do what we can. We keep off strangers and the foolhardy; and we train and we teach, we walk and we weed.

'We are tree-herds, we old Ents. Few enough of us are left now. Sheep get like shepherd, and shepherds like sheep, it is said; but slowly, and neither have long in the world. It is

＊ See Appendix F under *Ents*.

quicker and closer with trees and Ents, and they walk down the ages together. For Ents are more like Elves: less interested in themselves than Men are, and better at getting inside other things. And yet again Ents are more like Men, more change-able than Elves are, and quicker at taking the colour of the outside, you might say. Or better than both: for they are steadier and keep their minds on things longer.

'Some of my kin look just like trees now, and need some-thing great to rouse them; and they speak only in whispers. But some of my trees are limb-lithe, and many can talk to me. Elves began it, of course, waking trees up and teaching them to speak and learning their tree-talk. They always wished to talk to everything, the old Elves did. But then the Great Darkness came, and they passed away over the Sea, or fled into far valleys, and hid themselves, and made songs about days that would never come again. Never again. Aye, aye, there was all one wood once upon a time from here to the Mountains of Lune, and this was just the East End.

'Those were the broad days! Time was when I could walk and sing all day and hear no more than the echo of my own voice in the hollow hills. The woods were like the woods of Lothlórien, only thicker, stronger, younger. And the smell of the air! I used to spend a week just breathing.'

Treebeard fell silent, striding along, and yet making hardly a sound with his great feet. Then he began to hum again, and passed into a murmuring chant. Gradually the hobbits became aware that he was chanting to them:

> *In the willow-meads of Tasarinan I walked in the Spring.*
> *Ah! the sight and the smell of the Spring in Nan-tasarion!*
> *And I said that was good.*
> *I wandered in Summer in the elm-woods of Ossiriand.*
> *Ah! the light and the music in the Summer by the Seven*
> *   Rivers of Ossir!*
> *And I thought that was best.*
> *To the beeches of Neldoreth I came in the Autumn.*

Ah! the gold and the red and the sighing of leaves in the
  Autumn in Taur-na-neldor!
It was more than my desire.
To the pine-trees upon the highland of Dorthonion I climbed
  in the Winter.
Ah! the wind and the whiteness and the black branches of
  Winter upon Orod-na-Thôn!
My voice went up and sang in the sky.
And now all those lands lie under the wave,
And I walk in Ambaróna, in Tauremorna, in Aldalómë,
In my own land, in the country of Fangorn,
Where the roots are long,
And the years lie thicker than the leaves
In Tauremornalómë.

He ended, and strode on silently, and in all the wood, as far
as ear could reach, there was not a sound.

The day waned, and dusk was twined about the boles of
the trees. At last the hobbits saw, rising dimly before them,
a steep dark land: they had come to the feet of the mountains,
and to the green roots of tall Methedras. Down the hillside
the young Entwash, leaping from its springs high above, ran
noisily from step to step to meet them. On the right of the
stream there was a long slope, clad with grass, now grey in
the twilight. No trees grew there and it was open to the sky;
stars were shining already in lakes between shores of cloud.
Treebeard strode up the slope, hardly slackening his pace.
Suddenly before them the hobbits saw a wide opening. Two
great trees stood there, one on either side, like living gate-
posts; but there was no gate save their crossing and inter-
woven boughs. As the old Ent approached, the trees lifted
up their branches, and all their leaves quivered and rustled.
For they were evergreen trees, and their leaves were dark and
polished, and gleamed in the twilight. Beyond them was a
wide level space, as though the floor of a great hall had been
cut in the side of the hill. On either hand the walls sloped

upwards, until they were fifty feet high or more, and along each wall stood an aisle of trees that also increased in height as they marched inwards.

At the far end the rock-wall was sheer, but at the bottom it had been hollowed back into a shallow bay with an arched roof: the only roof of the hall, save the branches of the trees, which at the inner end overshadowed all the ground leaving only a broad open path in the middle. A little stream escaped from the springs above, and leaving the main water, fell tinkling down the sheer face of the wall, pouring in silver drops, like a fine curtain in front of the arched bay. The water was gathered again into a stone basin in the floor between the trees, and thence it spilled and flowed away beside the open path, out to rejoin the Entwash in its journey through the forest.

'Hm! Here we are!' said Treebeard, breaking his long silence. 'I have brought you about seventy thousand entstrides, but what that comes to in the measurement of your land I do not know. Anyhow we are near the roots of the Last Mountain. Part of the name of this place might be Wellinghall, if it were turned into your language. I like it. We will stay here tonight.' He set them down on the grass between the aisles of the trees, and they followed him towards the great arch. The hobbits now noticed that as he walked his knees hardly bent, but his legs opened in a great stride. He planted his big toes (and they were indeed big, and very broad) on the ground first, before any other part of his feet.

For a moment Treebeard stood under the rain of the falling spring, and took a deep breath; then he laughed, and passed inside. A great stone table stood there, but no chairs. At the back of the bay it was already quite dark. Treebeard lifted two great vessels and stood them on the table. They seemed to be filled with water; but he held his hands over them, and immediately they began to glow, one with a golden and the other with a rich green light; and the blending of the two lights lit the bay, as if the sun of summer was shining through a roof of young leaves. Looking back, the hobbits saw that the trees in the court had also begun to glow, faintly at first, but steadily quickening, until every leaf was edged with light: some green, some gold, some red as copper; while the tree-trunks looked like pillars moulded out of luminous stone.

'Well, well, now we can talk again,' said Treebeard. 'You are thirsty, I expect. Perhaps you are also tired. Drink this!' He went to the back of the bay, and then they saw that several tall stone jars stood there, with heavy lids. He removed one of the lids, and dipped in a great ladle, and with it filled three bowls, one very large bowl, and two smaller ones.

'This is an ent-house,' he said, 'and there are no seats, I fear. But you may sit on the table.' Picking up the hobbits he set them on the great stone slab, six feet above the ground, and there they sat dangling their legs, and drinking in sips.

The drink was like water, indeed very like the taste of the draughts they had drunk from the Entwash near the borders of the forest, and yet there was some scent or savour in it which they could not describe: it was faint, but it reminded them of the smell of a distant wood borne from afar by a cool breeze at night. The effect of the draught began at the toes, and rose steadily through every limb, bringing refreshment and vigour as it coursed upwards, right to the tips of the hair. Indeed the hobbits felt that the hair on their heads was actually standing up, waving and curling and growing. As for Treebeard, he first laved his feet in the basin beyond the arch, and then he drained his bowl at one draught, one long, slow draught. The hobbits thought he would never stop.

At last he set the bowl down again. 'Ah – ah,' he sighed. 'Hm, hoom, now we can talk easier. You can sit on the floor, and I will lie down; that will prevent this drink from rising to my head and sending me to sleep.'

On the right side of the bay there was a great bed on low legs, not more than a couple of feet high, covered deep in dried grass and bracken. Treebeard lowered himself slowly on to this (with only the slightest sign of bending at his middle), until he lay at full length, with his arms behind his head, looking up at the ceiling, upon which lights were flickering, like the play of leaves in the sunshine. Merry and Pippin sat beside him on pillows of grass.

'Now tell me your tale, and do not hurry!' said Treebeard.

The hobbits began to tell him the story of their adventures ever since they left Hobbiton. They followed no very clear order, for they interrupted one another continually, and Treebeard often stopped the speaker, and went back to some earlier point, or jumped forward asking questions about later events. They said nothing whatever about the Ring, and did not tell him why they set out or where they were going to; and he did not ask for any reasons.

He was immensely interested in everything: in the Black Riders, in Elrond, and Rivendell, in the Old Forest, and Tom Bombadil, in the Mines of Moria, and in Lothlórien and Galadriel. He made them describe the Shire and its country over and over again. He said an odd thing at this point. 'You never see any, hm, any Ents round there, do you?' he asked. 'Well, not Ents, *Entwives* I should really say.'

'*Entwives?*' said Pippin. 'Are they like you at all?'

'Yes, hm, well no: I do not really know now,' said Tree-beard thoughtfully. 'But they would like your country, so I just wondered.'

Treebeard was however especially interested in everything that concerned Gandalf; and most interested of all in Saruman's doings. The hobbits regretted very much that they knew so little about them: only a rather vague report by Sam of what Gandalf had told the Council. But they were clear at any rate that Uglúk and his troop came from Isengard, and spoke of Saruman as their master.

'Hm, hoom!' said Treebeard, when at last their story had wound and wandered down to the battle of the Orcs and the Riders of Rohan. 'Well, well! That is a bundle of news and no mistake. You have not told me all, no indeed, not by a long way. But I do not doubt that you are doing as Gandalf would wish. There is something very big going on, that I can see, and what it is maybe I shall learn in good time, or in bad time. By root and twig, but it is a strange business: up sprout a little folk that are not in the old lists, and behold! the Nine forgotten Riders reappear to hunt them, and Gandalf takes them on a great journey, and Galadriel harbours them in Caras Galadhon, and Orcs pursue them down all the leagues of Wilderland: indeed they seem to be caught up in a great storm. I hope they weather it!'

'And what about yourself?' asked Merry.

'Hoom, hm, I have not troubled about the Great Wars,' said Treebeard; 'they mostly concern Elves and Men. That is the business of Wizards: Wizards are always troubled about the future. I do not like worrying about the future. I am not altogether on anybody's *side*, because nobody is altogether on my *side*, if you understand me: nobody cares for the woods as I care for them, not even Elves nowadays. Still, I take more kindly to Elves than to others: it was the Elves that cured us of dumbness long ago, and that was a great gift that cannot be forgotten, though our ways have parted since. And there are some things, of course, whose side I am altogether *not* on; I am against them altogether: these – *burárum*' (he again made a deep rumble of disgust) '——these Orcs, and their masters.

'I used to be anxious when the shadow lay on Mirkwood, but when it removed to Mordor, I did not trouble for a while: Mordor is a long way away. But it seems that the wind is setting East, and the withering of all woods may be drawing near. There is naught that an old Ent can do to hold back that storm: he must weather it or crack.

'But Saruman now! Saruman is a neighbour: I cannot overlook him. I must do something, I suppose. I have often wondered lately what I should do about Saruman.'

'Who is Saruman?' asked Pippin. 'Do you know anything about his history?'

'Saruman is a Wizard,' answered Treebeard. 'More than that I cannot say. I do not know the history of Wizards. They appeared first after the Great Ships came over the Sea; but if they came with the Ships I never can tell. Saruman was reckoned great among them, I believe. He gave up wandering about and minding the affairs of Men and Elves, some time ago – you would call it a very long time ago; and he settled down at Angrenost, or Isengard as the Men of Rohan call it. He was very quiet to begin with, but his fame began to grow. He was chosen to be the head of the White Council, they say; but that did not turn out too well. I wonder now if even then Saruman was not turning to evil ways. But at any rate he used to give no trouble to his neighbours. I used to talk to him. There was a time when he was always walking about my woods. He was polite in those days, always asking my leave (at least when he met me); and always eager to listen. I told him many things that he would never have found out by himself; but he never repaid me in like kind. I cannot remember that he ever told me anything. And he got more and more like that; his face, as I remember it – I have not seen it for many a day – became like windows in a stone wall: windows with shutters inside.

'I think that I now understand what he is up to. He is plotting to become a Power. He has a mind of metal and wheels; and he does not care for growing things, except as far as they serve him for the moment. And now it is clear that he is a black traitor. He has taken up with foul folk, with the Orcs. Brm, hoom! Worse than that: he has been doing something to them; something dangerous. For these Isen-garders are more like wicked Men. It is a mark of evil things that came in the Great Darkness that they cannot abide the Sun; but Saruman's Orcs can endure it, even if they hate it. I wonder what he has done? Are they Men he has ruined, or has he blended the races of Orcs and Men? That would be a black evil!'

Treebeard rumbled for a moment, as if he were pronoun-cing some deep, subterranean Entish malediction. 'Some time ago I began to wonder how Orcs dared to pass through my woods so freely,' he went on. 'Only lately did I guess that Saruman was to blame, and that long ago he had been spying out all the ways, and discovering my secrets. He and his foul folk are making havoc now. Down on the borders they are felling trees – good trees. Some of the trees they just cut down and leave to rot – orc-mischief that; but most are hewn up and carried off to feed the fires of Orthanc. There is always a smoke rising from Isengard these days.

'Curse him, root and branch! Many of those trees were my friends, creatures I had known from nut and acorn; many had voices of their own that are lost for ever now. And there are wastes of stump and bramble where once there were singing groves. I have been idle. I have let things slip. It must stop!'

Treebeard raised himself from his bed with a jerk, stood up, and thumped his hand on the table. The vessels of light trembled and sent up two jets of flame. There was a flicker like green fire in his eyes, and his beard stood out stiff as a great besom.

'I will stop it!' he boomed. 'And you shall come with me. You may be able to help me. You will be helping your own friends that way, too; for if Saruman is not checked Rohan and Gondor will have an enemy behind as well as in front. Our roads go together – to Isengard!'

'We will come with you,' said Merry. 'We will do what we can.'

'Yes!' said Pippin. 'I should like to see the White Hand overthrown. I should like to be there, even if I could not be of much use: I shall never forget Uglúk and the crossing of Rohan.'

'Good! Good!' said Treebeard. 'But I spoke hastily. We must not be hasty. I have become too hot. I must cool myself and think; for it is easier to shout *stop!* than to do it.'

He strode to the archway and stood for some time under the falling rain of the spring. Then he laughed and shook himself, and wherever the drops of water fell glittering from him to the ground they glinted like red and green sparks. He came back and laid himself on the bed again and was silent.

*   *   *

After some time the hobbits heard him murmuring again. He seemed to be counting on his fingers. 'Fangorn, Finglas, Fladrif, aye, aye,' he sighed. 'The trouble is that there are so few of us left,' he said turning towards the hobbits. 'Only three remain of the first Ents that walked in the woods before the Darkness: only myself, Fangorn, and Finglas and Fladrif – to give them their Elvish names; you may call them Leaflock and Skinbark if you like that better. And of us three, Leaflock and Skinbark are not much use for this business. Leaflock has grown sleepy, almost tree-ish, you might say: he has taken to standing by himself half-asleep all through the summer with the deep grass of the meadows round his knees. Covered with leafy hair he is. He used to rouse up in winter; but of late he has been too drowsy to walk far even then. Skinbark lived on the mountain-slopes west of Isengard. That is where the worst trouble has been. He was wounded by the Orcs, and many of his folk and his tree-herds have been murdered and destroyed. He has gone up into the high places, among the birches that he loves best, and he will not come down. Still, I daresay I could get together a fair company of our younger folks – if I could make them understand the need; if I could rouse them: we are not a hasty folk. What a pity there are so few of us!'

'Why are there so few, when you have lived in this country so long?' asked Pippin. 'Have a great many died?'

'Oh, no!' said Treebeard. 'None have died from inside, as you might say. Some have fallen in the evil chances of the long years, of course; and more have grown tree-ish. But there were never many of us and we have not increased. There have been no Entings – no children, you would say, not for a terrible long count of years. You see, we lost the Entwives.'

'How very sad!' said Pippin. 'How was it that they all died?'

'They did not *die*!' said Treebeard. 'I never said *died*. We lost them, I said. We lost them and we cannot find them.' He sighed. 'I thought most folk knew that. There were songs about the hunt of the Ents for the Entwives sung among

Elves and Men from Mirkwood to Gondor. They cannot be quite forgotten.'

'Well, I am afraid the songs have not come west over the Mountains to the Shire,' said Merry. 'Won't you tell us some more, or sing us one of the songs?'

'Yes, I will indeed,' said Treebeard, seeming pleased with the request. 'But I cannot tell it properly, only in short; and then we must end our talk: tomorrow we have councils to call, and work to do, and maybe a journey to begin.'

'It is rather a strange and sad story,' he went on after a pause. 'When the world was young, and the woods were wide and wild, the Ents and the Entwives – and there were Entmaidens then: ah! the loveliness of Fimbrethil, of Wand-limb the lightfooted, in the days of our youth! – they walked together and they housed together. But our hearts did not go on growing in the same way: the Ents gave their love to things that they met in the world, and the Entwives gave their thought to other things, for the Ents loved the great trees, and the wild woods, and the slopes of the high hills; and they drank of the mountain-streams, and ate only such fruit as the trees let fall in their path; and they learned of the Elves and spoke with the Trees. But the Entwives gave their minds to the lesser trees, and to the meads in the sunshine beyond the feet of the forests; and they saw the sloe in the thicket, and the wild apple and the cherry blossoming in spring, and the green herbs in the waterlands in summer, and the seeding grasses in the autumn fields. They did not desire to speak with these things; but they wished them to hear and obey what was said to them. The Entwives ordered them to grow according to their wishes, and bear leaf and fruit to their liking; for the Entwives desired order, and plenty, and peace (by which they meant that things should remain where they had set them). So the Entwives made gardens to live in. But we Ents went on wandering, and we only came to the gardens now and again. Then when the Darkness came in the North, the Entwives crossed the Great River, and made new gardens, and tilled new fields, and we saw them more seldom. After the Darkness was overthrown the land of the Entwives blossomed richly, and their fields were full of corn. Many men learned the crafts of the Entwives and honoured them greatly; but we were only a legend to them, a secret in the heart of the forest. Yet here we still are, while all the gardens of the Entwives are wasted: Men call them the Brown Lands now.

'I remember it was long ago – in the time of the war between Sauron and the Men of the Sea – desire came over me to see Fimbrethil again. Very fair she was still in my eyes, when I had last seen her, though little like the Entmaiden of old. For the Entwives were bent and browned by their labour; their hair parched by the sun to the hue of ripe corn and their cheeks like red apples. Yet their eyes were still the eyes of our own people. We crossed over Anduin and came to their land; but we found a desert: it was all burned and uprooted, for war had passed over it. But the Entwives were not there. Long we called, and long we searched; and we asked all folk that we met which way the Entwives had gone. Some said they had never seen them; and some said that they had seen them walking away west, and some said east, and others south. But nowhere that we went could we find them. Our sorrow was very great. Yet the wild wood called, and we returned to it. For many years we used to go out every now and again and look for the Entwives, walking far and wide and calling them by their beautiful names. But as time passed we went more seldom and wandered less far. And now the Entwives are only a memory for us, and our beards are long and grey. The Elves made many songs concerning the Search of the Ents, and some of the songs passed into the tongues of Men. But we made no songs about it, being content to chant their beautiful names when we thought of the Entwives. We believe that we may meet again in a time to come, and perhaps we shall find somewhere a land where we can live together and both be content. But it is foreboded that that will only be when

we have both lost all that we now have. And it may well be
that that time is drawing near at last. For if Sauron of old
destroyed the gardens, the Enemy today seems likely to
wither all the woods.

'There was an Elvish song that spoke of this, or at least so
I understand it. It used to be sung up and down the Great
River. It was never an Entish song, mark you: it would
have been a very long song in Entish! But we know it by
heart, and hum it now and again. This is how it runs in your
tongue:

ENT. When Spring unfolds the beechen leaf, and sap
        is in the bough;
     When light is on the wild-wood stream, and
        wind is on the brow;
     When stride is long, and breath is deep, and
        keen the mountain-air,
     Come back to me! Come back to me, and say
        my land is fair!

ENTWIFE. When Spring is come to garth and field, and
        corn is in the blade;
     When blossom like a shining snow is on the
        orchard laid;
     When shower and Sun upon the Earth with
        fragrance fill the air,
     I'll linger here, and will not come, because my
        land is fair.

ENT. When Summer lies upon the world, and in a
        noon of gold
     Beneath the roof of sleeping leaves the dreams of
        trees unfold;
     When woodland halls are green and cool, and
        wind is in the West,
     Come back to me! Come back to me, and say
        my land is best!

ENTWIFE. When Summer warms the hanging fruit and
        burns the berry brown;

> When straw is gold, and ear is white, and
>   harvest comes to town;
> When honey spills, and apple swells, though
>   wind be in the West,
> I'll linger here beneath the Sun, because my
>   land is best!

ENT.   When Winter comes, the winter wild that hill
>   and wood shall slay;
>   When trees shall fall and starless night devour
>   the sunless day;
>   When wind is in the deadly East, then in the
>   bitter rain
>   I'll look for thee, and call to thee; I'll come to
>   thee again!

ENTWIFE.   When Winter comes, and singing ends; when
>   darkness falls at last;
>   When broken is the barren bough, and light and
>   labour past;
>   I'll look for thee, and wait for thee, until we
>   meet again:
>   Together we will take the road beneath the bitter
>   rain!

BOTH.   Together we will take the road that leads into
>   the West,
>   And far away will find a land where both our
>   hearts may rest.'

Treebeard ended his song. 'That is how it goes,' he said. 'It is
Elvish, of course: lighthearted, quickworded, and soon over. I
daresay it is fair enough. But the Ents could say more on
their side, if they had time! But now I am going to stand up
and take a little sleep. Where will you stand?'

'We usually lie down to sleep,' said Merry. 'We shall be
all right where we are.'

'Lie down to sleep!' said Treebeard. 'Why of course you
do! Hm, hoom: I was forgetting: singing that song put me
in mind of old times; almost thought that I was talking to

young Entings, I did. Well, you can lie on the bed. I am going to stand in the rain. Good night!'

Merry and Pippin climbed on to the bed and curled up in the soft grass and fern. It was fresh, and sweet-scented, and warm. The lights died down, and the glow of the trees faded; but outside under the arch they could see old Treebeard standing, motionless, with his arms raised above his head. The bright stars peered out of the sky, and lit the falling water as it spilled on to his fingers and head, and dripped, dripped, in hundreds of silver drops on to his feet. Listening to the tinkling of the drops the hobbits fell asleep.

They woke to find a cool sun shining into the great court, and on to the floor of the bay. Shreds of high cloud were overhead, running on a stiff easterly wind. Treebeard was not to be seen; but while Merry and Pippin were bathing in the basin by the arch, they heard him humming and singing, as he came up the path between the trees.

'Hoo, ho! Good morning, Merry and Pippin!' he boomed, when he saw them. 'You sleep long. I have been many a hundred strides already today. Now we will have a drink, and go to Entmoot.'

He poured them out two full bowls from a stone jar; but from a different jar. The taste was not the same as it had been the night before: it was earthier and richer, more sustaining and food-like, so to speak. While the hobbits drank, sitting on the edge of the bed, and nibbling small pieces of elf-cake (more because they felt that eating was a necessary part of breakfast than because they felt hungry), Treebeard stood, humming in Entish or Elvish or some strange tongue, and looking up at the sky.

'Where is Entmoot?' Pippin ventured to ask.

'Hoo, eh? Entmoot?' said Treebeard, turning round. 'It is not a place, it is a gathering of Ents – which does not often happen nowadays. But I have managed to make a fair number promise to come. We shall meet in the place where we have always met: Derndingle Men call it. It is away south from here. We must be there before noon.'

Before long they set off. Treebeard carried the hobbits in his arms as on the previous day. At the entrance to the court he turned to the right, stepped over the stream, and strode away southwards along the feet of great tumbled slopes where trees were scanty. Above these the hobbits saw thickets of birch and rowan, and beyond them dark climbing pinewoods. Soon Treebeard turned a little away from the hills and plunged into deep groves, where the trees were larger, taller, and thicker than any that the hobbits had ever seen before. For a while they felt faintly the sense of stifling which they had noticed when they first ventured into Fangorn, but it soon passed. Treebeard did not talk to them. He hummed to himself deeply and thoughtfully, but Merry and Pippin caught no proper words: it sounded like *boom, boom, rumboom, boorar, boom boom, dahrar boom boom, dahrar boom,* and so on with a constant change of note and rhythm. Now and again they thought they heard an answer, a hum or a quiver of sound, that seemed to come out of the earth, or from boughs above their heads, or perhaps from the boles of the trees; but Treebeard did not stop or turn his head to either side.

They had been going for a long while – Pippin had tried to keep count of the 'ent-strides' but had failed, getting lost at about three thousand – when Treebeard began to slacken his pace. Suddenly he stopped, put the hobbits down, and raised his curled hands to his mouth so that they made a hollow tube; then he blew or called through them. A great *hoom, hom* rang out like a deep-throated horn in the woods, and seemed to echo from the trees. Far off there came from several directions a similar *hoom, hom, hoom* that was not an echo but an answer.

Treebeard now perched Merry and Pippin on his shoulders and strode on again, every now and then sending out another horn-call, and each time the answers came louder and nearer. In this way they came at last to what looked like an impenetrable wall of dark evergreen trees, trees of a kind that the hobbits had never seen before: they branched out right from the roots, and were densely clad in dark glossy leaves like thornless holly, and they bore many stiff upright flower-spikes with large shining olive-coloured buds.

Turning to the left and skirting this huge hedge Treebeard came in a few strides to a narrow entrance. Through it a worn path passed and dived suddenly down a long steep slope. The hobbits saw that they were descending into a great dingle, almost as round as a bowl, very wide and deep, crowned at the rim with the high dark evergreen hedge. It was smooth and grassclad inside, and there were no trees except three very tall and beautiful silver-birches that stood at the bottom of the bowl. Two other paths led down into the dingle: from the west and from the east.

Several Ents had already arrived. More were coming in down the other paths, and some were now following Treebeard. As they drew near the hobbits gazed at them. They had expected to see a number of creatures as much like Treebeard as one hobbit is like another (at any rate to a stranger's eye); and they were very much surprised to see nothing of the kind. The Ents were as different from one another as trees from trees: some as different as one tree is from another of the same name but quite different growth and history; and some as different as one tree-kind from another, as birch from beech, oak from fir. There were a few older Ents, bearded and gnarled like hale but ancient trees (though none looked as ancient as Treebeard); and there were tall strong Ents, clean-limbed and smooth-skinned like forest-trees in their prime; but there were no young Ents, no saplings. Altogether there were about two dozen standing on the wide grassy floor of the dingle, and as many more were marching in.

At first Merry and Pippin were struck chiefly by the variety that they saw: the many shapes, and colours, the differences in girth, and height, and length of leg and arm; and in the number of toes and fingers (anything from three to nine). A few seemed more or less related to Treebeard, and reminded them of beech-trees or oaks. But there were other kinds. Some recalled the chestnut: brown-skinned Ents with large splayfingered hands, and short thick legs. Some recalled the ash: tall straight grey Ents with many-fingered hands and long legs; some the fir (the tallest Ents), and others the birch, the rowan, and the linden. But when the Ents all gathered round Treebeard, bowing their heads slightly, murmuring in their slow musical voices, and looking long and intently at the strangers, then the hobbits saw that they were all of the same kindred, and all had the same eyes: not all so old or so deep as Treebeard's, but all with the same slow, steady, thoughtful expression, and the same green flicker.

As soon as the whole company was assembled, standing in a wide circle round Treebeard, a curious and unintelligible conversation began. The Ents began to murmur slowly: first one joined and then another, until they were all chanting together in a long rising and falling rhythm, now louder on one side of the ring, now dying away there and rising to a great boom on the other side. Though he could not catch or understand any of the words – he supposed the language was Entish – Pippin found the sound very pleasant to listen to at first; but gradually his attention wavered. After a long time (and the chant showed no signs of slackening) he found himself wondering, since Entish was such an 'unhasty' language, whether they had yet got further than *Good Morning*; and if Treebeard was to call the roll, how many days it would take to sing all their names. 'I wonder what the Entish is for *yes* or *no*,' he thought. He yawned.

Treebeard was immediately aware of him. '*Hm, ha, hey*, my Pippin!' he said, and the other Ents all stopped their chant. 'You are a hasty folk, I was forgetting; and anyway it is wearisome listening to a speech you do not understand. You may get down now. I have told your names to the Entmoot, and they have seen you, and they have agreed that you are not Orcs, and that a new line shall be put in the old lists. We have got no further yet, but that is quick work for

an Entmoot. You and Merry can stroll about in the dingle,
if you like. There is a well of good water, if you need
refreshing, away yonder in the north bank. There are still
some words to speak before the Moot really begins. I will
come and see you again, and tell you how things are going.'

He put the hobbits down. Before they walked away, they
bowed low. This feat seemed to amuse the Ents very much,
to judge by the tone of their murmurs, and the flicker of their
eyes; but they soon turned back to their own business. Merry
and Pippin climbed up the path that came in from the west,
and looked through the opening in the great hedge. Long
tree-clad slopes rose from the lip of the dingle, and away
beyond them, above the fir-trees of the furthest ridge there
rose, sharp and white, the peak of a high mountain.
Southwards to their left they could see the forest falling away
down into the grey distance. There far away there was a pale
green glimmer that Merry guessed to be a glimpse of the
plains of Rohan.

'I wonder where Isengard is?' said Pippin.

'I don't know quite where we are,' said Merry; 'but that
peak is probably Methedras, and as far as I can remember
the ring of Isengard lies in a fork or deep cleft at the end of
the mountains. It is probably down behind this great ridge.
There seems to be a smoke or haze over there, left of the
peak, don't you think?'

'What is Isengard like?' said Pippin. 'I wonder what Ents
can do about it anyway.'

'So do I,' said Merry. 'Isengard is a sort of ring of rocks
or hills, I think, with a flat space inside and an island or pillar
of rock in the middle, called Orthanc. Saruman has a tower
on it. There is a gate, perhaps more than one, in the encircling
wall, and I believe there is a stream running through it; it
comes out of the mountains, and flows on across the Gap of
Rohan. It does not seem the sort of place for Ents to tackle.
But I have an odd feeling about these Ents: somehow I don't
think they are quite as safe and, well, funny as they seem.

They seem slow, queer, and patient, almost sad; and yet I believe they *could* be roused. If that happened, I would rather not be on the other side.'

'Yes!' said Pippin. 'I know what you mean. There might be all the difference between an old cow sitting and thoughtfully chewing, and a bull charging; and the change might come suddenly. I wonder if Treebeard will rouse them. I am sure he means to try. But they don't like being roused. Treebeard got roused himself last night, and then bottled it up again.'

The hobbits turned back. The voices of the Ents were still rising and falling in their conclave. The sun had now risen high enough to look over the high hedge: it gleamed on the tops of the birches and lit the northward side of the dingle with a cool yellow light. There they saw a little glittering fountain. They walked along the rim of the great bowl at the feet of the evergreens – it was pleasant to feel cool grass about their toes again, and not to be in a hurry – and then they climbed down to the gushing water. They drank a little, a clean, cold, sharp draught, and sat down on a mossy stone, watching the patches of sun on the grass and the shadows of the sailing clouds passing over the floor of the dingle. The murmur of the Ents went on. It seemed a very strange and remote place, outside their world, and far from everything that had ever happened to them. A great longing came over them for the faces and voices of their companions, especially for Frodo and Sam, and for Strider.

At last there came a pause in the Ent-voices; and looking up they saw Treebeard coming towards them, with another Ent at his side.

'Hm, hoom, here I am again,' said Treebeard. 'Are you getting weary, or feeling impatient, hmm, eh? Well, I am afraid that you must not get impatient yet. We have finished the first stage now; but I have still got to explain things again to those that live a long way off, far from Isengard, and those that I could not get round to before the Moot, and after that we shall have to decide what to do. However, deciding what to do does not take Ents so long as going over all the facts and events that they have to make up their minds about. Still, it is no use denying, we shall be here a long time yet: a couple of days very likely. So I have brought you a companion. He has an ent-house nearby. Bregalad is his Elvish name. He says he has already made up his mind and does not need to remain at the Moot. Hm, hm, he is the nearest thing among us to a hasty Ent. You ought to get on together. Good-bye!' Treebeard turned and left them.

Bregalad stood for some time surveying the hobbits solemnly; and they looked at him, wondering when he would show any signs of 'hastiness'. He was tall, and seemed to be one of the younger Ents; he had smooth shining skin on his arms and legs; his lips were ruddy, and his hair was grey-green. He could bend and sway like a slender tree in the wind. At last he spoke, and his voice though resonant was higher and clearer than Treebeard's.

'Ha, hmm, my friends, let us go for a walk!' he said. 'I am Bregalad, that is Quickbeam in your language. But it is only a nickname, of course. They have called me that ever since I said *yes* to an elder Ent before he had finished his question. Also I drink quickly, and go out while some are still wetting their beards. Come with me!'

He reached down two shapely arms and gave a long-fingered hand to each of the hobbits. All that day they walked about, in the woods with him, singing, and laughing; for Quickbeam often laughed. He laughed if the sun came out from behind a cloud, he laughed if they came upon a stream or spring: then he stooped and splashed his feet and head with water; he laughed sometimes at some sound or whisper in the trees. Whenever he saw a rowan-tree he halted a while with his arms stretched out, and sang, and swayed as he sang.

At nightfall he brought them to his ent-house: nothing more than a mossy stone set upon turves under a green bank. Rowan-trees grew in a circle about it, and there was water (as in all ent-houses), a spring bubbling out from the bank. They talked for a while as darkness fell on the forest. Not far away the voices of the Entmoot could be heard still going on; but now they seemed deeper and less leisurely, and every now and again one great voice would rise in a high and quickening music, while all the others died away. But beside them Bregalad spoke gently in their own tongue, almost whispering; and they learned that he belonged to Skinbark's people, and the country where they had lived had been ravaged. That seemed to the hobbits quite enough to explain his 'hastiness', at least in the matter of Orcs.

'There were rowan-trees in my home,' said Bregalad, softly and sadly, 'rowan-trees that took root when I was an Enting, many many years ago in the quiet of the world. The oldest were planted by the Ents to try and please the Entwives; but they looked at them and smiled and said that they knew where whiter blossom and richer fruit were growing. Yet there are no trees of all that race, the people of the Rose, that are so beautiful to me. And these trees grew and grew, till the shadow of each was like a green hall, and their red berries in the autumn were a burden, and a beauty and a wonder. Birds used to flock there. I like birds, even when they chatter; and the rowan has enough and to spare. But the birds became unfriendly and greedy and tore at the trees, and threw the fruit down and did not eat it. Then Orcs came with axes and cut down my trees. I came and called them by their long names, but they did not quiver, they did not hear or answer: they lay dead.

> O Orofarnë, Lassemista, Carnimirië!
> O rowan fair, upon your hair how white the blossom lay!
> O rowan mine, I saw you shine upon a summer's day,
> Your rind so bright, your leaves so light, your voice so cool
>   and soft:
> Upon your head how golden-red the crown you bore aloft!
> O rowan dead, upon your head your hair is dry and grey;
> Your crown is spilled, your voice is stilled for ever and a
>   day.
> O Orofarnë, Lassemista, Carnimirië!'

The hobbits fell asleep to the sound of the soft singing of Bregalad, that seemed to lament in many tongues the fall of trees that he had loved.

The next day they spent also in his company, but they did not go far from his 'house'. Most of the time they sat silent under the shelter of the bank; for the wind was colder, and the clouds closer and greyer; there was little sunshine, and in the distance the voices of the Ents at the Moot still rose and fell, sometimes loud and strong, sometimes low and sad, sometimes quickening, sometimes slow and solemn as a dirge. A second night came and still the Ents held conclave under hurrying clouds and fitful stars.

The third day broke, bleak and windy. At sunrise the Ents' voices rose to a great clamour and then died down again. As the morning wore on the wind fell and the air grew heavy with expectancy. The hobbits could see that Bregalad was now listening intently, although to them, down in the dell of his ent-house, the sound of the Moot was faint.

The afternoon came, and the sun, going west towards the mountains, sent out long yellow beams between the cracks and fissures of the clouds. Suddenly they were aware that everything was very quiet; the whole forest stood in listening silence. Of course, the Ent-voices had stopped. What did that mean? Bregalad was standing up erect and tense, looking back northwards towards Derndingle.

Then with a crash came a great ringing shout: *ra-hoom-rah!* The trees quivered and bent as if a gust had struck them. There was another pause, and then a marching music began like solemn drums, and above the rolling beats and booms there welled voices singing high and strong.

> *We come, we come with roll of drum: ta-runda runda*
> *runda rom!*

The Ents were coming: ever nearer and louder rose their song:

*We come, we come with horn and drum: ta-rūna rūna
rūna rom!*

Bregalad picked up the hobbits and strode from his house.

Before long they saw the marching line approaching: the
Ents were swinging along with great strides down the slope
towards them. Treebeard was at their head, and some fifty
followers were behind him, two abreast, keeping step with
their feet and beating time with their hands upon their flanks.
As they drew near the flash and flicker of their eyes could
be seen.

'Hoom, hom! Here we come with a boom, here we come
at last!' called Treebeard when he caught sight of Bregalad
and the hobbits. 'Come, join the Moot! We are off. We are
off to Isengard!'

'To Isengard!' the Ents cried in many voices.
'To Isengard!'

*To Isengard! Though Isengard be ringed and barred with
   doors of stone;*
*Though Isengard be strong and hard, as cold as stone and
   bare as bone,*
*We go, we go, we go to war, to hew the stone and break the
   door;*
*For bole and bough are burning now, the furnace roars – we
   go to war!*
*To land of gloom with tramp of doom, with roll of drum, we
   come, we come;*
   To Isengard with doom we come!
   With doom we come, with doom we come!

So they sang as they marched southwards.

Bregalad, his eyes shining, swung into the line beside
Treebeard. The old Ent now took the hobbits back, and set
them on his shoulders again, and so they rode proudly at the

head of the singing company with beating hearts and heads
held high. Though they had expected something to happen
eventually, they were amazed at the change that had come
over the Ents. It seemed now as sudden as the bursting of a
flood that had long been held back by a dike.

'The Ents made up their minds rather quickly, after all,
didn't they?' Pippin ventured to say after some time, when
for a moment the singing paused, and only the beating of
hands and feet was heard.

'Quickly?' said Treebeard. 'Hoom! Yes, indeed. Quicker
than I expected. Indeed I have not seen them roused like this
for many an age. We Ents do not like being roused; and we
never are roused unless it is clear to us that our trees and
our lives are in great danger. That has not happened in this
Forest since the wars of Sauron and the Men of the Sea. It
is the orc-work, the wanton hewing – *rárum* – without even
the bad excuse of feeding the fires, that has so angered us;
and the treachery of a neighbour, who should have helped
us. Wizards ought to know better: they do know better. There
is no curse in Elvish, Entish, or the tongues of Men bad
enough for such treachery. Down with Saruman!'

'Will you really break the doors of Isengard?' asked Merry.

'Ho, hm, well, we could, you know! You do not know,
perhaps, how strong we are. Maybe you have heard of Trolls?
They are mighty strong. But Trolls are only counterfeits,
made by the Enemy in the Great Darkness, in mockery of
Ents, as Orcs were of Elves. We are stronger than Trolls.
We are made of the bones of the earth. We can split stone
like the roots of trees, only quicker, far quicker, if our minds
are roused! If we are not hewn down, or destroyed by fire
or blast of sorcery, we could split Isengard into splinters and
crack its walls into rubble.'

'But Saruman will try to stop you, won't he?'

'Hm, ah, yes, that is so. I have not forgotten it. Indeed I
have thought long about it. But, you see, many of the Ents
are younger than I am, by many lives of trees. They are all
roused now, and their mind is all on one thing: breaking

Isengard. But they will start thinking again before long; they will cool down a little, when we take our evening drink. What a thirst we shall have! But let them march now and sing! We have a long way to go, and there is time ahead for thought. It is something to have started.'

Treebeard marched on, singing with the others for a while. But after a time his voice died to a murmur and fell silent again. Pippin could see that his old brow was wrinkled and knotted. At last he looked up, and Pippin could see a sad look in his eyes, sad but not unhappy. There was a light in them, as if the green flame had sunk deeper into the dark wells of his thought.

'Of course, it is likely enough, my friends,' he said slowly, 'likely enough that we are going to our doom: the last march of the Ents. But if we stayed at home and did nothing, doom would find us anyway, sooner or later. That thought has long been growing in our hearts; and that is why we are marching now. It was not a hasty resolve. Now at least the last march of the Ents may be worth a song. Aye,' he sighed, 'we may help the other peoples before we pass away. Still, I should have liked to see the songs come true about the Entwives. I should dearly have liked to see Fimbrethil again. But there, my friends, songs like trees bear fruit only in their own time and their own way: and sometimes they are withered untimely.'

The Ents went striding on at a great pace. They had descended into a long fold of the land that fell away southward; now they began to climb up, and up, on to the high western ridge. The woods fell away and they came to scattered groups of birch, and then to bare slopes where only a few gaunt pine-trees grew. The sun sank behind the dark hill-back in front. Grey dusk fell.

Pippin looked behind. The number of the Ents had grown – or what was happening? Where the dim bare slopes that they had crossed should lie, he thought he saw groves of trees. But they were moving! Could it be that the trees of

Fangorn were awake, and the forest was rising, marching over the hills to war? He rubbed his eyes wondering if sleep and shadow had deceived him; but the great grey shapes moved steadily onward. There was a noise like wind in many branches. The Ents were drawing near the crest of the ridge now, and all song had ceased. Night fell, and there was silence: nothing was to be heard save a faint quiver of the earth beneath the feet of the Ents, and a rustle, the shade of a whisper as of many drifting leaves. At last they stood upon the summit, and looked down into a dark pit: the great cleft at the end of the mountains: Nan Curunír, the Valley of Saruman.

'Night lies over Isengard,' said Treebeard.

CHAPTER V

THE WHITE RIDER

'My very bones are chilled,' said Gimli, flapping his arms and stamping his feet. Day had come at last. At dawn the companions had made such breakfast as they could; now in the growing light they were getting ready to search the ground again for signs of the hobbits.

'And do not forget that old man!' said Gimli. 'I should be happier if I could see the print of a boot.'

'Why would that make you happy?' said Legolas.

'Because an old man with feet that leave marks might be no more than he seemed,' answered the Dwarf.

'Maybe,' said the Elf; 'but a heavy boot might leave no print here: the grass is deep and springy.'

'That would not baffle a Ranger,' said Gimli. 'A bent blade is enough for Aragorn to read. But I do not expect him to find any traces. It was an evil phantom of Saruman that we saw last night. I am sure of it, even under the light of morning. His eyes are looking out on us from Fangorn even now, maybe.'

'It is likely enough,' said Aragorn; 'yet I am not sure. I am thinking of the horses. You said last night, Gimli, that they were scared away. But I did not think so. Did you hear them, Legolas? Did they sound to you like beasts in terror?'

'No,' said Legolas. 'I heard them clearly. But for the darkness and our own fear I should have guessed that they were beasts wild with some sudden gladness. They spoke as horses will when they meet a friend that they have long missed.'

'So I thought,' said Aragorn; 'but I cannot read the riddle, unless they return. Come! The light is growing fast. Let us look first and guess later! We should begin here, near to our own camping-ground, searching carefully all about, and working up the slope towards the forest. To find the hobbits is our errand, whatever we may think of our visitor in the night. If they escaped by some chance, then they must have hidden in the trees, or they would have been seen. If we find nothing between here and the eaves of the wood, then we will make a last search upon the battle-field and among the ashes. But there is little hope there: the horsemen of Rohan did their work too well.'

For some time the companions crawled and groped upon the ground. The tree stood mournfully above them, its dry leaves now hanging limp, and rattling in the chill easterly wind. Aragorn moved slowly away. He came to the ashes of the watch-fire near the river-bank, and then began to retrace the ground back towards the knoll where the battle had been fought. Suddenly he stooped and bent low with his face almost in the grass. Then he called to the others. They came running up.

'Here at last we find news!' said Aragorn. He lifted up a broken leaf for them to see, a large pale leaf of golden hue, now fading and turning brown. 'Here is a mallorn-leaf of Lórien, and there are small crumbs on it, and a few more crumbs in the grass. And see! there are some pieces of cut cord lying nearby!'

'And here is the knife that cut them!' said Gimli. He stooped and drew out of a tussock, into which some heavy foot had trampled it, a short jagged blade. The haft from which it had been snapped was beside it. 'It was an orc-weapon,' he said, holding it gingerly, and looking with disgust at the carved handle: it had been shaped like a hideous head with squinting eyes and leering mouth.

'Well, here is the strangest riddle that we have yet found!' exclaimed Legolas. 'A bound prisoner escapes both from the Orcs and from the surrounding horsemen. He then stops, while still in the open, and cuts his bonds with an orc-knife. But how and why? For if his legs were tied, how did he walk? And if his arms were tied, how did he use the knife? And if neither were tied, why did he cut the cords at all? Being pleased with his skill, he then sat down and quietly ate some waybread! That at least is enough to show that he was a hobbit, without the mallorn-leaf. After that, I suppose, he turned his arms into wings and flew away singing into the trees. It should be easy to find him: we only need wings ourselves!'

'There was sorcery here right enough,' said Gimli. 'What was that old man doing? What have you to say, Aragorn, to the reading of Legolas. Can you better it?'

'Maybe, I could,' said Aragorn, smiling. 'There are some other signs near at hand that you have not considered. I agree that the prisoner was a hobbit and must have had either legs or hands free, before he came here. I guess that it was hands, because the riddle then becomes easier, and also because, as I read the marks, he was *carried* to this point by an Orc. Blood was spilled there, a few paces away, orc-blood. There are deep prints of hoofs all about this spot, and signs that a heavy thing was dragged away. The Orc was slain by horsemen, and later his body was hauled to the fire. But the hobbit was not seen: he was not "in the open", for it was night and he still had his elven-cloak. He was exhausted and hungry, and it is not to be wondered at that, when he had cut his bonds with the knife of his fallen enemy, he rested and ate a little before he crept away. But it is a comfort to know that he had some *lembas* in his pocket, even though he ran away without gear or pack; that, perhaps, is like a hobbit. I say *he*, though I hope and guess that both Merry and Pippin were here together. There is, however, nothing to show that for certain.'

'And how do you suppose that either of our friends came to have a hand free?' asked Gimli.

'I do not know how it happened,' answered Aragorn. 'Nor do I know why an Orc was carrying them away. Not to help them to escape, we may be sure. Nay, rather I think that I now begin to understand a matter that has puzzled me from the beginning: why when Boromir had fallen were the Orcs content with the capture of Merry and Pippin? They did not seek out the rest of us, nor attack our camp; but instead they went with all speed towards Isengard. Did they suppose they had captured the Ring-bearer and his faithful comrade? I think not. Their masters would not dare to give such plain orders to Orcs, even if they knew so much themselves; they would not speak openly to them of the Ring: they are not trusty servants. But I think the Orcs had been commanded to capture *hobbits*, alive, at all costs. An attempt was made to slip out with the precious prisoners before the battle. Treachery perhaps, likely enough with such folk; some large and bold Orc may have been trying to escape with the prize alone, for his own ends. There, that is my tale. Others might be devised. But on this we may count in any case: one at least of our friends escaped. It is our task to find him and help him before we return to Rohan. We must not be daunted by Fangorn, since need drove him into that dark place.'

'I do not know which daunts me more: Fangorn, or the thought of the long road through Rohan on foot,' said Gimli.

'Then let us go to the forest,' said Aragorn.

It was not long before Aragorn found fresh signs. At one point, near the bank of the Entwash, he came upon footprints: hobbit-prints, but too light for much to be made of them. Then again beneath the bole of a great tree on the very edge of the wood more prints were discovered. The earth was bare and dry, and did not reveal much.

'One hobbit at least stood here for a while and looked back; and then he turned away into the forest,' said Aragorn.

'Then we must go in, too,' said Gimli. 'But I do not like the look of this Fangorn; and we were warned against it. I wish the chase had led anywhere else!'

'I do not think the wood feels evil, whatever tales may say,' said Legolas. He stood under the eaves of the forest, stooping forward, as if he were listening, and peering with wide eyes into the shadows. 'No, it is not evil; or what evil is in it is far away. I catch only the faintest echoes of dark places where the hearts of the trees are black. There is no malice near us; but there is watchfulness, and anger.'

'Well, it has no cause to be angry with me,' said Gimli. 'I have done it no harm.'

'That is just as well,' said Legolas. 'But nonetheless it has suffered harm. There is something happening inside, or going to happen. Do you not feel the tenseness? It takes my breath.'

'I feel the air is stuffy,' said the Dwarf. 'This wood is lighter than Mirkwood, but it is musty and shabby.'

'It is old, very old,' said the Elf. 'So old that almost I feel young again, as I have not felt since I journeyed with you children. It is old and full of memory. I could have been happy here, if I had come in days of peace.'

'I dare say you could,' snorted Gimli. 'You are a Wood-elf, anyway, though Elves of any kind are strange folk. Yet you comfort me. Where you go, I will go. But keep your bow ready to hand, and I will keep my axe loose in my belt. Not for use on trees,' he added hastily, looking up at the tree under which they stood. 'I do not wish to meet that old man at unawares without an argument ready to hand, that is all. Let us go!'

With that the three hunters plunged into the forest of Fangorn. Legolas and Gimli left the tracking to Aragorn. There was little for him to see. The floor of the forest was dry and covered with a drift of leaves; but guessing that the fugitives would stay near the water, he returned often to the banks of the stream. So it was that he came upon the place where Merry and Pippin had drunk and bathed their feet. There plain for all to see were the footprints of two hobbits, one somewhat smaller than the other.

'This is good tidings,' said Aragorn. 'Yet the marks are two days old. And it seems that at this point the hobbits left the water-side.'

'Then what shall we do now?' said Gimli. 'We cannot pursue them through the whole fastness of Fangorn. We have come ill supplied. If we do not find them soon, we shall be of no use to them, except to sit down beside them and show our friendship by starving together.'

'If that is indeed all we can do, then we must do that,' said Aragorn. 'Let us go on.'

They came at length to the steep abrupt end of Treebeard's Hill, and looked up at the rock-wall with its rough steps leading to the high shelf. Gleams of sun were striking through the hurrying clouds, and the forest now looked less grey and drear.

'Let us go up and look about us!' said Legolas. 'I still feel my breath short. I should like to taste a freer air for a while.'

The companions climbed up. Aragorn came last, moving slowly: he was scanning the steps and ledges closely.

'I am almost sure that the hobbits have been up here,' he said. 'But there are other marks, very strange marks, which I do not understand. I wonder if we can see anything from this ledge which will help us to guess which way they went next?'

He stood up and looked about, but he saw nothing that was of any use. The shelf faced southward and eastward; but only on the east was the view open. There he could see the heads of the trees descending in ranks towards the plain from which they had come.

'We have journeyed a long way round,' said Legolas. 'We could have all come here safe together, if we had left the Great River on the second or third day and struck west. Few can foresee whither their road will lead them, till they come to its end.'

'But we did not wish to come to Fangorn,' said Gimli.

'Yet here we are – and nicely caught in the net,' said Legolas. 'Look!'

'Look at what?' said Gimli.

'There in the trees.'

'Where? I have not elf-eyes.'

'Hush! Speak more softly! Look!' said Legolas pointing. 'Down in the wood, back in the way that we have just come.

It is he. Cannot you see him, passing from tree to tree?'

'I see, I see now!' hissed Gimli. 'Look, Aragorn! Did I not warn you? There is the old man. All in dirty grey rags: that is why I could not see him at first.'

Aragorn looked and beheld a bent figure moving slowly. It was not far away. It looked like an old beggar-man, walking wearily, leaning on a rough staff. His head was bowed, and he did not look towards them. In other lands they would have greeted him with kind words; but now they stood silent, each feeling a strange expectancy: something was approaching that held a hidden power – or menace.

Gimli gazed with wide eyes for a while, as step by step the figure drew nearer. Then suddenly, unable to contain himself longer, he burst out: 'Your bow, Legolas! Bend it! Get ready! It is Saruman. Do not let him speak, or put a spell upon us! Shoot first!'

Legolas took his bow and bent it, slowly and as if some other will resisted him. He held an arrow loosely in his hand but did not fit it to the string. Aragorn stood silent, his face was watchful and intent.

'Why are you waiting? What is the matter with you?' said Gimli in a hissing whisper.

'Legolas is right,' said Aragorn quietly. 'We may not shoot an old man so, at unawares and unchallenged, whatever fear or doubt be on us. Watch and wait!'

At that moment the old man quickened his pace and came with surprising speed to the foot of the rock-wall. Then suddenly he looked up, while they stood motionless looking down. There was no sound.

They could not see his face: he was hooded, and above the hood he wore a wide-brimmed hat, so that all his features were overshadowed, except for the end of his nose and his grey beard. Yet it seemed to Aragorn that he caught the gleam of eyes keen and bright from within the shadow of the hooded brows.

At last the old man broke the silence. 'Well met indeed,

my friends,' he said in a soft voice. 'I wish to speak to you. Will you come down, or shall I come up?' Without waiting for an answer he began to climb.

'Now!' cried Gimli. 'Stop him, Legolas!'

'Did I not say that I wished to speak to you?' said the old man. 'Put away that bow, Master Elf!'

The bow and arrow fell from Legolas' hands, and his arms hung loose at his sides.

'And you, Master Dwarf, pray take your hand from your axe-haft, till I am up! You will not need such arguments.'

Gimli started and then stood still as stone, staring, while the old man sprang up the rough steps as nimbly as a goat. All weariness seemed to have left him. As he stepped up on to the shelf there was a gleam, too brief for certainty, a quick glint of white, as if some garment shrouded by the grey rags had been for an instant revealed. The intake of Gimli's breath could be heard as a loud hiss in the silence.

'Well met, I say again!' said the old man, coming towards them. When he was a few feet away, he stood, stooping over his staff, with his head thrust forward, peering at them from under his hood. 'And what may you be doing in these parts? An Elf, a Man, and a Dwarf, all clad in elvish fashion. No doubt there is a tale worth hearing behind it all. Such things are not often seen here.'

'You speak as one that knows Fangorn well,' said Aragorn. 'Is that so?'

'Not well,' said the old man: 'that would be the study of many lives. But I come here now and again.'

'Might we know your name, and then hear what it is that you have to say to us?' said Aragorn. 'The morning passes, and we have an errand that will not wait.'

'As for what I wished to say, I have said it: What may you be doing, and what tale can you tell of yourselves? As for my name!' He broke off, laughing long and softly. Aragorn felt a shudder run through him at the sound, a strange cold thrill; and yet it was not fear or terror that he felt: rather it was like the sudden bite of a keen air, or the slap of a cold rain that wakes an uneasy sleeper.

'My name!' said the old man again. 'Have you not guessed it already? You have heard it before, I think. Yes, you have heard it before. But come now, what of your tale?'

The three companions stood silent and made no answer.

'There are some who would begin to doubt whether your errand is fit to tell,' said the old man. 'Happily I know something of it. You are tracking the footsteps of two young hobbits, I believe. Yes, hobbits. Don't stare, as if you had never heard the strange name before. You have, and so have I. Well, they climbed up here the day before yesterday; and they met someone that they did not expect. Does that comfort you? And now you would like to know where they were taken? Well, well, maybe I can give you some news about that. But why are we standing? Your errand, you see, is no longer as urgent as you thought. Let us sit down and be more at ease.'

The old man turned away and went towards a heap of fallen stones and rock at the foot of the cliff behind. Immediately, as if a spell had been removed, the others relaxed and stirred. Gimli's hand went at once to his axe-haft. Aragorn drew his sword. Legolas picked up his bow.

The old man took no notice, but stooped and sat himself on a low flat stone. Then his grey cloak drew apart, and they saw, beyond doubt, that he was clothed beneath all in white.

'Saruman!' cried Gimli, springing towards him with axe in hand. 'Speak! Tell us where you have hidden our friends! What have you done with them? Speak, or I will make a dint in your hat that even a wizard will find it hard to deal with!'

The old man was too quick for him. He sprang to his feet and leaped to the top of a large rock. There he stood, grown suddenly tall, towering above them. His hood and his grey rags were flung away. His white garments shone. He lifted up his staff, and Gimli's axe leaped from his grasp and fell ringing on the ground. The sword of Aragorn, stiff in his motionless hand, blazed with a sudden fire. Legolas gave a great shout and shot an arrow high into the air: it vanished in a flash of flame.

'Mithrandir!' he cried. 'Mithrandir!'

'Well met, I say to you again, Legolas!' said the old man.

They all gazed at him. His hair was white as snow in the sunshine; and gleaming white was his robe; the eyes under his deep brows were bright, piercing as the rays of the sun; power was in his hand. Between wonder, joy, and fear they stood and found no words to say.

At last Aragorn stirred. 'Gandalf!' he said. 'Beyond all hope you return to us in our need! What veil was over my sight? Gandalf!' Gimli said nothing, but sank to his knees, shading his eyes.

'Gandalf,' the old man repeated, as if recalling from old memory a long disused word. 'Yes, that was the name. I was Gandalf.'

He stepped down from the rock, and picking up his grey cloak wrapped it about him: it seemed as if the sun had been shining, but now was hid in cloud again. 'Yes, you may still call me Gandalf,' he said, and the voice was the voice of their old friend and guide. 'Get up, my good Gimli! No blame to you, and no harm done to me. Indeed my friends, none of you have any weapon that could hurt me. Be merry! We meet again. At the turn of the tide. The great storm is coming, but the tide has turned.'

He laid his hand on Gimli's head, and the Dwarf looked up and laughed suddenly. 'Gandalf!' he said. 'But you are all in white!'

'Yes, I am white now,' said Gandalf. 'Indeed I *am* Saruman, one might almost say, Saruman as he should have been. But come now, tell me of yourselves! I have passed through fire and deep water, since we parted. I have forgotten much that I thought I knew, and learned again much that I had forgotten. I can see many things far off, but many things that are close at hand I cannot see. Tell me of yourselves!'

* * *

'What do you wish to know?' said Aragorn. 'All that has happened since we parted on the bridge would be a long tale. Will you not first give us news of the hobbits? Did you find them, and are they safe?'

'No, I did not find them,' said Gandalf. 'There was a darkness over the valleys of the Emyn Muil, and I did not know of their captivity, until the eagle told me.'

'The eagle!' said Legolas. 'I have seen an eagle high and far off: the last time was three days ago, above the Emyn Muil.'

'Yes,' said Gandalf, 'that was Gwaihir the Windlord, who rescued me from Orthanc. I sent him before me to watch the River and gather tidings. His sight is keen, but he cannot see all that passes under hill and tree. Some things he has seen, and others I have seen myself. The Ring now has passed beyond my help, or the help of any of the Company that set out from Rivendell. Very nearly it was revealed to the Enemy, but it escaped. I had some part in that: for I sat in a high place, and I strove with the Dark Tower; and the Shadow passed. Then I was weary, very weary; and I walked long in dark thought.'

'Then you know about Frodo!' said Gimli. 'How do things go with him?'

'I cannot say. He was saved from a great peril, but many lie before him still. He resolved to go alone to Mordor, and he set out: that is all that I can say.'

'Not alone,' said Legolas. 'We think that Sam went with him.'

'Did he!' said Gandalf, and there was a gleam in his eye and a smile on his face. 'Did he indeed? It is news to me, yet it does not surprise me. Good! Very good! You lighten my heart. You must tell me more. Now sit by me and tell me the tale of your journey.'

The companions sat on the ground at his feet, and Aragorn took up the tale. For a long while Gandalf said nothing, and he asked no questions. His hands were spread upon his knees, and his eyes were closed. At last when Aragorn spoke of the death of Boromir and of his last journey upon the Great River, the old man sighed.

'You have not said all that you know or guess, Aragorn my friend,' he said quietly. 'Poor Boromir! I could not see what happened to him. It was a sore trial for such a man: a warrior, and a lord of men. Galadriel told me that he was in peril. But he escaped in the end. I am glad. It was not in vain that the young hobbits came with us, if only for Boromir's sake. But that is not the only part they have to play. They were brought to Fangorn, and their coming was like the falling of small stones that starts an avalanche in the mountains. Even as we talk here, I hear the first rumblings. Saruman had best not be caught away from home when the dam bursts!'

'In one thing you have not changed, dear friend,' said Aragorn: 'you still speak in riddles.'

'What? In riddles?' said Gandalf. 'No! For I was talking aloud to myself. A habit of the old: they choose the wisest person present to speak to; the long explanations needed by the young are wearying.' He laughed, but the sound now seemed warm and kindly as a gleam of sunshine.

'I am no longer young even in the reckoning of Men of the Ancient Houses,' said Aragorn. 'Will you not open your mind more clearly to me?'

'What then shall I say?' said Gandalf, and paused for a while in thought. 'This in brief is how I see things at the moment, if you wish to have a piece of my mind as plain as possible. The Enemy, of course, has long known that the Ring is abroad, and that it is borne by a hobbit. He knows now the number of our Company that set out from Rivendell, and the kind of each of us. But he does not yet perceive our purpose clearly. He supposes that we were all going to Minas Tirith; for that is what he would himself have done in our place. And according to his wisdom it would have been a heavy stroke against his power. Indeed he is in great fear, not knowing what mighty one may suddenly appear, wielding the Ring, and assailing him with war, seeking to cast him down and take his place. That we should wish to cast him down and have *no* one in his place is not a thought that occurs to his mind. That we should try to destroy the Ring itself has not yet entered into his darkest dream. In which no doubt you will see our good fortune and our hope. For imagining war he has let loose war, believing that he has no time to waste; for he that strikes the first blow, if he strikes it hard enough, may need to strike no more. So the forces that he has long been preparing he is now setting in motion, sooner than he intended. Wise fool. For if he had used all his power to guard Mordor, so that none could enter, and bent all his guile to the hunting of the Ring, then indeed hope would have faded: neither Ring nor bearer could long have eluded him. But now his eye gazes abroad rather than near at home; and mostly he looks towards Minas Tirith. Very soon now his strength will fall upon it like a storm.

'For already he knows that the messengers that he sent to waylay the Company have failed again. They have not found the Ring. Neither have they brought away any hobbits as hostages. Had they done even so much as that, it would have been a heavy blow to us, and it might have been fatal. But let us not darken our hearts by imagining the trial of their gentle loyalty in the Dark Tower. For the Enemy has failed – so far. Thanks to Saruman.'

'Then is not Saruman a traitor?' said Gimli.

'Indeed yes,' said Gandalf. 'Doubly. And is not that strange? Nothing that we have endured of late has seemed so grievous as the treason of Isengard. Even reckoned as a lord and captain Saruman has grown very strong. He threatens the Men of Rohan and draws off their help from Minas Tirith, even as the main blow is approaching from the East. Yet a treacherous weapon is ever a danger to the hand. Saruman also had a mind to capture the Ring, for himself, or at least to snare some hobbits for his evil purposes. So between them our enemies have contrived only to bring Merry and Pippin with marvellous speed, and in the nick of time, to Fangorn, where otherwise they would never have come at all!

'Also they have filled themselves with new doubts that disturb their plans. No tidings of the battle will come to Mordor, thanks to the horsemen of Rohan; but the Dark Lord knows that two hobbits were taken in the Emyn Muil and borne away towards Isengard against the will of his own servants. He now has Isengard to fear as well as Minas Tirith. If Minas Tirith falls, it will go ill with Saruman.'

'It is a pity that our friends lie in between,' said Gimli. 'If no land divided Isengard and Mordor, then they could fight while we watched and waited.'

'The victor would emerge stronger than either, and free from doubt,' said Gandalf. 'But Isengard cannot fight Mordor, unless Saruman first obtains the Ring. That he will never do now. He does not yet know his peril. There is much that he does not know. He was so eager to lay his hands on his prey that he could not wait at home, and he came forth to meet and to spy on his messengers. But he came too late, for once, and the battle was over and beyond his help before he reached these parts. He did not remain here long. I look into his mind and I see his doubt. He has no woodcraft. He believes that the horsemen slew and burned all upon the field of battle; but he does not know whether the Orcs were bringing any prisoners or not. And he does not know of the quarrel between his servants and the Orcs of Mordor; nor does he know of the Winged Messenger.'

'The Winged Messenger!' cried Legolas. 'I shot at him with the bow of Galadriel above Sarn Gebir, and I felled him from the sky. He filled us all with fear. What new terror is this?'

'One that you cannot slay with arrows,' said Gandalf. 'You only slew his steed. It was a good deed; but the Rider was soon horsed again. For he was a Nazgûl, one of the Nine, who ride now upon winged steeds. Soon their terror will overshadow the last armies of our friends, cutting off the sun. But they have not yet been allowed to cross the River, and Saruman does not know of this new shape in which the Ringwraiths have been clad. His thought is ever on the Ring. Was it present in the battle? Was it found? What if Théoden, Lord of the Mark, should come by it and learn of its power? That is the danger that he sees, and he has fled back to Isengard to double and treble his assault on Rohan. And all the time there is another danger, close at hand, which he does not see, busy with his fiery thoughts. He has forgotten Treebeard.'

'Now you speak to yourself again,' said Aragorn with a smile. 'Treebeard is not known to me. And I have guessed part of Saruman's double treachery; yet I do not see in what way the coming of two hobbits to Fangorn has served, save to give us a long and fruitless chase.'

'Wait a minute!' cried Gimli. 'There is another thing that I should like to know first. Was it you, Gandalf, or Saruman that we saw last night?'

'You certainly did not see me,' answered Gandalf, 'therefore I must guess that you saw Saruman. Evidently we look so much alike that your desire to make an incurable dent in my hat must be excused.'

'Good, good!' said Gimli. 'I am glad that it was not you.'

Gandalf laughed again. 'Yes, my good Dwarf,' he said, 'it is a comfort not to be mistaken at all points. Do I not know it only too well! But, of course, I never blamed you for your welcome of me. How could I do so, who have so often counselled my friends to suspect even their own hands when dealing with the Enemy. Bless you, Gimli, son of Glóin! Maybe you will see us both together one day and judge between us!'

'But the hobbits!' Legolas broke in. 'We have come far to seek them, and you seem to know where they are. Where are they now?'

'With Treebeard and the Ents,' said Gandalf.

'The Ents!' exclaimed Aragorn. 'Then there is truth in the old legends about the dwellers in the deep forests and the giant shepherds of the trees? Are there still Ents in the world?

I thought they were only a memory of ancient days, if indeed they were ever more than a legend of Rohan.'

'A legend of Rohan!' cried Legolas. 'Nay, every Elf in Wilderland has sung songs of the old Onodrim and their long sorrow. Yet even among us they are only a memory. If I were to meet one still walking in this world, then indeed I should feel young again! But Treebeard: that is only a rendering of Fangorn into the Common Speech; yet you seem to speak of a person. Who is this Treebeard?'

'Ah! now you are asking much,' said Gandalf. 'The little that I know of his long slow story would make a tale for which we have no time now. Treebeard is Fangorn, the guardian of the forest; he is the oldest of the Ents, the oldest living thing that still walks beneath the Sun upon this Middle-earth. I hope indeed, Legolas, that you may yet meet him. Merry and Pippin have been fortunate: they met him here, even where we sit. For he came here two days ago and bore them away to his dwelling far off by the roots of the mountains. He often comes here, especially when his mind is uneasy, and rumours of the world outside trouble him. I saw him four days ago striding among the trees, and I think he saw me, for he paused; but I did not speak, for I was heavy with thought, and weary after my struggle with the Eye of Mordor; and he did not speak either, nor call my name.'

'Perhaps he also thought that you were Saruman,' said Gimli. 'But you speak of him as if he was a friend. I thought Fangorn was dangerous.

'Dangerous!' cried Gandalf. 'And so am I, very dangerous: more dangerous than anything you will ever meet, unless you are brought alive before the seat of the Dark Lord. And Aragorn is dangerous, and Legolas is dangerous. You are beset with dangers, Gimli son of Glóin; for you are dangerous yourself, in your own fashion. Certainly the forest of Fangorn is perilous – not least to those that are too ready with their axes; and Fangorn himself, he is perilous too; yet he is wise and kindly nonetheless. But now his long slow wrath is brimming over, and all the forest is filled with it. The coming of the hobbits and the tidings that they brought have spilled it: it will soon be running like a flood; but its tide is turned against Saruman and the axes of Isengard. A thing is about to happen which has not happened since the Elder Days: the Ents are going to wake up and find that they are strong.'

'What will they do?' asked Legolas in astonishment.

'I do not know,' said Gandalf. 'I do not think they know themselves. I wonder.' He fell silent, his head bowed in thought.

The others looked at him. A gleam of sun through fleeting clouds fell on his hands, which lay now upturned on his lap: they seemed to be filled with light as a cup is with water. At last he looked up and gazed straight at the sun.

'The morning is wearing away,' he said. 'Soon we must go.'

'Do we go to find our friends and to see Treebeard?' asked Aragorn.

'No,' said Gandalf. 'That is not the road that you must take. I have spoken words of hope. But only of hope. Hope is not victory. War is upon us and all our friends, a war in which only the use of the Ring could give us surety of victory. It fills me with great sorrow and great fear: for much shall be destroyed and all may be lost. I am Gandalf, Gandalf the White, but Black is mightier still.'

He rose and gazed out eastward, shading his eyes, as if he saw things far away that none of them could see. Then he shook his head. 'No,' he said in a soft voice, 'it has gone beyond our reach. Of that at least let us be glad. We can no longer be tempted to use the Ring. We must go down to face a peril near despair, yet that deadly peril is removed.'

He turned. 'Come, Aragorn son of Arathorn!' he said. 'Do not regret your choice in the valley of the Emyn Muil, nor call it a vain pursuit. You chose amid doubts the path that seemed right: the choice was just, and it has been rewarded. For so we have met in time, who otherwise might have met too late. But the quest of your companions is over. Your next journey is marked by your given word. You must go to Edoras and seek out Théoden in his hall. For you are needed. The light of Andúril must now be uncovered in the battle for which it has so long waited. There is war in Rohan, and worse evil: it goes ill with Théoden.'

'Then are we not to see the merry young hobbits again?' said Legolas.

'I did not say so,' said Gandalf. 'Who knows? Have patience. Go where you must go, and hope! To Edoras! I go thither also.'

'It is a long way for a man to walk, young or old,' said Aragorn. 'I fear the battle will be over long ere I come there.'

'We shall see, we shall see,' said Gandalf. 'Will you come now with me?'

'Yes, we will set out together,' said Aragorn. 'But I do not doubt that you will come there before me, if you wish.' He rose and looked long at Gandalf. The others gazed at them in silence as they stood there facing one another. The grey figure of the Man, Aragorn son of Arathorn, was tall, and stern as stone, his hand upon the hilt of his sword; he looked as if some king out of the mists of the sea had stepped upon the shores of lesser men. Before him stooped the old figure, white, shining now as if with some light kindled within, bent, laden with years, but holding a power beyond the strength of kings.

'Do I not say truly, Gandalf,' said Aragorn at last, 'that you could go whithersoever you wished quicker than I? And this I also say: you are our captain and our banner. The Dark Lord has Nine. But we have One, mightier than they: the White Rider. He has passed through the fire and the abyss, and they shall fear him. We will go where he leads.'

'Yes, together we will follow you,' said Legolas. 'But first, it would ease my heart, Gandalf, to hear what befell you in Moria. Will you not tell us? Can you not stay even to tell your friends how you were delivered?'

'I have stayed already too long,' answered Gandalf. 'Time

is short. But if there were a year to spend, I would not tell you all.'

'Then tell us what you will, and time allows!' said Gimli. 'Come, Gandalf, tell us how you fared with the Balrog!'

'Name him not!' said Gandalf, and for a moment it seemed that a cloud of pain passed over his face, and he sat silent, looking old as death. 'Long time I fell,' he said at last, slowly, as if thinking back with difficulty. 'Long I fell, and he fell with me. His fire was about me. I was burned. Then we plunged into the deep water and all was dark. Cold it was as the tide of death: almost it froze my heart.'

'Deep is the abyss that is spanned by Durin's Bridge, and none has measured it,' said Gimli.

'Yet it has a bottom, beyond light and knowledge,' said Gandalf. 'Thither I came at last, to the uttermost foundations of stone. He was with me still. His fire was quenched, but now he was a thing of slime, stronger than a strangling snake.

'We fought far under the living earth, where time is not counted. Ever he clutched me, and ever I hewed him, till at last he fled into dark tunnels. They were not made by Durin's folk, Gimli son of Glóin. Far, far below the deepest delvings of the Dwarves, the world is gnawed by nameless things. Even Sauron knows them not. They are older than he. Now I have walked there, but I will bring no report to darken the light of day. In that despair my enemy was my only hope, and I pursued him, clutching at his heel. Thus he brought me back at last to the secret ways of Khazad-dûm: too well he knew them all. Ever up now we went, until we came to the Endless Stair.'

'Long has that been lost,' said Gimli. 'Many have said that it was never made save in legend, but others say that it was destroyed.'

'It was made, and it had not been destroyed,' said Gandalf. 'From the lowest dungeon to the highest peak it climbed, ascending in unbroken spiral in many thousand steps, until it issued at last in Durin's Tower carved in the living rock of Zirakzigil, the pinnacle of the Silvertine.

'There upon Celebdil was a lonely window in the snow, and before it lay a narrow space, a dizzy eyrie above the mists of the world. The sun shone fiercely there, but all below was wrapped in cloud. Out he sprang, and even as I came behind, he burst into new flame. There was none to see, or perhaps in after ages songs would still be sung of the Battle of the Peak.' Suddenly Gandalf laughed. 'But what would they say in song? Those that looked up from afar thought that the mountain was crowned with storm. Thunder they heard, and lightning, they said, smote upon Celebdil, and leaped back broken into tongues of fire. Is not that enough? A great smoke rose about us, vapour and steam. Ice fell like rain. I threw down my enemy, and he fell from the high place and broke the mountain-side where he smote it in his ruin. Then darkness took me, and I strayed out of thought and time, and I wandered far on roads that I will not tell.

'Naked I was sent back – for a brief time, until my task is done. And naked I lay upon the mountain-top. The tower behind was crumbled into dust, the window gone; the ruined stair was choked with burned and broken stone. I was alone, forgotten, without escape upon the hard horn of the world. There I lay staring upward, while the stars wheeled over, and each day was as long as a life-age of the earth. Faint to my ears came the gathered rumour of all lands: the springing and the dying, the song and the weeping, and the slow ever-lasting groan of overburdened stone. And so at the last Gwaihir the Windlord found me again, and he took me up and bore me away.

'"Ever am I fated to be your burden, friend at need," I said.

'"A burden you have been," he answered, "but not so now. Light as a swan's feather in my claw you are. The Sun shines through you. Indeed I do not think you need me any more: were I to let you fall, you would float upon the wind."

'"Do not let me fall!" I gasped, for I felt life in me again. "Bear me to Lothlórien!"

' "That indeed is the command of the Lady Galadriel who sent me to look for you," he answered.

'Thus it was that I came to Caras Galadhon and found you but lately gone. I tarried there in the ageless time of that land where days bring healing not decay. Healing I found, and I was clothed in white. Counsel I gave and counsel took. Thence by strange roads I came, and messages I bring to some of you. To Aragorn I was bidden to say this:

> *Where now are the Dúnedain, Elessar, Elessar?*
> *Why do thy kinsfolk wander afar?*
> *Near is the hour when the Lost should come forth,*
> *And the Grey Company ride from the North.*
> *But dark is the path appointed for thee:*
> *The Dead watch the road that leads to the Sea.*

To Legolas she sent this word:

> *Legolas Greenleaf long under tree*
> *In joy thou hast lived. Beware of the Sea!*
> *If thou hearest the cry of the gull on the shore,*
> *Thy heart shall then rest in the forest no more.*'

Gandalf fell silent and shut his eyes.

'Then she sent me no message?' said Gimli and bent his head.

'Dark are her words,' said Legolas, 'and little do they mean to those that receive them.'

'That is no comfort,' said Gimli.

'What then?' said Legolas. 'Would you have her speak openly to you of your death?'

'Yes, if she had nought else to say.'

'What is that?' said Gandalf, opening his eyes. 'Yes, I think I can guess what her words may mean. Your pardon, Gimli! I was pondering the messages once again. But indeed she sent words to you, and neither dark nor sad.

' "To Gimli son of Glóin," she said, "give his Lady's greeting. Lockbearer, wherever thou goest my thought goes with thee. But have a care to lay thine axe to the right tree!"'

'In happy hour you have returned to us, Gandalf,' cried the Dwarf, capering as he sang loudly in the strange dwarf-tongue. 'Come, come!' he shouted, swinging his axe. 'Since Gandalf's head is now sacred, let us find one that it is right to cleave!'

'That will not be far to seek,' said Gandalf, rising from his seat. 'Come! We have spent all the time that is allowed to a meeting of parted friends. Now there is need of haste.'

He wrapped himself again in his old tattered cloak, and led the way. Following him they descended quickly from the high shelf and made their way back through the forest, down the bank of the Entwash. They spoke no more words, until they stood again upon the grass beyond the eaves of Fangorn. There was no sign of their horses to be seen.

'They have not returned,' said Legolas. 'It will be a weary walk!'

'I shall not walk. Time presses,' said Gandalf. Then lifting up his head he gave a long whistle. So clear and piercing was the note that the others stood amazed to hear such a sound come from those old bearded lips. Three times he whistled; and then faint and far off it seemed to them that they heard the whinny of a horse borne up from the plains upon the eastern wind. They waited wondering. Before long there came the sound of hoofs, at first hardly more than a tremor of the ground perceptible only to Aragorn as he lay upon the grass, then growing steadily louder and clearer to a quick beat.

'There is more than one horse coming,' said Aragorn.

'Certainly,' said Gandalf. 'We are too great a burden for one.'

'There are three,' said Legolas, gazing out over the plain. 'See how they run! There is Hasufel, and there is my friend Arod beside him! But there is another that strides ahead: a very great horse. I have not seen his like before.'

'Nor will you again,' said Gandalf. 'That is Shadowfax. He is the chief of the *Mearas*, lords of horses, and not even Théoden, King of Rohan, has ever looked on a better. Does he not shine like silver, and run as smoothly as a swift stream? He has come for me: the horse of the White Rider. We are going to battle together.'

Even as the old wizard spoke, the great horse came striding up the slope towards them; his coat was glistening and his mane flowing in the wind of his speed. The two others followed, now far behind. As soon as Shadowfax saw Gandalf, he checked his pace and whinnied loudly; then trotting gently forward he stooped his proud head and nuzzled his great nostrils against the old man's neck.

Gandalf caressed him. 'It is a long way from Rivendell, my friend,' he said; 'but you are wise and swift and come at need. Far let us ride now together, and part not in this world again!'

Soon the other horses came up and stood quietly by, as if awaiting orders. 'We go at once to Meduseld, the hall of your master, Théoden,' said Gandalf, addressing them gravely. They bowed their heads. 'Time presses, so with your leave, my friends, we will ride. We beg you to use all the speed that you can. Hasufel shall bear Aragorn and Arod Legolas. I will set Gimli before me, and by his leave Shadowfax shall bear us both. We will wait now only to drink a little.'

'Now I understand a part of last night's riddle,' said Legolas as he sprang lightly upon Arod's back. 'Whether they fled at first in fear, or not, our horses met Shadowfax, their chieftain, and greeted him with joy. Did you know that he was at hand, Gandalf?'

'Yes, I knew,' said the wizard. 'I bent my thought upon him, bidding him to make haste; for yesterday he was far away in the south of this land. Swiftly may he bear me back again!'

Gandalf spoke now to Shadowfax, and the horse set off at a good pace, yet not beyond the measure of the others. After a little while he turned suddenly, and choosing a place where the banks were lower, he waded the river, and then led them away due south into a flat land, treeless and wide. The wind went like grey waves through the endless miles of grass. There was no sign of road or track, but Shadowfax did not stay or falter.

'He is steering a straight course now for the halls of Théoden under the slopes of the White Mountains,' said Gandalf. 'It will be quicker so. The ground is firmer in the Eastemnet, where the chief northward track lies, across the river, but Shadowfax knows the way through every fen and hollow.'

For many hours they rode on through the meads and riverlands. Often the grass was so high that it reached above the knees of the riders, and their steeds seemed to be swimming in a grey-green sea. They came upon many hidden pools, and broad acres of sedge waving above wet and treacherous bogs; but Shadowfax found the way, and the other horses followed in his swath. Slowly the sun fell from the sky down into the West. Looking out over the great plain, far away the riders saw it for a moment like a red fire sinking into the grass. Low upon the edge of sight shoulders of the mountains glinted red upon either side. A smoke seemed to rise up and darken the sun's disc to the hue of blood, as if it had kindled the grass as it passed down under the rim of earth.

'There lies the Gap of Rohan,' said Gandalf. 'It is now almost due west of us. That way lies Isengard.'

'I see a great smoke,' said Legolas. 'What may that be?'

'Battle and war!' said Gandalf. 'Ride on!'

CHAPTER VI

THE KING OF THE GOLDEN HALL

They rode on through sunset, and slow dusk, and gathering night. When at last they halted and dismounted, even Aragorn was stiff and weary. Gandalf only allowed them a few hours' rest. Legolas and Gimli slept, and Aragorn lay flat, stretched upon his back; but Gandalf stood, leaning on his staff, gazing into the darkness, east and west. All was silent, and there was no sign or sound of living thing. The night was barred with long clouds, fleeting on a chill wind, when they arose again. Under the cold moon they went on once more, as swift as by the light of day.

Hours passed and still they rode on. Gimli nodded and would have fallen from his seat, if Gandalf had not clutched and shaken him. Hasufel and Arod, weary but proud, followed their tireless leader, a grey shadow before them hardly to be seen. The miles went by. The waxing moon sank into the cloudy West.

A bitter chill came into the air. Slowly in the East the dark faded to a cold grey. Red shafts of light leapt above the black walls of the Emyn Muil far away upon their left. Dawn came clear and bright; a wind swept across their path, rushing through the bent grasses. Suddenly Shadowfax stood still and neighed. Gandalf pointed ahead.

'Look!' he cried, and they lifted their tired eyes. Before them stood the mountains of the South: white-tipped and streaked with black. The grass-lands rolled against the hills that clustered at their feet, and flowed up into many valleys still dim and dark, untouched by the light of dawn, winding their way into the heart of the great mountains. Immediately before the travellers the widest of these glens opened like a long gulf among the hills. Far inward they glimpsed a tumbled mountain-mass with one tall peak; at the mouth of the vale there stood like a sentinel a lonely height. About its feet there flowed, as a thread of silver, the stream that issued from the dale; upon its brow they caught, still far away, a glint in the rising sun, a glimmer of gold.

'Speak, Legolas!' said Gandalf. 'Tell us what you see there before us!'

Legolas gazed ahead, shading his eyes from the level shafts of the new-risen sun. 'I see a white stream that comes down from the snows,' he said. 'Where it issues from the shadow of the vale a green hill rises upon the east. A dike and mighty wall and thorny fence encircle it. Within there rise the roofs of houses; and in the midst, set upon a green terrace, there stands aloft a great hall of Men. And it seems to my eyes that it is thatched with gold. The light of it shines far over the land. Golden, too, are the posts of its doors. There men in bright mail stand; but all else within the courts are yet asleep.'

'Edoras those courts are called,' said Gandalf, 'and Meduseld is that golden hall. There dwells Théoden son of Thengel, King of the Mark of Rohan. We are come with the rising of the day. Now the road lies plain to see before us. But we must ride more warily; for war is abroad, and the Rohirrim, the Horse-lords, do not sleep, even if it seem so from afar. Draw no weapon, speak no haughty word, I counsel you all, until we are come before Théoden's seat.'

The morning was bright and clear about them, and birds were singing, when the travellers came to the stream. It ran down swiftly into the plain, and beyond the feet of the hills turned across their path in a wide bend, flowing away east to feed the Entwash far off in its reed-choked beds. The land was green: in the wet meads and along the grassy borders of the stream grew many willow-trees. Already in this southern land they were blushing red at their fingertips, feeling the approach of spring. Over the stream there was a ford between low banks much trampled by the passage of horses. The travellers passed over and came upon a wide rutted track leading towards the uplands.

At the foot of the walled hill the way ran under the shadow of many mounds, high and green. Upon their western sides the grass was white as with a drifted snow: small flowers sprang there like countless stars amid the turf.

'Look!' said Gandalf. 'How fair are the bright eyes in the grass! Evermind they are called, *simbelmynë* in this land of Men, for they blossom in all the seasons of the year, and grow where dead men rest. Behold! we are come to the great barrows where the sires of Théoden sleep.'

'Seven mounds upon the left, and nine upon the right,' said Aragorn. 'Many long lives of men it is since the golden hall was built.'

'Five hundred times have the red leaves fallen in Mirkwood in my home since then,' said Legolas, 'and but a little while does that seem to us.'

'But to the Riders of the Mark it seems so long ago,' said Aragorn, 'that the raising of this house is but a memory of song, and the years before are lost in the mist of time. Now they call this land their home, their own, and their speech is sundered from their northern kin.' Then he began to chant softly in a slow tongue unknown to the Elf and Dwarf; yet they listened, for there was a strong music in it.

'That, I guess, is the language of the Rohirrim,' said Legolas; 'for it is like to this land itself; rich and rolling in part, and else hard and stern as the mountains. But I cannot guess what it means, save that it is laden with the sadness of Mortal Men.'

'It runs thus in the Common Speech,' said Aragorn, 'as near as I can make it.

> *Where now the horse and the rider? Where is the horn that*
> *was blowing?*
> *Where is the helm and the hauberk, and the bright hair*
> *flowing?*

Where is the hand on the harpstring, and the red fire
  glowing?
Where is the spring and the harvest and the tall corn
  growing?
They have passed like rain on the mountain, like a wind in
  the meadow;
The days have gone down in the West behind the hills into
  shadow.
Who shall gather the smoke of the dead wood burning,
Or behold the flowing years from the Sea returning?

Thus spoke a forgotten poet long ago in Rohan, recalling how tall and fair was Eorl the Young, who rode down out of the North; and there were wings upon the feet of his steed, Felaróf, father of horses. So men still sing in the evening.'

With these words the travellers passed the silent mounds. Following the winding way up the green shoulders of the hills, they came at last to the wide wind-swept walls and the gates of Edoras.

There sat many men in bright mail, who sprang at once to their feet and barred the way with spears. 'Stay, strangers here unknown!' they cried in the tongue of the Riddermark, demanding the names and errand of the strangers. Wonder was in their eyes but little friendliness; and they looked darkly upon Gandalf.

'Well do I understand your speech,' he answered in the same language; 'yet few strangers do so. Why then do you not speak in the Common Tongue, as is the custom in the West, if you wish to be answered?'

'It is the will of Théoden King that none should enter his gates, save those who know our tongue and are our friends,' replied one of the guards. 'None are welcome here in days of war but our own folk, and those that come from Mundburg in the land of Gondor. Who are you that come heedless over the plain thus strangely clad, riding horses like to our own horses? Long have we kept guard here, and we have watched you from afar. Never have we seen other riders so strange, nor any horse more proud than is one of these that bear you. He is one of the *Mearas*, unless our eyes are cheated by some spell. Say, are you not a wizard, some spy from Saruman, or phantoms of his craft? Speak now and be swift!'

'We are no phantoms,' said Aragorn, 'nor do your eyes cheat you. For indeed these are your own horses that we ride, as you knew well ere you asked, I guess. But seldom does thief ride home to the stable. Here are Hasufel and Arod, that Éomer, the Third Marshal of the Mark, lent to us, only two days ago. We bring them back now, even as we promised him. Has not Éomer then returned and given warning of our coming?'

A troubled look came into the guard's eyes. 'Of Éomer I have naught to say,' he answered. 'If what you tell me is truth, then doubtless Théoden will have heard of it. Maybe your coming was not wholly unlooked-for. It is but two nights ago that Wormtongue came to us and said that by the will of Théoden no stranger should pass these gates.'

'Wormtongue?' said Gandalf, looking sharply at the guard. 'Say no more! My errand is not to Wormtongue, but to the Lord of the Mark himself. I am in haste. Will you not go or send to say that we are come?' His eyes glinted under his deep brows as he bent his gaze upon the man.

'Yes, I will go,' he answered slowly. 'But what names shall I report? And what shall I say of you? Old and weary you seem now, and yet you are fell and grim beneath, I deem.'

'Well do you see and speak,' said the wizard. 'For I am Gandalf. I have returned. And behold! I too bring back a horse. Here is Shadowfax the Great, whom no other hand can tame. And here beside me is Aragorn son of Arathorn, the heir of Kings, and it is to Mundburg that he goes. Here also are Legolas the Elf and Gimli the Dwarf, our comrades. Go now and say to your master that we are at his gates and would have speech with him, if he will permit us to come into his hall.'

'Strange names you give indeed! But I will report them as you bid, and learn my master's will,' said the guard. 'Wait here a little while, and I will bring you such answer as seems good to him. Do not hope too much! These are dark days.' He went swiftly away, leaving the strangers in the watchful keeping of his comrades.

After some time he returned. 'Follow me!' he said. 'Théoden gives you leave to enter; but any weapon that you bear, be it only a staff, you must leave on the threshold. The doorwardens will keep them.'

The dark gates were swung open. The travellers entered, walking in file behind their guide. They found a broad path, paved with hewn stones, now winding upward, now climbing in short flights of well-laid steps. Many houses built of wood and many dark doors they passed. Beside the way in a stone channel a stream of clear water flowed, sparkling and chattering. At length they came to the crown of the hill. There stood a high platform above a green terrace, at the foot of which a bright spring gushed from a stone carved in the likeness of a horse's head; beneath was a wide basin from which the water spilled and fed the falling stream. Up the green terrace went a stair of stone, high and broad, and on either side of the topmost step were stone-hewn seats. There sat other guards, with drawn swords laid upon their knees. Their golden hair was braided on their shoulders; the sun was blazoned upon their green shields, their long corslets were burnished bright, and when they rose taller they seemed than mortal men.

'There are the doors before you,' said the guide. 'I must return now to my duty at the gate. Farewell! And may the Lord of the Mark be gracious to you!'

He turned and went swiftly back down the road. The others climbed the long stair under the eyes of the tall watchmen. Silent they stood now above and spoke no word, until Gandalf stepped out upon the paved terrace at the stair's head. Then suddenly with clear voices they spoke a courteous greeting in their own tongue.

'Hail, comers from afar!' they said, and they turned the hilts of their swords towards the travellers in token of peace. Green gems flashed in the sunlight. Then one of the guards stepped forward and spoke in the Common Speech.

'I am the Doorward of Théoden,' he said. 'Háma is my name. Here I must bid you lay aside your weapons before you enter.'

Then Legolas gave into his hand his silver-hafted knife, his quiver, and his bow. 'Keep these well,' he said, 'for they come from the Golden Wood and the Lady of Lothlórien gave them to me.'

Wonder came into the man's eyes, and he laid the weapons hastily by the wall, as if he feared to handle them. 'No man will touch them, I promise you,' he said.

Aragorn stood a while hesitating. 'It is not my will,' he said, 'to put aside my sword or to deliver Andúril to the hand of any other man.'

'It is the will of Théoden,' said Háma.

'It is not clear to me that the will of Théoden son of Thengel, even though he be lord of the Mark, should prevail over the will of Aragorn son of Arathorn, Elendil's heir of Gondor.'

'This is the house of Théoden, not of Aragorn, even were he King of Gondor in the seat of Denethor,' said Háma, stepping swiftly before the doors and barring the way. His sword was now in his hand and the point towards the strangers.

'This is idle talk,' said Gandalf. 'Needless is Théoden's demand, but it is useless to refuse. A king will have his way in his own hall, be it folly or wisdom.'

'Truly,' said Aragorn. 'And I would do as the master of the house bade me, were this only a woodman's cot, if I bore now any sword but Andúril.'

'Whatever its name may be,' said Háma, 'here you shall lay it, if you would not fight alone against all the men in Edoras.'

'Not alone!' said Gimli, fingering the blade of his axe, and looking darkly up at the guard, as if he were a young tree that Gimli had a mind to fell. 'Not alone!'

'Come, come!' said Gandalf. 'We are all friends here. Or should be; for the laughter of Mordor will be our only reward, if we quarrel. My errand is pressing. Here at least is *my* sword, goodman Háma. Keep it well. Glamdring it is called, for the Elves made it long ago. Now let me pass. Come, Aragorn!'

Slowly Aragorn unbuckled his belt and himself set his sword upright against the wall. 'Here I set it,' he said; 'but I command you not to touch it, nor to permit any other to lay hand on it. In this elvish sheath dwells the Blade that was Broken and has been made again. Telchar first wrought it in the deeps of time. Death shall come to any man that draws Elendil's sword save Elendil's heir.'

The guard stepped back and looked with amazement on Aragorn. 'It seems that you are come on the wings of song out of the forgotten days,' he said. 'It shall be, lord, as you command.'

'Well,' said Gimli, 'if it has Andúril to keep it company, my axe may stay here, too, without shame'; and he laid it on the floor. 'Now then, if all is as you wish, let us go and speak with your master.'

The guard still hesitated. 'Your staff,' he said to Gandalf. 'Forgive me, but that too must be left at the doors.'

'Foolishness!' said Gandalf. 'Prudence is one thing, but discourtesy is another. I am old. If I may not lean on my stick as I go, then I will sit out here, until it pleases Théoden to hobble out himself to speak with me.'

Aragorn laughed. 'Every man has something too dear to trust to another. But would you part an old man from his support? Come, will you not let us enter?'

'The staff in the hand of a wizard may be more than a prop for age,' said Háma. He looked hard at the ash-staff on which Gandalf leaned. 'Yet in doubt a man of worth will trust to his own wisdom. I believe you are friends and folk worthy of honour, who have no evil purpose. You may go in.'

The guards now lifted the heavy bars of the doors and swung them slowly inwards grumbling on their great hinges. The travellers entered. Inside it seemed dark and warm after the clear air upon the hill. The hall was long and wide and filled with shadows and half lights; mighty pillars upheld its lofty roof. But here and there bright sunbeams fell in glimmering shafts from the eastern windows, high under the deep eaves. Through the louver in the roof, above the thin wisps of issuing smoke, the sky showed pale and blue. As their eyes changed, the travellers perceived that the floor was paved with stones of many hues; branching runes and strange devices intertwined beneath their feet. They saw now that the pillars were richly carved, gleaming dully with gold and half-seen colours. Many woven cloths were hung upon the walls, and over their wide spaces marched figures of ancient legend, some dim with years, some darkling in the shade. But upon one form the sunlight fell: a young man upon a white horse. He was blowing a great horn, and his yellow hair was flying in the wind. The horse's head was lifted, and its nostrils were wide and red as it neighed, smelling battle afar. Foaming water, green and white, rushed and curled about its knees.

'Behold Eorl the Young!' said Aragorn. 'Thus he rode out of the North to the Battle of the Field of Celebrant.'

Now the four companions went forward, past the clear wood-fire burning upon the long hearth in the midst of the hall. Then they halted. At the far end of the house, beyond the hearth and facing north towards the doors, was a dais with three steps; and in the middle of the dais was a great gilded chair. Upon it sat a man so bent with age that he seemed almost a dwarf; but his white hair was long and thick and fell in great braids from beneath a thin golden circlet set upon his brow. In the centre upon his forehead shone a single white diamond. His beard was laid like snow upon his knees; but his eyes still burned with a bright light, glinting as he gazed at the strangers. Behind his chair stood a woman clad in white. At his feet upon the steps sat a wizened figure of a man, with a pale wise face and heavy-lidded eyes.

There was a silence. The old man did not move in his chair. At length Gandalf spoke. 'Hail, Théoden son of Thengel! I have returned. For behold! the storm comes, and now all friends should gather together, lest each singly be destroyed.'

Slowly the old man rose to his feet, leaning heavily upon a short black staff with a handle of white bone; and now the strangers saw that, bent though he was, he was still tall and must in youth have been high and proud indeed.

'I greet you,' he said, 'and maybe you look for welcome. But truth to tell your welcome is doubtful here, Master Gandalf. You have ever been a herald of woe. Troubles follow you like crows, and ever the oftener the worse. I will not deceive you: when I heard that Shadowfax had come back riderless, I rejoiced at the return of the horse, but still more at the lack of the rider; and when Éomer brought the tidings that you had gone at last to your long home, I did not mourn. But news from afar is seldom sooth. Here you come again! And with you come evils worse than before, as might be expected. Why should I welcome you, Gandalf Stormcrow? Tell me that.' Slowly he sat down again in his chair.

'You speak justly, lord,' said the pale man sitting upon the steps of the dais. 'It is not yet five days since the bitter tidings came that Théodred your son was slain upon the West Marches: your right-hand, Second Marshal of the Mark. In Éomer there is little trust. Few men would be left to guard your walls, if he had been allowed to rule. And even now we learn from Gondor that the Dark Lord is stirring in the East. Such is the hour in which this wanderer chooses to return. Why indeed should we welcome you, Master Stormcrow? *Láthspell* I name you, Ill-news; and ill news is an ill guest they say.' He laughed grimly, as he lifted his heavy lids for a moment and gazed on the strangers with dark eyes.

'You are held wise, my friend Wormtongue, and are doubtless a great support to your master,' answered Gandalf in a soft voice. 'Yet in two ways may a man come with evil tidings. He may be a worker of evil; or he may be such as leaves well alone, and comes only to bring aid in time of need.'

'That is so,' said Wormtongue; 'but there is a third kind: pickers of bones, meddlers in other men's sorrows, carrionfowl that grow fat on war. What aid have you ever brought, Stormcrow? And what aid do you bring now? It was aid from us that you sought last time that you were here. Then my lord bade you choose any horse that you would and be gone; and to the wonder of all you took Shadowfax in your insolence. My lord was sorely grieved; yet to some it seemed that to speed you from the land the price was not too great. I guess that it is likely to turn out the same once more: you will seek aid rather than render it. Do you bring men? Do you bring horses, swords, spears? That I would call aid; that is our present need. But who are these that follow at your tail? Three ragged wanderers in grey, and you yourself the most beggar-like of the four!'

'The courtesy of your hall is somewhat lessened of late, Théoden son of Thengel,' said Gandalf. 'Has not the messenger from your gate reported the names of my companions? Seldom has any lord of Rohan received three such guests. Weapons they have laid at your doors that are worth many a mortal man, even the mightiest. Grey is their raiment, for the Elves clad them, and thus they have passed through the shadow of great perils to your hall.'

'Then it is true, as Éomer reported, that you are in league with the Sorceress of the Golden Wood?' said Wormtongue. 'It is not to be wondered at: webs of deceit were ever woven in Dwimordene.'

Gimli strode a pace forward, but felt suddenly the hand of Gandalf clutch him by the shoulder, and he halted, standing stiff as stone.

In Dwimordene, in Lórien
Seldom have walked the feet of Men,
Few mortal eyes have seen the light
That lies there ever, long and bright.
Galadriel! Galadriel!
Clear is the water of your well;
White is the star in your white hand;
Unmarred, unstained is leaf and land
In Dwimordene, in Lórien
More fair than thoughts of Mortal Men.

Thus Gandalf softly sang, and then suddenly he changed. Casting his tattered cloak aside, he stood up and leaned no longer on his staff; and he spoke in a clear cold voice.

'The wise speak only of what they know, Gríma son of Gálmód. A witless worm have you become. Therefore be silent, and keep your forked tongue behind your teeth. I have not passed through fire and death to bandy crooked words with a serving-man till the lightning falls.'

He raised his staff. There was a roll of thunder. The sunlight was blotted out from the eastern windows; the whole hall became suddenly dark as night. The fire faded to sullen embers. Only Gandalf could be seen, standing white and tall before the blackened hearth.

In the gloom they heard the hiss of Wormtongue's voice: 'Did I not counsel you, lord, to forbid his staff? That fool, Háma, has betrayed us!' There was a flash as if lightning had cloven the roof. Then all was silent. Wormtongue sprawled on his face.

'Now Théoden son of Thengel, will you hearken to me?' said Gandalf. 'Do you ask for help?' He lifted his staff and pointed to a high window. There the darkness seemed to clear, and through the opening could be seen, high and far, a patch of shining sky. 'Not all is dark. Take courage, Lord of the Mark; for better help you will not find. No counsel have I to give to those that despair. Yet counsel I could give,

and words I could speak to you. Will you hear them? They
are not for all ears. I bid you come out before your doors
and look abroad. Too long have you sat in shadows and
trusted to twisted tales and crooked promptings.'

Slowly Théoden left his chair. A faint light grew in the hall
again. The woman hastened to the king's side, taking his
arm, and with faltering steps the old man came down from
the dais and paced softly through the hall. Wormtongue
remained lying on the floor. They came to the doors and
Gandalf knocked.

'Open!' he cried. 'The Lord of the Mark comes forth!'

The doors rolled back and a keen air came whistling in. A
wind was blowing on the hill.

'Send your guards down to the stairs' foot,' said Gandalf.
'And you, lady, leave him a while with me. I will care for him.'

'Go, Éowyn sister-daughter!' said the old king. 'The time
for fear is past.'

The woman turned and went slowly into the house. As
she passed the doors she turned and looked back. Grave and
thoughtful was her glance, as she looked on the king with
cool pity in her eyes. Very fair was her face, and her long
hair was like a river of gold. Slender and tall she was in her
white robe girt with silver; but strong she seemed and stern
as steel, a daughter of kings. Thus Aragorn for the first time
in the full light of day beheld Éowyn, Lady of Rohan, and
thought her fair, fair and cold, like a morning of pale spring
that is not yet come to womanhood. And she now was suddenly aware of him: tall heir of kings, wise with many winters,
greycloaked, hiding a power that yet she felt. For a moment
still as stone she stood, then turning swiftly she was gone.

'Now, lord,' said Gandalf, 'look out upon your land!
Breathe the free air again!'

From the porch upon the top of the high terrace they could
see beyond the stream the green fields of Rohan fading into
distant grey. Curtains of wind-blown rain were slanting
down. The sky above and to the west was still dark with
thunder, and lightning far away flickered among the tops of

hidden hills. But the wind had shifted to the north, and already the storm that had come out of the East was receding, rolling away southward to the sea. Suddenly through a rent in the clouds behind them a shaft of sun stabbed down. The falling showers gleamed like silver, and far away the river glittered like a shimmering glass.

'It is not so dark here,' said Théoden.

'No,' said Gandalf. 'Nor does age lie so heavily on your shoulders as some would have you think. Cast aside your prop!'

From the king's hand the black staff fell clattering on the stones. He drew himself up, slowly, as a man that is stiff from long bending over some dull toil. Now tall and straight he stood, and his eyes were blue as he looked into the opening sky.

'Dark have been my dreams of late,' he said, 'but I feel as one new-awakened. I would now that you had come before, Gandalf. For I fear that already you have come too late, only to see the last days of my house. Not long now shall stand the high hall which Brego son of Eorl built. Fire shall devour the high seat. What is to be done?'

'Much,' said Gandalf. 'But first send for Éomer. Do I not guess rightly that you hold him prisoner, by the counsel of Gríma, of him that all save you name the Wormtongue?'

'It is true,' said Théoden. 'He had rebelled against my commands, and threatened death to Gríma in my hall.'

'A man may love you and yet not love Wormtongue or his counsels,' said Gandalf.

'That may be. I will do as you ask. Call Háma to me. Since he proved untrusty as a doorward, let him become an errand-runner. The guilty shall bring the guilty to judgement,' said Théoden, and his voice was grim, yet he looked at Gandalf and smiled and as he did so many lines of care were smoothed away and did not return.

When Háma had been summoned and had gone, Gandalf led Théoden to a stone seat, and then sat himself before the king upon the topmost stair. Aragorn and his companions stood nearby.

'There is no time to tell all that you should hear,' said Gandalf. 'Yet if my hope is not cheated, a time will come ere long when I can speak more fully. Behold! you are come into a peril greater even than the wit of Wormtongue could weave into your dreams. But see! you dream no longer. You live. Gondor and Rohan do not stand alone. The enemy is strong beyond our reckoning, yet we have a hope at which he has not guessed.'

Quickly now Gandalf spoke. His voice was low and secret, and none save the king heard what he said. But ever as he spoke the light shone brighter in Théoden's eye, and at the last he rose from his seat to his full height, and Gandalf beside him, and together they looked out from the high place towards the East.

'Verily,' said Gandalf, now in a loud voice, keen and clear, 'that way lies our hope, where sits our greatest fear. Doom hangs still on a thread. Yet hope there is still, if we can but stand unconquered for a little while.'

The others too now turned their eyes eastward. Over the sundering leagues of land, far away they gazed to the edge of sight, and hope and fear bore their thoughts still on, beyond dark mountains to the Land of Shadow. Where now was the Ring-bearer? How thin indeed was the thread upon which doom still hung! It seemed to Legolas, as he strained his farseeing eyes, that he caught a glint of white: far away perchance the sun twinkled on a pinnacle of the Tower of Guard. And further still, endlessly remote and yet a present threat, there was a tiny tongue of flame.

Slowly Théoden sat down again, as if weariness still struggled to master him against the will of Gandalf. He turned and looked at his great house. 'Alas!' he said, 'that these evil days should be mine, and should come in my old age instead of that peace which I have earned. Alas for Boromir the brave! The young perish and the old linger, withering.' He clutched his knees with his wrinkled hands.

'Your fingers would remember their old strength better, if they grasped a sword-hilt,' said Gandalf.

Théoden rose and put his hand to his side; but no sword hung at his belt. 'Where has Gríma stowed it?' he muttered under his breath.

'Take this, dear lord!' said a clear voice. 'It was ever at your service.' Two men had come softly up the stair and stood now a few steps from the top. Éomer was there. No helm was on his head, no mail was on his breast, but in his hand he held a drawn sword; and as he knelt he offered the hilt to his master.

'How comes this?' said Théoden sternly. He turned towards Éomer, and the men looked in wonder at him, standing now proud and erect. Where was the old man whom they had left crouching in his chair or leaning on his stick?

'It is my doing, lord,' said Háma, trembling. 'I understood that Éomer was to be set free. Such joy was in my heart that maybe I have erred. Yet, since he was free again, and he a Marshal of the Mark, I brought him his sword as he bade me.'

'To lay at your feet, my lord,' said Éomer.

For a moment of silence Théoden stood looking down at Éomer as he knelt still before him. Neither moved.

'Will you not take the sword?' said Gandalf.

Slowly Théoden stretched forth his hand. As his fingers took the hilt, it seemed to the watchers that firmness and strength returned to his thin arm. Suddenly he lifted the blade and swung it shimmering and whistling in the air. Then he gave a great cry. His voice rang clear as he chanted in the tongue of Rohan a call to arms.

> *Arise now, arise, Riders of Théoden!*
> *Dire deeds awake, dark is it eastward.*
> *Let horse be bridled, horn be sounded!*
> *Forth Eorlingas!*

The guards, thinking that they were summoned, sprang up the stair. They looked at their lord in amazement, and then as one man they drew their swords and laid them at his feet. 'Command us!' they said.

'*Westu Théoden hál!*' cried Éomer. 'It is a joy to us to see you return into your own. Never again shall it be said, Gandalf, that you come only with grief!'

'Take back your sword, Éomer, sister-son!' said the king. 'Go, Háma, and seek my own sword! Gríma has it in his keeping. Bring him to me also. Now, Gandalf, you said that you had counsel to give, if I would hear it. What is your counsel?'

'You have yourself already taken it,' answered Gandalf. 'To put your trust in Éomer, rather than in a man of crooked mind. To cast aside regret and fear. To do the deed at hand. Every man that can ride should be sent west at once, as Éomer counselled you: we must first destroy the threat of Saruman, while we have time. If we fail, we fall. If we succeed – then we will face the next task. Meanwhile your people that are left, the women and the children and the old, should fly to the refuges that you have in the mountains. Were they not prepared against just such an evil day as this? Let them take provision, but delay not, nor burden themselves with treasures, great or small. It is their lives that are at stake.'

'This counsel seems good to me now,' said Théoden. 'Let all my folk get ready! But you my guests – truly you said, Gandalf, that the courtesy of my hall is lessened. You have ridden through the night, and the morning wears away. You have had neither sleep nor food. A guest-house shall be made ready: there you shall sleep, when you have eaten.'

'Nay, lord,' said Aragorn. 'There is no rest yet for the weary. The men of Rohan must ride forth today, and we will ride with them, axe, sword, and bow. We did not bring them to rest against your wall, Lord of the Mark. And I promised Éomer that my sword and his should be drawn together.'

'Now indeed there is hope of victory!' said Éomer.

'Hope, yes,' said Gandalf. 'But Isengard is strong. And other perils draw ever nearer. Do not delay, Théoden, when we are gone. Lead your people swiftly to the Hold of Dun-harrow in the hills!'

'Nay, Gandalf!' said the king. 'You do not know your own skill in healing. It shall not be so. I myself will go to war, to fall in the front of the battle, if it must be. Thus shall I sleep better.'

'Then even the defeat of Rohan will be glorious in song,' said Aragorn. The armed men that stood near clashed their weapons, crying: 'The Lord of the Mark will ride! Forth Eorlingas!'

'But your people must not be both unarmed and shepherd-less,' said Gandalf. 'Who shall guide them and govern them in your place?'

'I will take thought for that ere I go,' answered Théoden. 'Here comes my counsellor.'

At that moment Háma came again from the hall. Behind him cringing between two other men, came Gríma the Wormtongue. His face was very white. His eyes blinked in the sunlight. Háma knelt and presented to Théoden a long sword in a scabbard clasped with gold and set with green gems.

'Here, lord, is Herugrim, your ancient blade,' he said. 'It was found in his chest. Loth was he to render up the keys. Many other things are there which men have missed.'

'You lie,' said Wormtongue. 'And this sword your master himself gave into my keeping.'

'And he now requires it of you again,' said Théoden. 'Does that displease you?'

'Assuredly not, lord,' said Wormtongue. 'I care for you and yours as best I may. But do not weary yourself, or tax too heavily your strength. Let others deal with these irksome guests. Your meat is about to be set on the board. Will you not go to it?'

'I will,' said Théoden. 'And let food for my guests be set on the board beside me. The host rides today. Send the heralds forth! Let them summon all who dwell nigh! Every man and strong lad able to bear arms, all who have horses, let them be ready in the saddle at the gate ere the second hour from noon!'

'Dear lord!' cried Wormtongue. 'It is as I feared. This wizard has bewitched you. Are none to be left to defend the Golden Hall of your fathers, and all your treasure? None to guard the Lord of the Mark?'

'If this is bewitchment,' said Théoden, 'it seems to me more wholesome than your whisperings. Your leechcraft ere long would have had me walking on all fours like a beast. No, not one shall be left, not even Gríma. Gríma shall ride too. Go! You have yet time to clean the rust from your sword.'

'Mercy, lord!' whined Wormtongue, grovelling on the ground. 'Have pity on one worn out in your service. Send me not from your side! I at least will stand by you when all others have gone. Do not send your faithful Gríma away!'

'You have my pity,' said Théoden. 'And I do not send you from my side. I go myself to war with my men. I bid you come with me and prove your faith.'

Wormtongue looked from face to face. In his eyes was the hunted look of a beast seeking some gap in the ring of his enemies. He licked his lips with a long pale tongue. 'Such a resolve might be expected from a lord of the House of Eorl, old though he be,' he said. 'But those who truly love him would spare his failing years. Yet I see that I come too late. Others, whom the death of my lord would perhaps grieve less, have already persuaded him. If I cannot undo their work, hear me at least in this, lord! One who knows your mind and honours your commands should be left in Edoras. Appoint a faithful steward. Let your counsellor Gríma keep all things till your return – and I pray that we may see it, though no wise man will deem it hopeful.'

Éomer laughed. 'And if that plea does not excuse you from war, most noble Wormtongue,' he said, 'what office of less honour would you accept? To carry a sack of meal up into the mountains – if any man would trust you with it?'

'Nay, Éomer, you do not fully understand the mind of Master Wormtongue,' said Gandalf, turning his piercing glance upon him. 'He is bold and cunning. Even now he plays a game with peril and wins a throw. Hours of my precious time he has wasted already. Down, snake!' he said suddenly in a terrible voice. 'Down on your belly! How long is it since Saruman bought you? What was the promised price? When all the men were dead, you were to pick your share of the treasure, and take the woman you desire? Too long have you watched her under your eyelids and haunted her steps.'

Éomer grasped his sword. 'That I knew already,' he muttered. 'For that reason I would have slain him before, forgetting the law of the hall. But there are other reasons.' He stepped forward, but Gandalf stayed him with his hand.

'Éowyn is safe now,' he said. 'But you, Wormtongue, you have done what you could for your true master. Some reward you have earned at least. Yet Saruman is apt to overlook his bargains. I should advise you to go quickly and remind him, lest he forget your faithful service.'

'You lie,' said Wormtongue.

'That word comes too oft and easy from your lips,' said Gandalf. 'I do not lie. See, Théoden, here is a snake! With safety you cannot take it with you, nor can you leave it behind. To slay it would be just. But it was not always as it now is. Once it was a man, and did you service in its fashion. Give him a horse and let him go at once, wherever he chooses. By his choice you shall judge him.'

'Do you hear this, Wormtongue?' said Théoden. 'This is your choice: to ride with me to war, and let us see in battle whether you are true; or to go now, whither you will. But then, if ever we meet again, I shall not be merciful.'

Slowly Wormtongue rose. He looked at them with half-closed eyes. Last of all he scanned Théoden's face and opened his mouth as if to speak. Then suddenly he drew himself up. His hands worked. His eyes glittered. Such malice was in them that men stepped back from him. He bared his teeth; and then with a hissing breath he spat before the king's feet, and darting to one side, he fled down the stair.

'After him!' said Théoden. 'See that he does no harm to any, but do not hurt him or hinder him. Give him a horse, if he wishes it.'

'And if any will bear him,' said Éomer.

One of the guards ran down the stair. Another went to the well at the foot of the terrace and in his helm drew water. With it he washed clean the stones that Wormtongue had defiled.

'Now my guests, come!' said Théoden. 'Come and take such refreshment as haste allows.'

They passed back into the great house. Already they heard below them in the town the heralds crying and the war-horns blowing. For the king was to ride forth as soon as the men of the town and those dwelling near could be armed and assembled.

At the king's board sat Éomer and the four guests, and there also waiting upon the king was the lady Éowyn. They ate and drank swiftly. The others were silent while Théoden questioned Gandalf concerning Saruman.

'How far back his treachery goes, who can guess?' said Gandalf. 'He was not always evil. Once I do not doubt that he was the friend of Rohan; and even when his heart grew colder, he found you useful still. But for long now he has plotted your ruin, wearing the mask of friendship, until he was ready. In those years Wormtongue's task was easy, and all that you did was swiftly known in Isengard; for your land was open, and strangers came and went. And ever Wormtongue's whispering was in your ears, poisoning your thought, chilling your heart, weakening your limbs, while others watched and could do nothing, for your will was in his keeping.

'But when I escaped and warned you, then the mask was torn, for those who would see. After that Wormtongue played dangerously, always seeking to delay you, to prevent your full strength being gathered. He was crafty: dulling men's wariness, or working on their fears, as served the occasion. Do you not remember how eagerly he urged that no man should be spared on a wildgoose chase northward, when the immediate peril was westward? He persuaded you to forbid Éomer to pursue the raiding Orcs. If Éomer had not defied Wormtongue's voice speaking with your mouth, those Orcs would have reached Isengard by now, bearing a great prize. Not indeed that prize which Saruman desires above all else, but at the least two members of my Company, sharers of a secret hope, of which even to you, lord, I cannot yet speak openly. Dare you think of what they might now be suffering, or what Saruman might now have learned to our destruction?'

'I owe much to Éomer,' said Théoden. 'Faithful heart may have forward tongue.'

'Say also,' said Gandalf, 'that to crooked eyes truth may wear a wry face.'

'Indeed my eyes were almost blind,' said Théoden. 'Most of all I owe to you, my guest. Once again you have come in time. I would give you a gift ere we go, at your own choosing. You have only to name aught that is mine. I reserve now only my sword!'

'Whether I came in time or not is yet to be seen,' said Gandalf. 'But as for your gift, lord, I will choose one that will fit my need: swift and sure. Give me Shadowfax! He was only lent before, if loan we may call it. But now I shall ride him into great hazard, setting silver against black: I would not risk anything that is not my own. And already there is a bond of love between us.'

'You choose well,' said Théoden; 'and I give him now gladly. Yet it is a great gift. There is none like to Shadowfax. In him one of the mighty steeds of old has returned. None such shall return again. And to you my other guests I will offer such things as may be found in my armoury. Swords you do not need, but there are helms and coats of mail of cunning work, gifts to my fathers out of Gondor. Choose from these ere we go, and may they serve you well!'

Now men came bearing raiment of war from the king's hoard, and they arrayed Aragorn and Legolas in shining mail. Helms too they chose, and round shields: their bosses were overlaid with gold and set with gems, green and red and white. Gandalf took no armour; and Gimli needed no coat of rings, even if one had been found to match his stature, for there was no hauberk in the hoards of Edoras of better make than his short corslet forged beneath the Mountain in the North. But he chose a cap of iron and leather that fitted well upon his round head; and a small shield he also took. It bore the running horse, white upon green, that was the emblem of the House of Eorl.

'May it keep you well!' said Théoden. 'It was made for me in Thengel's day, while still I was a boy.'

Gimli bowed. 'I am proud, Lord of the Mark, to bear your device,' he said. 'Indeed sooner would I bear a horse than be borne by one. I love my feet better. But, maybe, I shall come yet where I can stand and fight.'

'It may well be so,' said Théoden.

The king now rose, and at once Éowyn came forward bearing wine. '*Ferthu Théoden hál!*' she said. 'Receive now this cup and drink in happy hour. Health be with thee at thy going and coming!'

Théoden drank from the cup, and she then proffered it to the guests. As she stood before Aragorn she paused suddenly and looked upon him, and her eyes were shining. And he looked down upon her fair face and smiled; but as he took the cup, his hand met hers, and he knew that she trembled at the touch. 'Hail Aragorn son of Arathorn!' she said. 'Hail Lady of Rohan!' he answered, but his face now was troubled and he did not smile.

When they had all drunk, the king went down the hall to the doors. There the guards awaited him, and heralds stood, and all the lords and chiefs were gathered together that remained in Edoras or dwelt nearby.

'Behold! I go forth, and it seems like to be my last riding,' said Théoden. 'I have no child. Théodred my son is slain. I name Éomer my sister-son to be my heir. If neither of us return, then choose a new lord as you will. But to some one I must now entrust my people that I leave behind, to rule them in my place. Which of you will stay?'

No man spoke.

'Is there none whom you would name? In whom do my people trust?'

'In the House of Eorl,' answered Háma.

'But Éomer I cannot spare, nor would he stay,' said the king; 'and he is the last of that House.'

'I said not Éomer,' answered Háma. 'And he is not the last. There is Éowyn, daughter of Éomund, his sister. She is fearless and high-hearted. All love her. Let her be as lord to the Eorlingas, while we are gone.'

'It shall be so,' said Théoden. 'Let the heralds announce to the folk that the Lady Éowyn will lead them!'

Then the king sat upon a seat before his doors, and Éowyn knelt before him and received from him a sword and a fair corslet. 'Farewell sister-daughter!' he said. 'Dark is the hour, yet maybe we shall return to the Golden Hall. But in Dunharrow the people may long defend themselves, and if the battle go ill, thither will come all who escape.'

'Speak not so!' she answered. 'A year shall I endure for every day that passes until your return.' But as she spoke her eyes went to Aragorn who stood nearby.

'The king shall come again,' he said. 'Fear not! Not West but East does our doom await us.'

The king now went down the stair with Gandalf beside him. The others followed. Aragorn looked back as they passed towards the gate. Alone Éowyn stood before the doors of the house at the stair's head; the sword was set upright before her, and her hands were laid upon the hilt. She was clad now in mail and shone like silver in the sun.

Gimli walked with Legolas, his axe on his shoulder. 'Well, at last we set off!' he said. 'Men need many words before deeds. My axe is restless in my hands. Though I doubt not that these Rohirrim are fell-handed when they come to it. Nonetheless this is not the warfare that suits me. How shall I come to the battle? I wish I could walk and not bump like a sack at Gandalf's saddlebow.'

'A safer seat than many, I guess,' said Legolas. 'Yet doubtless Gandalf will gladly put you down on your feet when blows begin; or Shadowfax himself. An axe is no weapon for a rider.'

'And a Dwarf is no horseman. It is orc-necks I would hew, not shave the scalps of Men,' said Gimli, patting the haft of his axe.

At the gate they found a great host of men, old and young, all ready in the saddle. More than a thousand were there mustered. Their spears were like a springing wood. Loudly and joyously they shouted as Théoden came forth. Some held in readiness the king's horse, Snowmane, and others held the horses of Aragorn and Legolas. Gimli stood ill at ease, frowning, but Éomer came up to him, leading his horse.

'Hail, Gimli Glóin's son!' he cried. 'I have not had time to learn gentle speech under your rod, as you promised. But shall we not put aside our quarrel? At least I will speak no evil again of the Lady of the Wood.'

'I will forget my wrath for a while, Éomer son of Éomund,' said Gimli; 'but if ever you chance to see the Lady Galadriel with your eyes, then you shall acknowledge her the fairest of ladies, or our friendship will end.'

'So be it!' said Éomer. 'But until that time pardon me, and in token of pardon ride with me, I beg. Gandalf will be at the head with the Lord of the Mark; but Firefoot, my horse, will bear us both, if you will.'

'I thank you indeed,' said Gimli greatly pleased. 'I will

gladly go with you, if Legolas, my comrade, may ride beside us.'

'It shall be so,' said Éomer. 'Legolas upon my left, and Aragorn upon my right, and none will dare to stand before us!'

'Where is Shadowfax?' said Gandalf.

'Running wild over the grass,' they answered. 'He will let no man handle him. There he goes, away down by the ford, like a shadow among the willows.'

Gandalf whistled and called aloud the horse's name, and far away he tossed his head and neighed, and turning sped towards the host like an arrow.

'Were the breath of the West Wind to take a body visible, even so would it appear,' said Éomer, as the great horse ran up, until he stood before the wizard.

'The gift seems already to be given,' said Théoden. 'But hearken all! Here now I name my guest, Gandalf Greyhame, wisest of counsellors, most welcome of wanderers, a lord of the Mark, a chieftain of the Eorlingas while our kin shall last; and I give to him Shadowfax, prince of horses.'

'I thank you, Théoden King,' said Gandalf. Then suddenly he threw back his grey cloak, and cast aside his hat, and leaped to horseback. He wore no helm nor mail. His snowy hair flew free in the wind, his white robes shone dazzling in the sun.

'Behold the White Rider!' cried Aragorn, and all took up the words.

'Our King and the White Rider!' they shouted. 'Forth Eorlingas!'

The trumpets sounded. The horses reared and neighed. Spear clashed on shield. Then the king raised his hand, and with a rush like the sudden onset of a great wind the last host of Rohan rode thundering into the West.

Far over the plain Éowyn saw the glitter of their spears, as she stood still, alone before the doors of the silent house.

CHAPTER VII

HELM'S DEEP

The sun was already westering as they rode from Edoras, and the light of it was in their eyes, turning all the rolling fields of Rohan to a golden haze. There was a beaten way, north-westward along the foot-hills of the White Mountains, and this they followed, up and down in a green country, crossing small swift streams by many fords. Far ahead and to their right the Misty Mountains loomed; ever darker and taller they grew as the miles went by. The sun went slowly down before them. Evening came behind.

The host rode on. Need drove them. Fearing to come too late, they rode with all the speed they could, pausing seldom. Swift and enduring were the steeds of Rohan, but there were many leagues to go. Forty leagues and more it was, as a bird flies, from Edoras to the fords of the Isen, where they hoped to find the king's men that held back the hosts of Saruman.

Night closed about them. At last they halted to make their camp. They had ridden for some five hours and were far out upon the western plain, yet more than half their journey lay still before them. In a great circle, under the starry sky and the waxing moon, they now made their bivouac. They lit no fires, for they were uncertain of events; but they set a ring of mounted guards about them, and scouts rode out far ahead, passing like shadows in the folds of the land. The slow night passed without tidings or alarm. At dawn the horns sounded, and within an hour they took the road again.

There were no clouds overhead yet, but a heaviness was in the air; it was hot for the season of the year. The rising sun was hazy, and behind it, following it slowly up the sky, there was a growing darkness, as of a great storm moving

out of the East. And away in the North-west there seemed
to be another darkness brooding about the feet of the Misty
Mountains, a shadow that crept down slowly from the
Wizard's Vale.

Gandalf dropped back to where Legolas rode beside
Éomer. 'You have the keen eyes of your fair kindred,
Legolas,' he said; 'and they can tell a sparrow from a finch
a league off. Tell me, can you see anything away yonder
towards Isengard?'

'Many miles lie between,' said Legolas, gazing thither and
shading his eyes with his long hand. 'I can see a darkness.
There are shapes moving in it, great shapes far away upon
the bank of the river; but what they are I cannot tell. It is
not mist or cloud that defeats my eyes: there is a veiling
shadow that some power lays upon the land, and it marches
slowly down stream. It is as if the twilight under endless trees
were flowing downwards from the hills.'

'And behind us comes a very storm of Mordor,' said
Gandalf. 'It will be a black night.'

As the second day of their riding drew on, the heaviness
in the air increased. In the afternoon the dark clouds began
to overtake them: a sombre canopy with great billowing edges
flecked with dazzling light. The sun went down, blood-red
in a smoking haze. The spears of the Riders were tipped with
fire as the last shafts of light kindled the steep faces of the
peaks of Thrihyrne: now very near they stood on the north-
ernmost arm of the White Mountains, three jagged horns
staring at the sunset. In the last red glow men in the vanguard
saw a black speck, a horseman riding back towards them.
They halted awaiting him.

He came, a weary man with dinted helm and cloven shield.
Slowly he climbed from his horse and stood there a while
gasping. At length he spoke. 'Is Éomer here?' he asked. 'You
come at last, but too late, and with too little strength. Things
have gone evilly since Théodred fell. We were driven back
yesterday over the Isen with great loss; many perished at the

crossing. Then at night fresh forces came over the river against our camp. All Isengard must be emptied; and Saruman has armed the wild hillmen and herd-folk of Dunland beyond the rivers, and these also he loosed upon us. We were overmastered. The shield-wall was broken. Erkenbrand of Westfold has drawn off those men he could gather towards his fastness in Helm's Deep. The rest are scattered.

'Where is Éomer? Tell him there is no hope ahead. He should return to Edoras before the wolves of Isengard come there.'

Théoden had sat silent, hidden from the man's sight behind his guards; now he urged his horse forward. 'Come, stand before me, Ceorl!' he said. 'I am here. The last host of the Eorlingas has ridden forth. It will not return without battle.'

The man's face lightened with joy and wonder. He drew himself up. Then he knelt, offering his notched sword to the king. 'Command me, lord!' he cried. 'And pardon me! I thought——'

'You thought I remained in Meduseld bent like an old tree under winter snow. So it was when you rode to war. But a west wind has shaken the boughs,' said Théoden. 'Give this man a fresh horse! Let us ride to the help of Erkenbrand!'

While Théoden was speaking, Gandalf rode a short way ahead, and he sat there alone, gazing north to Isengard and west to the setting sun. Now he came back.

'Ride, Théoden!' he said. 'Ride to Helm's Deep! Go not to the Fords of Isen, and do not tarry in the plain! I must leave you for a while. Shadowfax must bear me now on a swift errand.' Turning to Aragorn and Éomer and the men of the king's household, he cried: 'Keep well the Lord of the Mark, till I return. Await me at Helm's Gate! Farewell!'

He spoke a word to Shadowfax, and like an arrow from the bow the great horse sprang away. Even as they looked he was gone: a flash of silver in the sunset, a wind over the grass, a shadow that fled and passed from sight. Snowmane snorted and reared, eager to follow; but only a swift bird on the wing could have overtaken him.

'What does that mean?' said one of the guard to Háma.

'That Gandalf Greyhame has need of haste,' answered Háma. 'Ever he goes and comes unlooked-for.'

'Wormtongue, were he here, would not find it hard to explain,' said the other.

'True enough,' said Háma; 'but for myself, I will wait until I see Gandalf again.'

'Maybe you will wait long,' said the other.

The host turned away now from the road to the Fords of Isen and bent their course southward. Night fell, and still they rode on. The hills drew near, but the tall peaks of Thrihyrne were already dim against the darkening sky. Still some miles away, on the far side of the Westfold Vale, lay a green coomb, a great bay in the mountains, out of which a gorge opened in the hills. Men of that land called it Helm's Deep, after a hero of old wars who had made his refuge there. Ever steeper and narrower it wound inward from the north under the shadow of the Thrihyrne, till the crowhaunted cliffs rose like mighty towers on either side, shutting out the light.

At Helm's Gate, before the mouth of the Deep, there was a heel of rock thrust outward by the northern cliff. There upon its spur stood high walls of ancient stone, and within them was a lofty tower. Men said that in the far-off days of the glory of Gondor the sea-kings had built here this fastness with the hands of giants. The Hornburg it was called, for a trumpet sounded upon the tower echoed in the Deep behind, as if armies long-forgotten were issuing to war from caves beneath the hills. A wall, too, the men of old had made from the Hornburg to the southern cliff, barring the entrance to the gorge. Beneath it by a wide culvert the Deeping-stream passed out. About the feet of the Hornrock it wound, and flowed then in a gully through the midst of a wide green gore, sloping gently down from Helm's Gate to Helm's Dike.

Thence it fell into the Deeping-coomb and out into the Westfold Vale. There in the Hornburg at Helm's Gate Erkenbrand, master of Westfold on the borders of the Mark, now dwelt. As the days darkened with threat of war, being wise, he had repaired the wall and made the fastness strong.

The Riders were still in the low valley before the mouth of the Coomb, when cries and hornblasts were heard from their scouts that went in front. Out of the darkness arrows whistled. Swiftly a scout rode back and reported that wolf-riders were abroad in the valley, and that a host of Orcs and wild men were hurrying southward from the Fords of Isen and seemed to be making for Helm's Deep.

'We have found many of our folk lying slain as they fled thither,' said the scout. 'And we have met scattered companies, going this way and that, leaderless. What has become of Erkenbrand none seem to know. It is likely that he will be overtaken ere he can reach Helm's Gate, if he has not already perished.'

'Has aught been seen of Gandalf?' asked Théoden.

'Yes, lord. Many have seen an old man in white upon a horse, passing hither and thither over the plains like wind in the grass. Some thought he was Saruman. It is said that he went away ere nightfall towards Isengard. Some say also that Wormtongue was seen earlier, going northward with a company of Orcs.'

'It will go ill with Wormtongue, if Gandalf comes upon him,' said Théoden. 'Nonetheless I miss now both my counsellors, the old and the new. But in this need we have no better choice than to go on, as Gandalf said, to Helm's Gate, whether Erkenbrand be there or no. Is it known how great is the host that comes from the North?'

'It is very great,' said the scout. 'He that flies counts every foeman twice, yet I have spoken to stouthearted men, and I do not doubt that the main strength of the enemy is many times as great as all that we have here.'

'Then let us be swift,' said Éomer. 'Let us drive through

such foes as are already between us and the fastness. There are caves in Helm's Deep where hundreds may lie hid; and secret ways lead thence up on to the hills.'

'Trust not to secret ways,' said the king. 'Saruman has long spied out this land. Still in that place our defence may last long. Let us go!'

Aragorn and Legolas went now with Éomer in the van. On through the dark night they rode, ever slower as the darkness deepened and their way climbed southward, higher and higher into the dim folds about the mountains' feet. They found few of the enemy before them. Here and there they came upon roving bands of Orcs; but they fled ere the Riders could take or slay them.

'It will not be long I fear,' said Éomer, 'ere the coming of the king's host will be known to the leader of our enemies, Saruman or whatever captain he has sent forth.'

The rumour of war grew behind them. Now they could hear, borne over the dark, the sound of harsh singing. They had climbed far up into the Deeping-coomb when they looked back. Then they saw torches, countless points of fiery light upon the black fields behind, scattered like red flowers, or winding up from the lowlands in long flickering lines. Here and there a larger blaze leapt up.

'It is a great host and follows us hard,' said Aragorn.

'They bring fire,' said Théoden, 'and they are burning as they come, rick, cot, and tree. This was a rich vale and had many homesteads. Alas for my folk!'

'Would that day was here and we might ride down upon them like a storm out of the mountains!' said Aragorn. 'It grieves me to fly before them.'

'We need not fly much further,' said Éomer. 'Not far ahead now lies Helm's Dike, an ancient trench and rampart scored across the coomb, two furlongs below Helm's Gate. There we can turn and give battle.'

'Nay, we are too few to defend the Dike,' said Théoden. 'It is a mile long or more, and the breach in it is wide.'

'At the breach our rearguard must stand, if we are pressed,' said Éomer.

There was neither star nor moon when the Riders came to the breach in the Dike, where the stream from above passed out, and the road beside it ran down from the Hornburg. The rampart loomed suddenly before them, a high shadow beyond a dark pit. As they rode up a sentinel challenged them.

'The Lord of the Mark rides to Helm's Gate,' Éomer answered. 'I, Éomer son of Éomund, speak.'

'This is good tidings beyond hope,' said the sentinel. 'Hasten! The enemy is on your heels.'

The host passed through the breach and halted on the sloping sward above. They now learned to their joy that Erkenbrand had left many men to hold Helm's Gate, and more had since escaped thither.

'Maybe, we have a thousand fit to fight on foot,' said Gamling, an old man, the leader of those that watched the Dike. 'But most of them have seen too many winters, as I have, or too few, as my son's son here. What news of Erkenbrand? Word came yesterday that he was retreating hither with all that is left of the best Riders of Westfold. But he has not come.'

'I fear that he will not come now,' said Éomer. 'Our scouts have gained no news of him, and the enemy fills all the valley behind us.'

'I would that he had escaped,' said Théoden. 'He was a mighty man. In him lived again the valour of Helm the Hammerhand. But we cannot await him here. We must draw all our forces now behind the walls. Are you well stored? We bring little provision, for we rode forth to open battle, not to a siege.'

'Behind us in the caves of the Deep are three parts of the folk of Westfold, old and young, children and women,' said Gamling. 'But great store of food, and many beasts and their fodder, have also been gathered there.'

'That is well,' said Éomer. 'They are burning or despoiling all that is left in the vale.'

'If they come to bargain for our goods at Helm's Gate, they will pay a high price,' said Gamling.

The king and his Riders passed on. Before the causeway that crossed the stream they dismounted. In a long file they led their horses up the ramp and passed within the gates of the Hornburg. There they were welcomed again with joy and renewed hope; for now there were men enough to man both the burg and the barrier wall.

Quickly Éomer set his men in readiness. The king and the men of his household were in the Hornburg, and there also were many of the Westfold-men. But on the Deeping Wall and its tower, and behind it, Éomer arrayed most of the strength that he had, for here the defence seemed more doubtful, if the assault were determined and in great force. The horses were led far up the Deep under such guard as could be spared.

The Deeping Wall was twenty feet high, and so thick that four men could walk abreast along the top, sheltered by a parapet over which only a tall man could look. Here and there were clefts in the stone through which men could shoot. This battlement could be reached by a stair running down from a door in the outer court of the Hornburg; three flights of steps led also up on to the wall from the Deep behind; but in front it was smooth, and the great stones of it were set with such skill that no foothold could be found at their joints, and at the top they hung over like a sea-delved cliff.

Gimli stood leaning against the breastwork upon the wall. Legolas sat above on the parapet, fingering his bow, and peering out into the gloom.

'This is more to my liking,' said the dwarf, stamping on the stones. 'Ever my heart rises as we draw near the mountains. There is good rock here. This country has tough bones.

I felt them in my feet as we came up from the dike. Give me a year and a hundred of my kin and I would make this a place that armies would break upon like water.'

'I do not doubt it,' said Legolas. 'But you are a dwarf, and dwarves are strange folk. I do not like this place, and I shall like it no more by the light of day. But you comfort me, Gimli, and I am glad to have you standing nigh with your stout legs and your hard axe. I wish there were more of your kin among us. But even more would I give for a hundred good archers of Mirkwood. We shall need them. The Rohir-rim have good bowmen after their fashion, but there are too few here, too few.'

'It is dark for archery,' said Gimli. 'Indeed it is time for sleep. Sleep! I feel the need of it, as never I thought any dwarf could. Riding is tiring work. Yet my axe is restless in my hand. Give me a row of orc-necks and room to swing and all weariness will fall from me!'

A slow time passed. Far down in the valley scattered fires still burned. The hosts of Isengard were advancing in silence now. Their torches could be seen winding up the coomb in many lines.

Suddenly from the Dike yells and screams, and the fierce battle-cries of men broke out. Flaming brands appeared over the brink and clustered thickly at the breach. Then they scat-tered and vanished. Men came galloping back over the field and up the ramp to the gate of the Hornburg. The rearguard of the Westfolders had been driven in.

'The enemy is at hand!' they said. 'We loosed every arrow that we had, and filled the Dike with Orcs. But it will not halt them long. Already they are scaling the bank at many points, thick as marching ants. But we have taught them not to carry torches.'

It was now past midnight. The sky was utterly dark, and the stillness of the heavy air foreboded storm. Suddenly the clouds were seared by a blinding flash. Branched lightning smote down upon the eastward hills. For a staring moment the watchers on the walls saw all the space between them and the Dike lit with white light: it was boiling and crawling with black shapes, some squat and broad, some tall and grim, with high helms and sable shields. Hundreds and hundreds more were pouring over the Dike and through the breach. The dark tide flowed up to the walls from cliff to cliff. Thunder rolled in the valley. Rain came lashing down.

Arrows thick as the rain came whistling over the battlements, and fell clinking and glancing on the stones. Some found a mark. The assault on Helm's Deep had begun, but no sound or challenge was heard within; no answering arrows came.

The assailing hosts halted, foiled by the silent menace of rock and wall. Ever and again the lightning tore aside the darkness. Then the Orcs screamed, waving spear and sword, and shooting a cloud of arrows at any that stood revealed upon the battlements; and the men of the Mark amazed looked out, as it seemed to them, upon a great field of dark corn, tossed by a tempest of war, and every ear glinted with barbed light.

Brazen trumpets sounded. The enemy surged forward, some against the Deeping Wall, others towards the causeway and the ramp that led up to the Hornburg-gates. There the hugest Orcs were mustered, and the wild men of the Dunland fells. A moment they hesitated and then on they came. The lightning flashed, and blazoned upon every helm and shield the ghastly hand of Isengard was seen. They reached the summit of the rock; they drove towards the gates.

Then at last an answer came: a storm of arrows met them, and a hail of stones. They wavered, broke, and fled back; and then charged again, broke and charged again; and each time, like the incoming sea, they halted at a higher point. Again trumpets rang, and a press of roaring men leaped forth. They held their great shields above them like a roof, while in their midst they bore two trunks of mighty trees. Behind them orc-archers crowded, sending a hail of darts against the bowmen on the walls. They gained the gates. The trees, swung by strong arms, smote the timbers with a rending boom. If any man fell, crushed by a stone hurtling from above, two others sprang to take his place. Again and again the great rams swung and crashed.

Éomer and Aragorn stood together on the Deeping Wall. They heard the roar of voices and the thudding of the rams; and then in a sudden flash of light they beheld the peril of the gates.

'Come!' said Aragorn. 'This is the hour when we draw swords together!'

Running like fire, they sped along the wall, and up the steps, and passed into the outer court upon the Rock. As they ran they gathered a handful of stout swordsmen. There was a small postern-door that opened in an angle of the burg-wall on the west, where the cliff stretched out to meet it. On that side a narrow path ran round towards the great gate, between the wall and the sheer brink of the Rock. Together Éomer and Aragorn sprang through the door, their men close behind. The two swords flashed from the sheath as one.

'Gúthwinë!' cried Éomer. 'Gúthwinë for the Mark!'

'Andúril!' cried Aragorn. 'Andúril for the Dúnedain!'

Charging from the side, they hurled themselves upon the wild men. Andúril rose and fell, gleaming with white fire. A shout went up from wall and tower: 'Andúril! Andúril goes to war. The Blade that was Broken shines again!'

Dismayed the rammers let fall the trees and turned to fight; but the wall of their shields was broken as by a lightning-stroke, and they were swept away, hewn down, or cast over the Rock into the stony stream below. The orc-archers shot wildly and then fled.

For a moment Éomer and Aragorn halted before the gates. The thunder was rumbling in the distance now. The lightning flickered still, far off among the mountains in the South. A keen wind was blowing from the North again. The clouds were torn and drifting, and stars peeped out; and above the hills of the Coomb-side the westering moon rode, glimmering yellow in the storm-wrack.

'We did not come too soon,' said Aragorn, looking at the gates. Their great hinges and iron bars were wrenched and bent; many of their timbers were cracked.

'Yet we cannot stay here beyond the walls to defend them,' said Éomer. 'Look!' He pointed to the causeway. Already a great press of Orcs and Men were gathering again beyond the stream. Arrows whined, and skipped on the stones about them. 'Come! We must get back and see what we can do to pile stone and beam across the gates within. Come now!'

They turned and ran. At that moment some dozen Orcs that had lain motionless among the slain leaped to their feet, and came silently and swiftly behind. Two flung themselves to the ground at Éomer's heels, tripped him, and in a moment they were on top of him. But a small dark figure that none had observed sprang out of the shadows and gave a hoarse shout: *Baruk Khazâd! Khazâd ai-mênu!* An axe swung and swept back. Two Orcs fell headless. The rest fled. Éomer struggled to his feet, even as Aragorn ran back to his aid.

The postern was closed again, the iron door was barred and piled inside with stones. When all were safe within, Éomer turned: 'I thank you, Gimli son of Glóin!' he said. 'I did not know that you were with us in the sortie. But oft the unbidden guest proves the best company. How came you there?'

'I followed you to shake off sleep,' said Gimli; 'but I looked on the hillmen and they seemed over large for me, so I sat beside a stone to see your sword-play.'

'I shall not find it easy to repay you,' said Éomer.

'There may be many a chance ere the night is over,' laughed the Dwarf. 'But I am content. Till now I have hewn naught but wood since I left Moria.'

*   *   *

'Two!' said Gimli, patting his axe. He had returned to his place on the wall.

'Two?' said Legolas. 'I have done better, though now I must grope for spent arrows; all mine are gone. Yet I make my tale twenty at the least. But that is only a few leaves in a forest.'

The sky now was quickly clearing and the sinking moon was shining brightly. But the light brought little hope to the Riders of the Mark. The enemy before them seemed to have grown rather than diminished, and still more were pressing up from the valley through the breach. The sortie upon the Rock gained only a brief respite. The assault on the gates was redoubled. Against the Deeping Wall the hosts of Isengard roared like a sea. Orcs and hillmen swarmed about its feet from end to end. Ropes with grappling hooks were hurled over the parapet faster than men could cut them or fling them back. Hundreds of long ladders were lifted up. Many were cast down in ruin, but many more replaced them, and Orcs sprang up them like apes in the dark forests of the South. Before the wall's foot the dead and broken were piled like shingle in a storm; ever higher rose the hideous mounds, and still the enemy came on.

The men of Rohan grew weary. All their arrows were spent, and every shaft was shot; their swords were notched, and their shields were riven. Three times Aragorn and Éomer rallied them, and three times Andúril flamed in a desperate charge that drove the enemy from the wall.

Then a clamour arose in the Deep behind. Orcs had crept like rats through the culvert through which the stream flowed out. There they had gathered in the shadow of the cliffs, until the assault above was hottest and nearly all the men of the defence had rushed to the wall's top. Then they sprang out. Already some had passed into the jaws of the Deep and were among the horses, fighting with the guards.

Down from the wall leapt Gimli with a fierce cry that

echoed in the cliffs. '*Khazâd! Khazâd!*' He soon had work enough.

'Ai-oi!' he shouted. 'The Orcs are behind the wall. Ai-oi! Come, Legolas! There are enough for us both. *Khazâd ai-mênu!*'

Gamling the Old looked down from the Hornburg, hearing the great voice of the dwarf above all the tumult. 'The Orcs are in the Deep!' he cried. 'Helm! Helm! Forth Helmingas!' he shouted as he leaped down the stair from the Rock with many men of Westfold at his back.

Their onset was fierce and sudden, and the Orcs gave way before them. Ere long they were hemmed in in the narrows of the gorge, and all were slain or driven shrieking into the chasm of the Deep to fall before the guardians of the hidden caves.

'Twenty-one!' cried Gimli. He hewed a two-handed stroke and laid the last Orc before his feet. 'Now my count passes Master Legolas again.'

'We must stop this rat-hole,' said Gamling. 'Dwarves are said to be cunning folk with stone. Lend us your aid, master!'

'We do not shape stone with battle-axes, nor with our finger-nails,' said Gimli. 'But I will help as I may.'

They gathered such small boulders and broken stones as they could find to hand, and under Gimli's direction the Westfold-men blocked up the inner end of the culvert, until only a narrow outlet remained. Then the Deeping-stream, swollen by the rain, churned and fretted in its choked path, and spread slowly in cold pools from cliff to cliff.

'It will be drier above,' said Gimli. 'Come, Gamling, let us see how things go on the wall!'

He climbed up and found Legolas beside Aragorn and Éomer. The elf was whetting his long knife. There was for a while a lull in the assault, since the attempt to break in through the culvert had been foiled.

'Twenty-one!' said Gimli.

'Good!' said Legolas. 'But my count is now two dozen. It has been knife-work up here.'

Éomer and Aragorn leant wearily on their swords. Away on the left the crash and clamour of the battle on the Rock rose loud again. But the Hornburg still held fast, like an island in the sea. Its gates lay in ruin; but over the barricade of beams and stones within no enemy as yet had passed.

Aragorn looked at the pale stars, and at the moon, now sloping behind the western hills that enclosed the valley. 'This is a night as long as years,' he said. 'How long will the day tarry?'

'Dawn is not far off,' said Gamling, who had now climbed up beside him. 'But dawn will not help us, I fear.'

'Yet dawn is ever the hope of men,' said Aragorn.

'But these creatures of Isengard, these half-orcs and goblin-men that the foul craft of Saruman has bred, they will not quail at the sun,' said Gamling. 'And neither will the wild men of the hills. Do you not hear their voices?'

'I hear them,' said Éomer; 'but they are only the scream of birds and the bellowing of beasts to my ears.'

'Yet there are many that cry in the Dunland tongue,' said Gamling. 'I know that tongue. It is an ancient speech of men, and once was spoken in many western valleys of the Mark. Hark! They hate us, and they are glad; for our doom seems certain to them. "The king, the king!" they cry. "We will take their king. Death to the Forgoil! Death to the Straw-heads! Death to the robbers of the North!" Such names they have for us. Not in half a thousand years have they forgotten their grievance that the lords of Gondor gave the Mark to Eorl the Young and made alliance with him. That old hatred Saruman has inflamed. They are fierce folk when roused. They will not give way now for dusk or dawn, until Théoden is taken, or they themselves are slain.'

'Nonetheless day will bring hope to me,' said Aragorn. 'Is it not said that no foe has ever taken the Hornburg, if men defended it?'

'So the minstrels say,' said Éomer.

'Then let us defend it, and hope!' said Aragorn.

Even as they spoke there came a blare of trumpets. Then there was a crash and a flash of flame and smoke. The waters of the Deeping-stream poured out hissing and foaming: they were choked no longer, a gaping hole was blasted in the wall. A host of dark shapes poured in.

'Devilry of Saruman!' cried Aragorn. 'They have crept in the culvert again, while we talked, and they have lit the fire of Orthanc beneath our feet. *Elendil, Elendil!*' he shouted, as he leaped down into the breach; but even as he did so a hundred ladders were raised against the battlements. Over the wall and under the wall the last assault came sweeping like a dark wave upon a hill of sand. The defence was swept away. Some of the Riders were driven back, further and further into the Deep, falling and fighting as they gave way, step by step, towards the caves. Others cut their way back towards the citadel.

A broad stairway climbed from the Deep up to the Rock and the rear-gate of the Hornburg. Near the bottom stood Aragorn. In his hand still Andúril gleamed, and the terror of the sword for a while held back the enemy, as one by one all who could gain the stair passed up towards the gate. Behind on the upper steps knelt Legolas. His bow was bent, but one gleaned arrow was all that he had left, and he peered out now, ready to shoot the first Orc that should dare to approach the stair.

'All who can have now got safe within, Aragorn,' he called. 'Come back!'

Aragorn turned and sped up the stair; but as he ran he stumbled in his weariness. At once his enemies leapt forward. Up came the Orcs, yelling, with their long arms stretched out to seize him. The foremost fell with Legolas' last arrow in his throat, but the rest sprang over him. Then a great boulder, cast from the outer wall above, crashed down upon the stair, and hurled them back into the Deep. Aragorn gained the door, and swiftly it clanged to behind him.

'Things go ill, my friends,' he said, wiping the sweat from his brow with his arm.

'Ill enough,' said Legolas, 'but not yet hopeless, while we have you with us. Where is Gimli?'

'I do not know,' said Aragorn. 'I last saw him fighting on the ground behind the wall, but the enemy swept us apart.'

'Alas! That is evil news,' said Legolas.

'He is stout and strong,' said Aragorn. 'Let us hope that he will escape back to the caves. There he would be safe for a while. Safer than we. Such a refuge would be to the liking of a dwarf.'

'That must be my hope,' said Legolas. 'But I wish that he had come this way. I desired to tell Master Gimli that my tale is now thirty-nine.'

'If he wins back to the caves, he will pass your count again,' laughed Aragorn. 'Never did I see an axe so wielded.'

'I must go and seek some arrows,' said Legolas. 'Would that this night would end, and I could have better light for shooting.'

Aragorn now passed into the citadel. There to his dismay he learned that Éomer had not reached the Hornburg.

'Nay, he did not come to the Rock,' said one of the Westfold-men. 'I last saw him gathering men about him and fighting in the mouth of the Deep. Gamling was with him, and the dwarf; but I could not come to them.'

Aragorn strode on through the inner court, and mounted to a high chamber in the tower. There stood the king, dark against a narrow window, looking out upon the vale.

'What is the news, Aragorn?' he said.

'The Deeping Wall is taken, lord, and all the defence swept away; but many have escaped hither to the Rock.'

'Is Éomer here?'

'No, lord. But many of your men retreated into the Deep; and some say that Éomer was amongst them. In the narrows they may hold back the enemy and come within the caves. What hope they may have then I do not know.'

'More than we. Good provision, it is said. And the air is wholesome there because of the outlets through fissures in the rock far above. None can force an entrance against determined men. They may hold out long.'

'But the Orcs have brought a devilry from Orthanc,' said Aragorn. 'They have a blasting fire, and with it they took the Wall. If they cannot come in the caves, they may seal up those that are inside. But now we must turn all our thought to our own defence.'

'I fret in this prison,' said Théoden. 'If I could have set a spear in rest, riding before my men upon the field, maybe I could have felt again the joy of battle, and so ended. But I serve little purpose here.'

'Here at least you are guarded in the strongest fastness of the Mark,' said Aragorn. 'More hope we have to defend you in the Hornburg than in Edoras, or even at Dunharrow in the mountains.'

'It is said that the Hornburg has never fallen to assault,' said Théoden; 'but now my heart is doubtful. The world changes, and all that once was strong now proves unsure. How shall any tower withstand such numbers and such reckless hate? Had I known that the strength of Isengard was grown so great, maybe I should not so rashly have ridden forth to meet it, for all the arts of Gandalf. His counsel seems not now so good as it did under the morning sun.'

'Do not judge the counsel of Gandalf, until all is over, lord,' said Aragorn.

'The end will not be long,' said the king. 'But I will not end here, taken like an old badger in a trap. Snowmane and Hasufel and the horses of my guard are in the inner court. When dawn comes, I will bid men sound Helm's horn, and I will ride forth. Will you ride with me then, son of Arathorn? Maybe we shall cleave a road, or make such an end as will be worth a song – if any be left to sing of us hereafter.'

'I will ride with you,' said Aragorn.

Taking his leave, he returned to the walls, and passed round all their circuit, enheartening the men, and lending aid wherever the assault was hot. Legolas went with him. Blasts of fire leaped up from below shaking the stones. Grappling-hooks were hurled, and ladders raised. Again and again the Orcs gained the summit of the outer wall, and again the defenders cast them down.

At last Aragorn stood above the great gates, heedless of the darts of the enemy. As he looked forth he saw the eastern sky grow pale. Then he raised his empty hand, palm outward in token of parley.

The Orcs yelled and jeered. 'Come down! Come down!' they cried. 'If you wish to speak to us, come down! Bring out your king! We are the fighting Uruk-hai. We will fetch him from his hole, if he does not come. Bring out your skulking king!'

'The king stays or comes at his own will,' said Aragorn.

'Then what are you doing here?' they answered. 'Why do you look out? Do you wish to see the greatness of our army? We are the fighting Uruk-hai.'

'I looked out to see the dawn,' said Aragorn.

'What of the dawn?' they jeered. 'We are the Uruk-hai: we do not stop the fight for night or day, for fair weather or for storm. We come to kill, by sun or moon. What of the dawn?'

'None knows what the new day shall bring him,' said Aragorn. 'Get you gone, ere it turn to your evil.'

'Get down or we will shoot you from the wall,' they cried. 'This is no parley. You have nothing to say.'

'I have still this to say,' answered Aragorn. 'No enemy has yet taken the Hornburg. Depart, or not one of you will be spared. Not one will be left alive to take back tidings to the North. You do not know your peril.'

So great a power and royalty was revealed in Aragorn, as he stood there alone above the ruined gates before the host of his enemies, that many of the wild men paused, and looked back over their shoulders to the valley, and some looked up doubtfully at the sky. But the Orcs laughed with loud voices; and a hail of darts and arrows whistled over the wall, as Aragorn leaped down.

There was a roar and a blast of fire. The archway of the gate above which he had stood a moment before crumbled and crashed in smoke and dust. The barricade was scattered as if by a thunderbolt. Aragorn ran to the king's tower.

But even as the gate fell, and the Orcs about it yelled, preparing to charge, a murmur arose behind them, like a wind in the distance, and it grew to a clamour of many voices crying strange news in the dawn. The Orcs upon the Rock, hearing the rumour of dismay, wavered and looked back. And then, sudden and terrible, from the tower above, the sound of the great horn of Helm rang out.

All that heard that sound trembled. Many of the Orcs cast themselves on their faces and covered their ears with their claws. Back from the Deep the echoes came, blast upon blast, as if on every cliff and hill a mighty herald stood. But on the walls men looked up, listening with wonder; for the echoes did not die. Ever the hornblasts wound on among the hills; nearer now and louder they answered one to another, blowing fierce and free.

'Helm! Helm!' the Riders shouted. 'Helm is arisen and comes back to war. Helm for Théoden King!'

And with that shout the king came. His horse was white as snow, golden was his shield, and his spear was long. At his right hand was Aragorn, Elendil's heir, behind him rode the lords of the House of Eorl the Young. Light sprang in the sky. Night departed.

'Forth Eorlingas!' With a cry and a great noise they charged. Down from the gates they roared, over the causeway they swept, and they drove through the hosts of Isengard as a wind among grass. Behind them from the Deep came the stern cries of men issuing from the caves, driving forth the enemy. Out poured all the men that were left upon the Rock. And ever the sound of blowing horns echoed in the hills.

On they rode, the king and his companions. Captains and champions fell or fled before them. Neither orc nor man withstood them. Their backs were to the swords and spears of the Riders, and their faces to the valley. They cried and wailed, for fear and great wonder had come upon them with the rising of the day.

So King Théoden rode from Helm's Gate and clove his path to the great Dike. There the company halted. Light grew bright about them. Shafts of the sun flared above the eastern hills and glimmered on their spears. But they sat silent on their horses, and they gazed down upon the Deeping-coomb. The land had changed. Where before the green dale had lain, its grassy slopes lapping the ever-mounting hills, there now a forest loomed. Great trees, bare and silent, stood, rank on rank, with tangled bough and hoary head; their twisted roots were buried in the long green grass. Darkness was under them. Between the Dike and the eaves of that nameless wood only two open furlongs lay. There now cowered the proud hosts of Saruman, in terror of the king and in terror of the trees. They streamed down from Helm's Gate until all above the Dike was empty of them, but below it they were packed like swarming flies. Vainly they crawled and clambered about the walls of the coomb, seeking to escape. Upon the east too sheer and stony was the valley's side; upon the left, from the west, their final doom approached.

There suddenly upon a ridge appeared a rider, clad in white, shining in the rising sun. Over the low hills the horns were sounding. Behind him, hastening down the long slopes, were a thousand men on foot; their swords were in their hands. Amid them strode a man tall and strong. His shield was red. As he came to the valley's brink, he set to his lips a great black horn and blew a ringing blast.

'Erkenbrand!' the Riders shouted. 'Erkenbrand!'
'Behold the White Rider!' cried Aragorn. 'Gandalf is come again!'

'Mithrandir, Mithrandir!' said Legolas. 'This is wizardry indeed! Come! I would look on this forest, ere the spell changes.'

The hosts of Isengard roared, swaying this way and that, turning from fear to fear. Again the horn sounded from the tower. Down through the breach of the Dike charged the king's company. Down from the hills leaped Erkenbrand, lord of Westfold. Down leaped Shadowfax, like a deer that runs surefooted in the mountains. The White Rider was upon them, and the terror of his coming filled the enemy with madness. The wild men fell on their faces before him. The Orcs reeled and screamed and cast aside both sword and spear. Like a black smoke driven by a mounting wind they fled. Wailing they passed under the waiting shadow of the trees; and from that shadow none ever came again.

CHAPTER VIII

THE ROAD TO ISENGARD

So it was that in the light of a fair morning King Théoden and Gandalf the White Rider met again upon the green grass beside the Deeping-stream. There was also Aragorn son of Arathorn, and Legolas the Elf, and Erkenbrand of Westfold, and the lords of the Golden House. About them were gathered the Rohirrim, the Riders of the Mark: wonder overcame their joy in victory, and their eyes were turned towards the wood.

Suddenly there was a great shout, and down from the Dike came those who had been driven back into the Deep. There came Gamling the Old, and Éomer son of Éomund, and beside them walked Gimli the dwarf. He had no helm, and about his head was a linen band stained with blood; but his voice was loud and strong.

'Forty-two, Master Legolas!' he cried. 'Alas! My axe is notched: the forty-second had an iron collar on his neck. How is it with you?'

'You have passed my score by one,' answered Legolas. 'But I do not grudge you the game, so glad am I to see you on your legs!'

'Welcome, Éomer, sister-son!' said Théoden. 'Now that I see you safe, I am glad indeed.'

'Hail, Lord of the Mark!' said Éomer. 'The dark night has passed, and day has come again. But the day has brought strange tidings.' He turned and gazed in wonder, first at the wood and then at Gandalf. 'Once more you come in the hour of need, unlooked-for,' he said.

'Unlooked-for?' said Gandalf. 'I said that I would return and meet you here.'

'But you did not name the hour, nor foretell the manner

of your coming. Strange help you bring. You are mighty in wizardry, Gandalf the White!'

'That may be. But if so, I have not shown it yet. I have but given good counsel in peril, and made use of the speed of Shadowfax. Your own valour has done more, and the stout legs of the Westfold-men marching through the night.'

Then they all gazed at Gandalf with still greater wonder. Some glanced darkly at the wood, and passed their hands over their brows, as if they thought their eyes saw otherwise than his.

Gandalf laughed long and merrily. 'The trees?' he said. 'Nay, I see the wood as plainly as do you. But that is no deed of mine. It is a thing beyond the counsel of the wise. Better than my design, and better even than my hope the event has proved.'

'Then if not yours, whose is the wizardry?' said Théoden. 'Not Saruman's, that is plain. Is there some mightier sage, of whom we have yet to learn?'

'It is not wizardry, but a power far older,' said Gandalf: 'a power that walked the earth, ere elf sang or hammer rang.

> *Ere iron was found or tree was hewn,*
> *When young was mountain under moon;*
> *Ere ring was made, or wrought was woe,*
> *It walked the forests long ago.'*

'And what may be the answer to your riddle?' said Théoden.

'If you would learn that, you should come with me to Isengard,' answered Gandalf.

'To Isengard?' they cried.

'Yes,' said Gandalf. 'I shall return to Isengard, and those who will may come with me. There we may see strange things.'

'But there are not men enough in the Mark, not if they were all gathered together and healed of wounds and weariness, to assault the stronghold of Saruman,' said Théoden.

'Nevertheless to Isengard I go,' said Gandalf. 'I shall not

stay there long. My way lies now eastward. Look for me in Edoras, ere the waning of the moon!'

'Nay!' said Théoden. 'In the dark hour before dawn I doubted, but we will not part now. I will come with you, if that is your counsel.'

'I wish to speak with Saruman, as soon as may be now,' said Gandalf, 'and since he has done you great injury, it would be fitting if you were there. But how soon and how swiftly will you ride?'

'My men are weary with battle,' said the King; 'and I am weary also. For I have ridden far and slept little. Alas! My old age is not feigned nor due only to the whisperings of Wormtongue. It is an ill that no leech can wholly cure, not even Gandalf.'

'Then let all who are to ride with me rest now,' said Gandalf. 'We will journey under the shadow of evening. It is as well; for it is my counsel that all our comings and goings should be as secret as may be, henceforth. But do not command many men to go with you, Théoden. We go to a parley not to a fight.'

The King then chose men that were unhurt and had swift horses, and he sent them forth with tidings of the victory into every vale of the Mark; and they bore his summons also, bidding all men, young and old, to come in haste to Edoras. There the Lord of the Mark would hold an assembly of all that could bear arms, on the second day after the full moon. To ride with him to Isengard the King chose Éomer and twenty men of his household. With Gandalf would go Aragorn, and Legolas, and Gimli. In spite of his hurt the dwarf would not stay behind.

'It was only a feeble blow and the cap turned it,' he said. 'It would take more than such an orc-scratch to keep me back.'

'I will tend it, while you rest,' said Aragorn.

The king now returned to the Hornburg, and slept, such a sleep of quiet as he had not known for many years, and the remainder of his chosen company rested also. But the others, all that were not hurt or wounded, began a great labour; for many had fallen in the battle and lay dead upon the field or in the Deep.

No Orcs remained alive; their bodies were uncounted. But a great many of the hillmen had given themselves up; and they were afraid, and cried for mercy.

The Men of the Mark took their weapons from them, and set them to work.

'Help now to repair the evil in which you have joined,' said Erkenbrand; 'and afterwards you shall take an oath never again to pass the Fords of Isen in arms, nor to march with the enemies of Men; and then you shall go free back to your land. For you have been deluded by Saruman. Many of you have got death as the reward of your trust in him; but had you conquered, little better would your wages have been.'

The men of Dunland were amazed; for Saruman had told them that the men of Rohan were cruel and burned their captives alive.

In the midst of the field before the Hornburg two mounds were raised, and beneath them were laid all the Riders of the Mark who fell in the defence, those of the East Dales upon one side, and those of Westfold upon the other. In a grave alone under the shadow of the Hornburg lay Háma, captain of the King's guard. He fell before the Gate.

The Orcs were piled in great heaps, away from the mounds of Men, not far from the eaves of the forest. And the people were troubled in their minds; for the heaps of carrion were too great for burial or for burning. They had little wood for firing, and none would have dared to take an axe to the strange trees, even if Gandalf had not warned them to hurt neither bark nor bough at their great peril.

'Let the Orcs lie,' said Gandalf. 'The morning may bring new counsel.'

In the afternoon the King's company prepared to depart. The work of burial was then but beginning; and Théoden mourned for the loss of Háma, his captain, and cast the first earth upon his grave. 'Great injury indeed has Saruman done to me and all this land,' he said; 'and I will remember it, when we meet.'

The sun was already drawing near the hills upon the west of the Coomb, when at last Théoden and Gandalf and their companions rode down from the Dike. Behind them were gathered a great host, both of the Riders and of the people of Westfold, old and young, women and children, who had come out from the caves. A song of victory they sang with clear voices; and then they fell silent, wondering what would chance, for their eyes were on the trees and they feared them.

The Riders came to the wood, and they halted; horse and man, they were unwilling to pass in. The trees were grey and menacing, and a shadow or a mist was about them. The ends of their long sweeping boughs hung down like searching fingers, their roots stood up from the ground like the limbs of strange monsters, and dark caverns opened beneath them. But Gandalf went forward, leading the company, and where the road from the Hornburg met the trees they saw now an opening like an arched gate under mighty boughs; and through it Gandalf passed, and they followed him. Then to their amazement they found that the road ran on, and the Deeping-stream beside it; and the sky was open above and full of golden light. But on either side the great aisles of the wood were already wrapped in dusk, stretching away into impenetrable shadows; and there they heard the creaking and groaning of boughs, and far cries, and a rumour of wordless voices, murmuring angrily. No Orc or other living creature could be seen.

Legolas and Gimli were now riding together upon one horse; and they kept close beside Gandalf, for Gimli was afraid of the wood.

'It is hot in here,' said Legolas to Gandalf. 'I feel a great wrath about me. Do you not feel the air throb in your ears?'

'Yes,' said Gandalf.

'What has become of the miserable Orcs?' said Legolas.

'That, I think, no one will ever know,' said Gandalf.

They rode in silence for a while; but Legolas was ever glancing from side to side, and would often have halted to listen to the sounds of the wood, if Gimli had allowed it.

'These are the strangest trees that ever I saw,' he said; 'and I have seen many an oak grow from acorn to ruinous age. I wish that there were leisure now to walk among them: they have voices, and in time I might come to understand their thought.'

'No, no!' said Gimli. 'Let us leave them! I guess their thought already: hatred of all that go on two legs; and their speech is of crushing and strangling.'

'Not of all that go on two legs,' said Legolas. 'There I think you are wrong. It is Orcs that they hate. For they do not belong here and know little of Elves and Men. Far away are the valleys where they sprang. From the deep dales of Fangorn, Gimli, that is whence they come, I guess.'

'Then that is the most perilous wood in Middle-earth,' said Gimli. 'I should be grateful for the part they have played, but I do not love them. You may think them wonderful, but I have seen a greater wonder in this land, more beautiful than any grove or glade that ever grew: my heart is still full of it.

'Strange are the ways of Men, Legolas! Here they have one of the marvels of the Northern World, and what do they say of it? Caves, they say! Caves! Holes to fly to in time of war, to store fodder in! My good Legolas, do you know that the caverns of Helm's Deep are vast and beautiful? There would be an endless pilgrimage of Dwarves, merely to gaze at them, if such things were known to be. Aye indeed, they would pay pure gold for a brief glance!'

'And I would give gold to be excused,' said Legolas; 'and double to be let out, if I strayed in!'

'You have not seen, so I forgive your jest,' said Gimli. 'But you speak like a fool. Do you think those halls are fair, where your King dwells under the hill in Mirkwood, and Dwarves

helped in their making long ago? They are but hovels compared with the caverns I have seen here: immeasurable halls,
filled with an everlasting music of water that tinkles into
pools, as fair as Kheled-zâram in the starlight.

'And, Legolas, when the torches are kindled and men walk
on the sandy floors under the echoing domes, ah! then, Legolas, gems and crystals and veins of precious ore glint in the
polished walls; and the light glows through folded marbles,
shell-like, translucent as the living hands of Queen Galadriel.
There are columns of white and saffron and dawn-rose, Legolas, fluted and twisted into dreamlike forms; they spring up
from many-coloured floors to meet the glistening pendants of
the roof: wings, ropes, curtains fine as frozen clouds; spears,
banners, pinnacles of suspended palaces! Still lakes mirror
them: a glimmering world looks up from dark pools covered
with clear glass; cities, such as the mind of Durin could scarce
have imagined in his sleep, stretch on through avenues and
pillared courts, on into the dark recesses where no light can
come. And plink! a silver drop falls, and the round wrinkles
in the glass make all the towers bend and waver like weeds
and corals in a grotto of the sea. Then evening comes: they
fade and twinkle out; the torches pass on into another
chamber and another dream. There is chamber after
chamber, Legolas; hall opening out of hall, dome after dome,
stair beyond stair; and still the winding paths lead on into
the mountains' heart. Caves! The Caverns of Helm's Deep!
Happy was the chance that drove me there! It makes me
weep to leave them.'

'Then I will wish you this fortune for your comfort, Gimli,'
said the Elf, 'that you may come safe from war and return to
see them again. But do not tell all your kindred! There seems
little left for them to do, from your account. Maybe the men
of this land are wise to say little: one family of busy dwarves
with hammer and chisel might mar more than they made.'

'No, you do not understand,' said Gimli. 'No dwarf could
be unmoved by such loveliness. None of Durin's race would
mine those caves for stones or ore, not if diamonds and gold

could be got there. Do you cut down groves of blossoming trees in the springtime for firewood? We would tend these glades of flowering stone, not quarry them. With cautious skill, tap by tap – a small chip of rock and no more, perhaps, in a whole anxious day – so we could work, and as the years went by, we should open up new ways, and display far chambers that are still dark, glimpsed only as a void beyond fissures in the rock. And lights, Legolas! We should make lights, such lamps as once shone in Khazad-dûm; and when we wished we would drive away the night that has lain there since the hills were made; and when we desired rest, we would let the night return.'

'You move me, Gimli,' said Legolas. 'I have never heard you speak like this before. Almost you make me regret that I have not seen these caves. Come! Let us make this bargain – if we both return safe out of the perils that await us, we will journey for a while together. You shall visit Fangorn with me, and then I will come with you to see Helm's Deep.'

'That would not be the way of return that I should choose,' said Gimli. 'But I will endure Fangorn, if I have your promise to come back to the caves and share their wonder with me.'

'You have my promise,' said Legolas. 'But alas! Now we must leave behind both cave and wood for a while. See! We are coming to the end of the trees. How far is it to Isengard, Gandalf?'

'About fifteen leagues, as the crows of Saruman make it,' said Gandalf: 'five from the mouth of Deeping-coomb to the Fords; and ten more from there to the gates of Isengard. But we shall not ride all the way this night.'

'And when we come there, what shall we see?' asked Gimli. 'You may know, but I cannot guess.'

'I do not know myself for certain,' answered the wizard. 'I was there at nightfall yesterday, but much may have happened since. Yet I think that you will not say that the journey was in vain – not though the Glittering Caves of Aglarond be left behind.'

*   *   *

At last the company passed through the trees, and found that they had come to the bottom of the Coomb, where the road from Helm's Deep branched, going one way east to Edoras, and the other north to the Fords of Isen. As they rode from under the eaves of the wood, Legolas halted and looked back with regret. Then he gave a sudden cry.

'There are eyes!' he said. 'Eyes looking out from the shadows of the boughs! I never saw such eyes before.'

The others, surprised by his cry, halted and turned; but Legolas started to ride back.

'No, no!' cried Gimli. 'Do as you please in your madness, but let me first get down from this horse! I wish to see no eyes!'

'Stay, Legolas Greenleaf!' said Gandalf. 'Do not go back into the wood, not yet! Now is not your time.'

Even as he spoke, there came forward out of the trees three strange shapes. As tall as trolls they were, twelve feet or more in height; their strong bodies, stout as young trees, seemed to be clad with raiment or with hide of close-fitting grey and brown. Their limbs were long, and their hands had many fingers; their hair was stiff, and their beards grey-green as moss. They gazed out with solemn eyes, but they were not looking at the riders: their eyes were bent northwards. Suddenly they lifted their long hands to their mouths, and sent forth ringing calls, clear as notes of a horn, but more musical and various. The calls were answered; and turning again, the riders saw other creatures of the same kind approaching, striding through the grass. They came swiftly from the North, walking like wading herons in their gait, but not in their speed; for their legs in their long paces beat quicker than the heron's wings. The riders cried aloud in wonder, and some set their hands upon their sword-hilts.

'You need no weapons,' said Gandalf. 'These are but herdsmen. They are not enemies, indeed they are not concerned with us at all.'

So it seemed to be; for as he spoke the tall creatures, without a glance at the riders, strode into the wood and vanished.

'Herdsmen!' said Théoden. 'Where are their flocks? What are they, Gandalf? For it is plain that to you, at any rate, they are not strange.'

'They are the shepherds of the trees,' answered Gandalf. 'Is it so long since you listened to tales by the fireside? There are children in your land who, out of the twisted threads of story, could pick the answer to your question. You have seen Ents, O King, Ents out of Fangorn Forest, which in your tongue you call the Entwood. Did you think that the name was given only in idle fancy? Nay, Théoden, it is otherwise: to them you are but the passing tale; all the years from Eorl the Young to Théoden the Old are of little count to them; and all the deeds of your house but a small matter.'

The king was silent. 'Ents!' he said at length. 'Out of the shadows of legend I begin a little to understand the marvel of the trees, I think. I have lived to see strange days. Long we have tended our beasts and our fields, built our houses, wrought our tools, or ridden away to help in the wars of Minas Tirith. And that we called the life of Men, the way of the world. We cared little for what lay beyond the borders of our land. Songs we have that tell of these things, but we are forgetting them, teaching them only to children, as a careless custom. And now the songs have come down among us out of strange places, and walk visible under the Sun.'

'You should be glad, Théoden King,' said Gandalf. 'For not only the little life of Men is now endangered, but the life also of those things which you have deemed the matter of legend. You are not without allies, even if you know them not.'

'Yet also I should be sad,' said Théoden. 'For however the fortune of war shall go, may it not so end that much that was fair and wonderful shall pass for ever out of Middle-earth?'

'It may,' said Gandalf. 'The evil of Sauron cannot be wholly cured, nor made as if it had not been. But to such days we are doomed. Let us now go on with the journey we have begun!'

*　　*　　*

The company turned then away from the Coomb and from the wood and took the road towards the Fords. Legolas followed reluctantly. The sun had set, already it had sunk behind the rim of the world; but as they rode out from the shadow of the hills and looked west to the Gap of Rohan the sky was still red, and a burning light was under the floating clouds. Dark against it there wheeled and flew many black-winged birds. Some passed overhead with mournful cries, returning to their homes among the rocks.

'The carrion-fowl have been busy about the battle-field,' said Éomer.

They rode now at an easy pace and dark came down upon the plains about them. The slow moon mounted, now waxing towards the full, and in its cold silver light the swelling grass-lands rose and fell like a wide grey sea. They had ridden for some four hours from the branching of the roads when they drew near to the Fords. Long slopes ran swiftly down to where the river spread in stony shoals between high grassy terraces. Borne upon the wind they heard the howling of wolves. Their hearts were heavy, remembering the many men that had fallen in battle in this place.

The road dipped between rising turf-banks, carving its way through the terraces to the river's edge, and up again upon the further side. There were three lines of flat stepping-stones across the stream, and between them fords for horses, that went from either brink to a bare eyot in the midst. The riders looked down upon the crossings, and it seemed strange to them; for the Fords had ever been a place full of the rush and chatter of water upon stones; but now they were silent. The beds of the stream were almost dry, a bare waste of shingles and grey sand.

'This is become a dreary place,' said Éomer. 'What sickness has befallen the river? Many fair things Saruman has destroyed: has he devoured the springs of Isen too?'

'So it would seem,' said Gandalf.

'Alas!' said Théoden. 'Must we pass this way, where the carrion-beasts devour so many good Riders of the Mark?'

'This is our way,' said Gandalf. 'Grievous is the fall of your men; but you shall see that at least the wolves of the mountains do not devour them. It is with their friends, the Orcs, that they hold their feast: such indeed is the friendship of their kind. Come!'

They rode down to the river, and as they came the wolves ceased their howling and slunk away. Fear fell on them seeing Gandalf in the moon, and Shadowfax his horse shining like silver. The riders passed over to the islet, and glittering eyes watched them wanly from the shadows of the banks.

'Look!' said Gandalf. 'Friends have laboured here.'

And they saw that in the midst of the eyot a mound was piled, ringed with stones, and set about with many spears.

'Here lie all the Men of the Mark that fell near this place,' said Gandalf.

'Here let them rest!' said Éomer. 'And when their spears have rotted and rusted, long still may their mound stand and guard the Fords of Isen!'

'Is this your work also, Gandalf, my friend?' said Théoden. 'You accomplished much in an evening and a night!'

'With the help of Shadowfax – and others,' said Gandalf. 'I rode fast and far. But here beside the mound I will say this for your comfort: many fell in the battles of the Fords, but fewer than rumour made them. More were scattered than were slain; I gathered together all that I could find. Some men I sent with Grimbold of Westfold to join Erkenbrand. Some I set to make this burial. They have now followed your marshal, Elfhelm. I sent him with many Riders to Edoras. Saruman I knew had despatched his full strength against you, and his servants had turned aside from all other errands and gone to Helm's Deep: the lands seemed empty of enemies; yet I feared that wolf-riders and plunderers might ride none-theless to Meduseld, while it was undefended. But now I think you need not fear: you will find your house to welcome your return.'

'And glad shall I be to see it again,' said Théoden, 'though brief now, I doubt not, shall be my abiding there.'

With that the company said farewell to the island and the mound, and passed over the river, and climbed the further bank. Then they rode on, glad to have left the mournful Fords. As they went the howling of the wolves broke out anew.

There was an ancient highway that ran down from Isengard to the crossings. For some way it took its course beside the river, bending with it east and then north; but at the last it turned away and went straight towards the gates of Isengard; and these were under the mountain-side in the west of the valley, sixteen miles or more from its mouth. This road they followed but they did not ride upon it; for the ground beside it was firm and level, covered for many miles about with short springing turf. They rode now more swiftly, and by midnight the Fords were nearly five leagues behind. Then they halted, ending their night's journey, for the King was weary. They were come to the feet of the Misty Mountains, and the long arms of Nan Curunír stretched down to meet them. Dark lay the vale before them, for the moon had passed into the West, and its light was hidden by the hills. But out of the deep shadow of the dale rose a vast spire of smoke and vapour; as it mounted, it caught the rays of the sinking moon, and spread in shimmering billows, black and silver, over the starry sky.

'What do you think of that, Gandalf?' asked Aragorn. 'One would say that all the Wizard's Vale was burning.'

'There is ever a fume above that valley in these days,' said Éomer: 'but I have never seen aught like this before. These are steams rather than smokes. Saruman is brewing some devilry to greet us. Maybe he is boiling all the waters of Isen, and that is why the river runs dry.'

'Maybe he is,' said Gandalf. 'Tomorrow we shall learn what he is doing. Now let us rest for a while, if we can.'

They camped beside the bed of the Isen river; it was still silent and empty. Some of them slept a little. But late in the night the watchmen cried out, and all awoke. The moon was gone. Stars were shining above; but over the ground there

crept a darkness blacker than the night. On both sides of the
river it rolled towards them, going northward.

'Stay where you are!' said Gandalf. 'Draw no weapons!
Wait! and it will pass you by!'

A mist gathered about them. Above them a few stars still
glimmered faintly; but on either side there arose walls of
impenetrable gloom; they were in a narrow lane between
moving towers of shadow. Voices they heard, whisperings
and groanings and an endless rustling sigh; the earth shook
under them. Long it seemed to them that they sat and were
afraid; but at last the darkness and the rumour passed, and
vanished between the mountain's arms.

Away south upon the Hornburg, in the middle night men
heard a great noise, as a wind in the valley, and the ground
trembled; and all were afraid and no one ventured to go
forth. But in the morning they went out and were amazed;
for the slain Orcs were gone, and the trees also. Far down
into the valley of the Deep the grass was crushed and
trampled brown, as if giant herdsmen had pastured great
droves of cattle there; but a mile below the Dike a huge pit
had been delved in the earth, and over it stones were piled
into a hill. Men believed that the Orcs whom they had slain
were buried there; but whether those who had fled into the
wood were with them, none could say, for no man ever set
foot upon that hill. The Death Down it was afterwards called,
and no grass would grow there. But the strange trees were
never seen in Deeping-coomb again; they had returned at
night, and had gone far away to the dark dales of Fangorn.
Thus they were revenged upon the Orcs.

The king and his company slept no more that night; but
they saw and heard no other strange thing, save one: the
voice of the river beside them suddenly awoke. There was a
rush of water hurrying down among the stones; and when it
had passed, the Isen flowed and bubbled in its bed again, as
it had ever done.

At dawn they made ready to go on. The light came grey and pale, and they did not see the rising of the sun. The air above was heavy with fog, and a reek lay on the land about them. They went slowly, riding now upon the highway. It was broad and hard, and well-tended. Dimly through the mists they could descry the long arm of the mountains rising on their left. They had passed into Nan Curunír, the Wizard's Vale. That was a sheltered valley, open only to the South. Once it had been fair and green, and through it the Isen flowed, already deep and strong before it found the plains; for it was fed by many springs and lesser streams among the rain-washed hills, and all about it there had lain a pleasant, fertile land.

It was not so now. Beneath the walls of Isengard there still were acres tilled by the slaves of Saruman; but most of the valley had become a wilderness of weeds and thorns. Brambles trailed upon the ground, or clambering over bush and bank, made shaggy caves where small beasts housed. No trees grew there; but among the rank grasses could still be seen the burned and axe-hewn stumps of ancient groves. It was a sad country, silent now but for the stony noise of quick waters. Smokes and steams drifted in sullen clouds and lurked in the hollows. The riders did not speak. Many doubted in their hearts, wondering to what dismal end their journey led.

After they had ridden for some miles, the highway became a wide street, paved with great flat stones, squared and laid with skill; no blade of grass was seen in any joint. Deep gutters, filled with trickling water, ran down on either side. Suddenly a tall pillar loomed up before them. It was black; and set upon it was a great stone, carved and painted in the likeness of a long White Hand. Its finger pointed north. Not far now they knew that the gates of Isengard must stand, and their hearts were heavy; but their eyes could not pierce the mists ahead.

Beneath the mountain's arm within the Wizard's Vale through years uncounted had stood that ancient place that

Men called Isengard. Partly it was shaped in the making of the mountains, but mighty works the Men of Westernesse had wrought there of old; and Saruman had dwelt there long and had not been idle.

This was its fashion, while Saruman was at his height, accounted by many the chief of Wizards. A great ring-wall of stone, like towering cliffs, stood out from the shelter of the mountain-side, from which it ran and then returned again. One entrance only was there made in it, a great arch delved in the southern wall. Here through the black rock a long tunnel had been hewn, closed at either end with mighty doors of iron. They were so wrought and poised upon their huge hinges, posts of steel driven into the living stone, that when unbarred they could be moved with a light thrust of the arms, noiselessly. One who passed in and came at length out of the echoing tunnel, beheld a plain, a great circle, somewhat hollowed like a vast shallow bowl: a mile it measured from rim to rim. Once it had been green and filled with avenues, and groves of fruitful trees, watered by streams that flowed from the mountains to a lake. But no green thing grew there in the latter days of Saruman. The roads were paved with stone-flags, dark and hard; and beside their borders instead of trees there marched long lines of pillars, some of marble, some of copper and of iron, joined by heavy chains.

Many houses there were, chambers, halls, and passages, cut and tunnelled back into the walls upon their inner side, so that all the open circle was overlooked by countless windows and dark doors. Thousands could dwell there, workers, servants, slaves, and warriors with great store of arms; wolves were fed and stabled in deep dens beneath. The plain, too, was bored and delved. Shafts were driven deep into the ground; their upper ends were covered by low mounds and domes of stone, so that in the moonlight the Ring of Isengard looked like a graveyard of unquiet dead. For the ground trembled. The shafts ran down by many slopes and spiral stairs to caverns far under; there Saruman had treasuries, store-houses, armouries, smithies, and great furnaces. Iron wheels revolved there endlessly, and hammers thudded. At night plumes of vapour steamed from the vents, lit from beneath with red light, or blue, or venomous green.

To the centre all the roads ran between their chains. There stood a tower of marvellous shape. It was fashioned by the builders of old, who smoothed the Ring of Isengard, and yet it seemed a thing not made by the craft of Men, but riven from the bones of the earth in the ancient torment of the hills. A peak and isle of rock it was, black and gleaming hard: four mighty piers of many-sided stone were welded into one, but near the summit they opened into gaping horns, their pinnacles sharp as the points of spears, keen-edged as knives. Between them was a narrow space, and there upon a floor of polished stone, written with strange signs, a man might stand five hundred feet above the plain. This was Orthanc, the citadel of Saruman, the name of which had (by design or chance) a twofold meaning; for in the Elvish speech *orthanc* signifies Mount Fang, but in the language of the Mark of old the Cunning Mind.

A strong place and wonderful was Isengard, and long it had been beautiful; and there great lords had dwelt, the wardens of Gondor upon the West, and wise men that watched the stars. But Saruman had slowly shaped it to his shifting purposes, and made it better, as he thought, being deceived – for all those arts and subtle devices, for which he forsook his former wisdom, and which fondly he imagined were his own, came but from Mordor; so that what he made was naught, only a little copy, a child's model or a slave's flattery, of that vast fortress, armoury, prison, furnace of great power, Barad-dûr, the Dark Tower, which suffered no rival, and laughed at flattery, biding its time, secure in its pride and its immeasurable strength.

This was the stronghold of Saruman, as fame reported it; for within living memory the men of Rohan had not passed its gates, save perhaps a few, such as Wormtongue, who came in secret and told no man what they saw.

*   *   *

Now Gandalf rode to the great pillar of the Hand, and passed it; and as he did so the Riders saw to their wonder that the Hand appeared no longer white. It was stained as with dried blood; and looking closer they perceived that its nails were red. Unheeding Gandalf rode on into the mist, and reluctantly they followed him. All about them now, as if there had been a sudden flood, wide pools of water lay beside the road, filling the hollows, and rills went trickling down among the stones.

At last Gandalf halted and beckoned to them; and they came, and saw that beyond him the mists had cleared, and a pale sunlight shone. The hour of noon had passed. They were come to the doors of Isengard.

But the doors lay hurled and twisted on the ground. And all about, stone, cracked and splintered into countless jagged shards, was scattered far and wide, or piled in ruinous heaps. The great arch still stood, but it opened now upon a roofless chasm: the tunnel was laid bare, and through the cliff-like walls on either side great rents and breaches had been torn; their towers were beaten into dust. If the Great Sea had risen in wrath and fallen on the hills with storm, it could have worked no greater ruin.

The ring beyond was filled with steaming water: a bubbling cauldron, in which there heaved and floated a wreckage of beams and spars, chests and casks and broken gear. Twisted and leaning pillars reared their splintered stems above the flood, but all the roads were drowned. Far off, it seemed, half veiled in winding cloud, there loomed the island rock. Still dark and tall, unbroken by the storm, the tower of Orthanc stood. Pale waters lapped about its feet.

The king and all his company sat silent on their horses, marvelling, perceiving that the power of Saruman was overthrown; but how they could not guess. And now they turned their eyes towards the archway and the ruined gates. There they saw close beside them a great rubble-heap; and suddenly they were aware of two small figures lying on it at their ease, grey-clad, hardly to be seen among the stones. There were bottles and bowls and platters laid beside them, as if they had just eaten well, and now rested from their labour. One seemed asleep; the other, with crossed legs and arms behind his head, leaned back against a broken rock and sent from his mouth long wisps and little rings of thin blue smoke.

For a moment Théoden and Éomer and all his men stared at them in wonder. Amid all the wreck of Isengard this seemed to them the strangest sight. But before the king could speak, the small smoke-breathing figure became suddenly aware of them, as they sat there silent on the edge of the mist. He sprang to his feet. A young man he looked, or like one, though not much more than half a man in height; his head of brown curling hair was uncovered, but he was clad in a travel-stained cloak of the same hue and shape as the companions of Gandalf had worn when they rode to Edoras. He bowed very low, putting his hand upon his breast. Then, seeming not to observe the wizard and his friends, he turned to Éomer and the king.

'Welcome, my lords, to Isengard!' he said. 'We are the doorwardens. Meriadoc, son of Saradoc is my name; and my companion, who, alas! is overcome with weariness' – here he gave the other a dig with his foot – 'is Peregrin, son of Paladin, of the house of Took. Far in the North is our home. The Lord Saruman is within; but at the moment he is closeted with one Wormtongue, or doubtless he would be here to welcome such honourable guests.'

'Doubtless he would!' laughed Gandalf. 'And was it Saruman that ordered you to guard his damaged doors, and watch for the arrival of guests, when your attention could be spared from plate and bottle?'

'No, good sir, the matter escaped him,' answered Merry gravely. 'He has been much occupied. Our orders came from Treebeard, who has taken over the management of Isengard. He commanded me to welcome the Lord of Rohan with fitting words. I have done my best.'

'And what about your companions? What about Legolas

and me?' cried Gimli, unable to contain himself longer. 'You rascals, you woolly-footed and wool-pated truants! A fine hunt you have led us! Two hundred leagues, through fen and forest, battle and death, to rescue you! And here we find you feasting and idling – and smoking! Smoking! Where did you come by the weed, you villains? Hammer and tongs! I am so torn between rage and joy, that if I do not burst, it will be a marvel!'

'You speak for me, Gimli,' laughed Legolas. 'Though I would sooner learn how they came by the wine.'

'One thing you have not found in your hunting, and that's brighter wits,' said Pippin, opening an eye. 'Here you find us sitting on a field of victory, amid the plunder of armies, and you wonder how we came by a few well-earned comforts!'

'Well-earned?' said Gimli. 'I cannot believe that!'

The Riders laughed. 'It cannot be doubted that we witness the meeting of dear friends,' said Théoden. 'So these are the lost ones of your company, Gandalf? The days are fated to be filled with marvels. Already I have seen many since I left my house; and now here before my eyes stand yet another of the folk of legend. Are not these the Halflings, that some among us call the Holbytlan?'

'Hobbits, if you please, lord,' said Pippin.

'Hobbits?' said Théoden. 'Your tongue is strangely changed; but the name sounds not unfitting so. Hobbits! No report that I have heard does justice to the truth.'

Merry bowed; and Pippin got up and bowed low. 'You are gracious, lord; or I hope that I may so take your words,' he said. 'And here is another marvel! I have wandered in many lands, since I left my home, and never till now have I found people that knew any story concerning hobbits.'

'My people came out of the North long ago,' said Théoden. 'But I will not deceive you: we know no tales about hobbits. All that is said among us is that far away, over many hills and rivers, live the halfling folk that dwell in holes in sand-dunes. But there are no legends of their deeds, for it is said that they do little, and avoid the sight of men, being able to vanish in a twinkling; and they can change their voices to resemble the piping of birds. But it seems that more could be said.'

'It could indeed, lord,' said Merry.

'For one thing,' said Théoden, 'I had not heard that they spouted smoke from their mouths.'

'That is not surprising,' answered Merry; 'for it is an art which we have not practised for more than a few generations. It was Tobold Hornblower, of Longbottom in the Southfarthing, who first grew the true pipe-weed in his gardens, about the year 1070 according to our reckoning. How old Toby came by the plant . . .'

'You do not know your danger, Théoden,' interrupted Gandalf. 'These hobbits will sit on the edge of ruin and discuss the pleasures of the table, or the small doings of their fathers, grandfathers, and great-grandfathers, and remoter cousins to the ninth degree, if you encourage them with undue patience. Some other time would be more fitting for the history of smoking. Where is Treebeard, Merry?'

'Away on the north side, I believe. He went to get a drink – of clean water. Most of the other Ents are with him, still busy at their work – over there.' Merry waved his hand towards the steaming lake; and as they looked, they heard a distant rumbling and rattling, as if an avalanche was falling from the mountain-side. Far away came a *hoom-hom*, as of horns blowing triumphantly.

'And is Orthanc then left unguarded?' asked Gandalf.

'There is the water,' said Merry. 'But Quickbeam and some others are watching it. Not all those posts and pillars in the plain are of Saruman's planting. Quickbeam, I think, is by the rock, near the foot of the stair.'

'Yes, a tall grey Ent is there,' said Legolas, 'but his arms are at his sides, and he stands as still as a door-tree.'

'It is past noon,' said Gandalf, 'and we at any rate have not eaten since early morning. Yet I wish to see Treebeard as soon as may be. Did he leave me no message, or has plate and bottle driven it from your mind?'

'He left a message,' said Merry, 'and I was coming to it, but I have been hindered by many other questions. I was to say that, if the Lord of the Mark and Gandalf will ride to the northern wall they will find Treebeard there, and he will welcome them. I may add that they will also find food of the best there, it was discovered and selected by your humble servants.' He bowed.

Gandalf laughed. 'That is better!' he said. 'Well, Théoden, will you ride with me to find Treebeard? We must go round about, but it is not far. When you see Treebeard, you will learn much. For Treebeard is Fangorn, and the eldest and chief of the Ents, and when you speak with him you will hear the speech of the oldest of all living things.'

'I will come with you,' said Théoden. 'Farewell, my hobbits! May we meet again in my house! There you shall sit beside me and tell me all that your hearts desire: the deeds of your grandsires, as far as you can reckon them; and we will speak also of Tobold the Old and his herb-lore. Farewell!'

The hobbits bowed low. 'So that is the King of Rohan!' said Pippin in an undertone. 'A fine old fellow. Very polite.'

CHAPTER IX

FLOTSAM AND JETSAM

Gandalf and the King's company rode away, turning eastward to make the circuit of the ruined walls of Isengard. But Aragorn, Gimli, and Legolas remained behind. Leaving Arod and Hasufel to stray in search of grass, they came and sat beside the hobbits.

'Well, well! The hunt is over, and we meet again at last, where none of us ever thought to come,' said Aragorn.

'And now that the great ones have gone to discuss high matters,' said Legolas, 'the hunters can perhaps learn the answers to their own small riddles. We tracked you as far as the forest, but there are still many things that I should like to know the truth of.'

'And there is a great deal, too, that we want to know about you,' said Merry. 'We have learnt a few things through Treebeard, the Old Ent, but that is not nearly enough.'

'All in good time,' said Legolas. 'We were the hunters, and you should give an account of yourselves to us first.'

'Or second,' said Gimli. 'It would go better after a meal. I have a sore head; and it is past mid-day. You truants might make amends by finding us some of the plunder that you spoke of. Food and drink would pay off some of my score against you.'

'Then you shall have it,' said Pippin. 'Will you have it here, or in more comfort in what's left of Saruman's guard-house – over there under the arch? We had to picnic out here, so as to keep an eye on the road.'

'Less than an eye!' said Gimli. 'But I will not go into any orc-house; nor touch Orcs' meat or anything that they have mauled.'

'We wouldn't ask you to,' said Merry. 'We have had

enough of Orcs ourselves to last a life-time. But there were many other folk in Isengard. Saruman kept enough wisdom not to trust his Orcs. He had Men to guard his gates: some of his most faithful servants, I suppose. Anyway they were favoured and got good provisions.'

'And pipe-weed?' asked Gimli.

'No, I don't think so,' Merry laughed. 'But that is another story, which can wait until after lunch.'

'Well let us go and have lunch then!' said the Dwarf.

The hobbits led the way; and they passed under the arch and came to a wide door upon the left, at the top of a stair. It opened direct into a large chamber, with other smaller doors at the far end, and a hearth and chimney at one side. The chamber was hewn out of the stone; and it must once have been dark, for its windows looked out only into the tunnel. But light came in now through the broken roof. On the hearth wood was burning.

'I lit a bit of fire,' said Pippin. 'It cheered us up in the fogs. There were few faggots about, and most of the wood we could find was wet. But there is a great draught in the chimney: it seems to wind away up through the rock, and fortunately it has not been blocked. A fire is handy. I will make you some toast. The bread is three or four days old, I am afraid.'

Aragorn and his companions sat themselves down at one end of a long table, and the hobbits disappeared through one of the inner doors.

'Store-room in there, and above the floods, luckily,' said Pippin, as they came back laden with dishes, bowls, cups, knives, and food of various sorts.

'And you need not turn up your nose at the provender, Master Gimli,' said Merry. 'This is not orc-stuff, but man-food, as Treebeard calls it. Will you have wine or beer? There's a barrel inside there – very passable. And this is first-rate salted pork. Or I can cut you some rashers of bacon and broil them, if you like. I am sorry there is no green stuff:

the deliveries have been rather interrupted in the last few days! I cannot offer you anything to follow but butter and honey for your bread. Are you content?'

'Indeed yes,' said Gimli. 'The score is much reduced.'

The three were soon busy with their meal; and the two hobbits, unabashed, set to a second time. 'We must keep our guests company,' they said.

'You are full of courtesy this morning,' laughed Legolas. 'But maybe, if we had not arrived, you would already have been keeping one another company again.'

'Maybe; and why not?' said Pippin. 'We had foul fare with the Orcs, and little enough for days before that. It seems a long while since we could eat to heart's content.'

'It does not seem to have done you any harm,' said Aragorn. 'Indeed you look in the bloom of health.'

'Aye, you do indeed,' said Gimli, looking them up and down over the top of his cup. 'Why, your hair is twice as thick and curly as when we parted; and I would swear that you have both grown somewhat, if that is possible for hobbits of your age. This Treebeard at any rate has not starved you.'

'He has not,' said Merry. 'But Ents only drink, and drink is not enough for content. Treebeard's draughts may be nourishing, but one feels the need of something solid. And even *lembas* is none the worse for a change.'

'You have drunk of the waters of the Ents, have you?' said Legolas. 'Ah, then I think it is likely that Gimli's eyes do not deceive him. Strange songs have been sung of the draughts of Fangorn.'

'Many strange tales have been told about that land,' said Aragorn. 'I have never entered it. Come, tell me more about it, and about the Ents!'

'Ents,' said Pippin, 'Ents are – well Ents are all different for one thing. But their eyes now, their eyes are very odd.' He tried a few fumbling words that trailed off into silence. 'Oh, well,' he went on, 'you have seen some at a distance, already – they saw you at any rate, and reported that you were on the way – and you will see many others, I expect, before you leave here. You must form your own ideas.'

'Now, now!' said Gimli. 'We are beginning the story in the middle. I should like a tale in the right order, starting with that strange day when our fellowship was broken.'

'You shall have it, if there is time,' said Merry. 'But first – if you have finished eating – you shall fill your pipes and light up. And then for a little while we can pretend that we are all back safe at Bree again, or in Rivendell.'

He produced a small leather bag full of tobacco. 'We have heaps of it,' he said; 'and you can all pack as much as you wish, when we go. We did some salvage-work this morning, Pippin and I. There are lots of things floating about. It was Pippin who found two small barrels, washed up out of some cellar or store-house, I suppose. When we opened them, we found they were filled with this: as fine a pipe-weed as you could wish for, and quite unspoilt.'

Gimli took some and rubbed it in his palms and sniffed it. 'It feels good, and it smells good,' he said.

'It is good!' said Merry. 'My dear Gimli, it is Longbottom Leaf! There were the Hornblower brandmarks on the barrels, as plain as plain. How it came here, I can't imagine. For Saruman's private use, I fancy. I never knew that it went so far abroad. But it comes in handy now!'

'It would,' said Gimli, 'if I had a pipe to go with it. Alas, I lost mine in Moria, or before. Is there no pipe in all your plunder?'

'No, I am afraid not,' said Merry. 'We have not found any, not even here in the guardrooms. Saruman kept this dainty to himself, it seems. And I don't think it would be any use knocking on the doors of Orthanc to beg a pipe of him! We shall have to share pipes, as good friends must at a pinch.'

'Half a moment!' said Pippin. Putting his hand inside the breast of his jacket he pulled out a little soft wallet on a string. 'I keep a treasure or two near my skin, as precious as Rings to me. Here's one: my old wooden pipe. And here's another: an unused one. I have carried it a long way, though I don't know why. I never really expected to find any pipe-weed on the journey, when my own ran out. But now it comes in useful after all.' He held up a small pipe with a wide flattened bowl, and handed it to Gimli. 'Does that settle the score between us?' he said.

'Settle it!' cried Gimli. 'Most noble hobbit, it leaves me deep in your debt.'

'Well, I am going back into the open air, to see what the wind and sky are doing!' said Legolas.

'We will come with you,' said Aragorn.

They went out and seated themselves upon the piled stones before the gateway. They could see far down into the valley now; the mists were lifting and floating away upon the breeze.

'Now let us take our ease here for a little!' said Aragorn. 'We will sit on the edge of ruin and talk, as Gandalf says, while he is busy elsewhere. I feel a weariness such as I have seldom felt before.' He wrapped his grey cloak about him, hiding his mail-shirt, and stretched out his long legs. Then he lay back and sent from his lips a thin stream of smoke.

'Look!' said Pippin. 'Strider the Ranger has come back!'

'He has never been away,' said Aragorn. 'I am Strider and Dúnadan too, and I belong both to Gondor and the North.'

They smoked in silence for a while, and the sun shone on them; slanting into the valley from among white clouds high in the West. Legolas lay still, looking up at the sun and sky with steady eyes, and singing softly to himself. At last he sat up. 'Come now!' he said. 'Time wears on, and the mists are blowing away, or would if you strange folk did not wreathe yourselves in smoke. What of the tale?'

'Well, my tale begins with waking up in the dark and find-ing myself all strung-up in an orc-camp,' said Pippin. 'Let me see, what is today?'

'The fifth of March in the Shire-reckoning,' said Aragorn. Pippin made some calculations on his fingers. 'Only nine days ago!' he said.* 'It seems a year since we were caught.

* Every month in the Shire-calendar had 30 days.

Well, though half of it was like a bad dream, I reckon that three very horrible days followed. Merry will correct me, if I forget anything important: I am not going into details: the whips and the filth and stench and all that; it does not bear remembering.' With that he plunged into an account of Boromir's last fight and the orc-march from Emyn Muil to the Forest. The others nodded as the various points were fitted in with their guesses.

'Here are some treasures that you let fall,' said Aragorn. 'You will be glad to have them back.' He loosened his belt from under his cloak, and took from it the two sheathed knives.

'Well!' said Merry. 'I never expected to see those again! I marked a few orcs with mine; but Uglúk took them from us. How he glared! At first I thought he was going to stab me, but he threw the things away as if they burned him.'

'And here also is your brooch, Pippin,' said Aragorn. 'I have kept it safe, for it is a very precious thing.'

'I know,' said Pippin. 'It was a wrench to let it go; but what else could I do?'

'Nothing else,' answered Aragorn. 'One who cannot cast away a treasure at need is in fetters. You did rightly.'

'The cutting of the bands on your wrists, that was smart work!' said Gimli. 'Luck served you there; but you seized your chance with both hands, one might say.'

'And set us a pretty riddle,' said Legolas. 'I wondered if you had grown wings!'

'Unfortunately not,' said Pippin. 'But you did not know about Grishnákh.' He shuddered and said no more, leaving Merry to tell of those last horrible moments: the pawing hands, the hot breath, and the dreadful strength of Grishnákh's hairy arms.

'All this about the Orcs of Barad-dûr, Lugbúrz as they call it, makes me uneasy,' said Aragorn. 'The Dark Lord already knew too much, and his servants also; and Grishnákh evidently sent some message across the River after the quarrel. The Red Eye will be looking towards Isengard. But

Saruman at any rate is in a cleft stick of his own cutting.'

'Yes, whichever side wins, his outlook is poor,' said Merry. 'Things began to go all wrong for him from the moment his Orcs set foot in Rohan.'

'We caught a glimpse of the old villain, or so Gandalf hints,' said Gimli. 'On the edge of the Forest.'

'When was that?' asked Pippin.

'Five nights ago,' said Aragorn.

'Let me see,' said Merry: 'five nights ago – now we come to a part of the story you know nothing about. We met Treebeard that morning after the battle; and that night we were at Wellinghall, one of his ent-houses. The next morning we went to Entmoot, a gathering of Ents, that is, and the queerest thing I have ever seen in my life. It lasted all that day and the next; and we spent the nights with an Ent called Quickbeam. And then late in the afternoon in the third day of their moot, the Ents suddenly blew up. It was amazing. The Forest had felt as tense as if a thunderstorm was brewing inside it: then all at once it exploded. I wish you could have heard their song as they marched.'

'If Saruman had heard it, he would be a hundred miles away by now, even if he had had to run on his own legs,' said Pippin.

> *'Though Isengard be strong and hard, as cold as stone and*
> *bare as bone,*
> *We go, we go, we go to war, to hew the stone and break*
> *the door!*

There was very much more. A great deal of the song had no words, and was like a music of horns and drums. It was very exciting. But I thought it was only marching music and no more, just a song – until I got here. I know better now.'

'We came down over the last ridge into Nan Curunír, after night had fallen,' Merry continued. 'It was then that I first had the feeling that the Forest itself was moving behind us. I thought I was dreaming an entish dream, but Pippin had noticed it too. We were both frightened; but we did not find out more about it until later.

'It was the Huorns, or so the Ents call them in "short language". Treebeard won't say much about them, but I think they are Ents that have become almost like trees, at least to look at. They stand here and there in the wood or under its eaves, silent, watching endlessly over the trees; but deep in the darkest dales there are hundreds and hundreds of them, I believe.

'There is a great power in them, and they seem able to wrap themselves in shadow: it is difficult to see them moving. But they do. They can move very quickly, if they are angry. You stand still looking at the weather, maybe, or listening to the rustling of the wind, and then suddenly you find that you are in the middle of a wood with great groping trees all around you. They still have voices, and can speak with the Ents – that is why they are called Huorns, Treebeard says – but they have become queer and wild. Dangerous. I should be terrified of meeting them, if there were no true Ents about to look after them.

'Well, in the early night we crept down a long ravine into the upper end of the Wizard's Vale, the Ents with all their rustling Huorns behind. We could not see them, of course, but the whole air was full of creaking. It was very dark, a cloudy night. They moved at a great speed as soon as they had left the hills, and made a noise like a rushing wind. The Moon did not appear through the clouds, and not long after midnight there was a tall wood all round the north side of Isengard. There was no sign of enemies nor of any challenge. There was a light gleaming from a high window in the tower, that was all.

'Treebeard and a few more Ents crept on, right round to within sight of the great gates. Pippin and I were with him. We were sitting on Treebeard's shoulders, and I could feel the quivering tenseness in him. But even when they are roused, Ents can be very cautious and patient. They stood still as carved stones, breathing and listening.

'Then all at once there was a tremendous stir. Trumpets blared, and the walls of Isengard echoed. We thought that we had been discovered, and that battle was going to begin. But nothing of the sort. All Saruman's people were marching away. I don't know much about this war, or about the Horse-men of Rohan, but Saruman seems to have meant to finish off the king and all his men with one final blow. He emptied Isengard. I saw the enemy go: endless lines of marching Orcs; and troops of them mounted on great wolves. And there were battalions of Men, too. Many of them carried torches, and in the flare I could see their faces. Most of them were ordinary men, rather tall and dark-haired, and grim but not particularly evil-looking. But there were some others that were horrible: man-high, but with goblin-faces, sallow, leering, squint-eyed. Do you know, they reminded me at once of that Southerner at Bree; only he was not so obviously orc-like as most of these were.'

'I thought of him too,' said Aragorn. 'We had many of these half-orcs to deal with at Helm's Deep. It seems plain now that that Southerner was a spy of Saruman's; but whether he was working with the Black Riders, or for Saruman alone, I do not know. It is difficult with these evil folk to know when they are in league, and when they are cheating one another.'

'Well, of all sorts together, there must have been ten thou-sand at the very least,' said Merry. 'They took an hour to pass out of the gates. Some went off down the highway to the Fords, and some turned away and went eastward. A bridge has been built down there, about a mile away, where the river runs in a very deep channel. You could see it now, if you stood up. They were all singing with harsh voices, and laughing, making a hideous din. I thought things looked very black for Rohan. But Treebeard did not move. He said: "My business is with Isengard tonight, with rock and stone."

'But, though I could not see what was happening in the dark, I believe that Huorns began to move south, as soon as the gates were shut again. Their business was with Orcs I

think. They were far down the valley in the morning; or at
any rate there was a shadow there that one couldn't see
through.

'As soon as Saruman had sent off all his army, our turn
came. Treebeard put us down, and went up to the gates, and
began hammering on the doors, and calling for Saruman.
There was no answer, except arrows and stones from the
walls. But arrows are no use against Ents. They hurt them,
of course, and infuriate them: like stinging flies. But an Ent
can be stuck as full of orc-arrows as a pin-cushion, and take
no serious harm. They cannot be poisoned, for one thing;
and their skin seems to be very thick, and tougher than bark.
It takes a very heavy axe-stroke to wound them seriously.
They don't like axes. But there would have to be a great
many axe-men to one Ent: a man that hacks once at an Ent
never gets a chance of a second blow. A punch from an
Ent-fist crumples up iron like thin tin.

'When Treebeard had got a few arrows in him, he began
to warm up, to get positively "hasty", as he would say. He
let out a great *hoom-hom*, and a dozen more Ents came striding up. An angry Ent is terrifying. Their fingers, and their
toes, just freeze on to rock; and they tear it up like bread-crust.
It was like watching the work of great tree-roots in a hundred
years, all packed into a few moments.

'They pushed, pulled, tore, shook, and hammered; and
clang-bang, *crash-crack*, in five minutes they had these huge
gates just lying in ruin; and some were already beginning to
eat into the walls, like rabbits in a sand-pit. I don't know
what Saruman thought was happening; but anyway he did
not know how to deal with it. His wizardry may have been
falling off lately, of course; but anyway I think he has not
much grit, not much plain courage alone in a tight place
without a lot of slaves and machines and things, if you know
what I mean. Very different from old Gandalf. I wonder if
his fame was not all along mainly due to his cleverness in
settling at Isengard.'

'No,' said Aragorn. 'Once he was as great as his fame made

him. His knowledge was deep, his thought was subtle, and his hands marvellously skilled; and he had a power over the minds of others. The wise he could persuade, and the smaller folk he could daunt. That power he certainly still keeps. There are not many in Middle-earth that I should say were safe, if they were left alone to talk with him, even now when he has suffered a defeat. Gandalf, Elrond, and Galadriel, perhaps, now that his wickedness has been laid bare, but very few others.'

'The Ents are safe,' said Pippin. 'He seems at one time to have got round them, but never again. And anyway he did not understand them; and he made the great mistake of leaving them out of his calculations. He had no plan for them, and there was no time to make any, once they had set to work. As soon as our attack began, the few remaining rats in Isengard started bolting through every hole that the Ents made. The Ents let the Men go, after they had questioned them, two or three dozen only down at this end. I don't think many orc-folk, of any size, escaped. Not from the Huorns: there was a wood full of them all round Isengard by that time, as well as those that had gone down the valley.

'When the Ents had reduced a large part of the southern walls to rubbish, and what was left of his people had bolted and deserted him, Saruman fled in a panic. He seems to have been at the gates when we arrived: I expect he came to watch his splendid army march out. When the Ents broke their way in, he left in a hurry. They did not spot him at first. But the night had opened out, and there was a great light of stars, quite enough for Ents to see by, and suddenly Quickbeam gave a cry "The tree-killer, the tree-killer!" Quickbeam is a gentle creature, but he hates Saruman all the more fiercely for that: his people suffered cruelly from orc-axes. He leapt down the path from the inner gate, and he can move like a wind when he is roused. There was a pale figure hurrying away in and out of the shadows of the pillars, and it had nearly reached the stairs to the tower-door. But it was a near thing. Quickbeam was so hot after him, that he was within a step or two of being caught and strangled when he slipped in through the door.

'When Saruman was safe back in Orthanc, it was not long before he set some of his precious machinery to work. By that time there were many Ents inside Isengard: some had followed Quickbeam, and others had burst in from the north and east; they were roaming about and doing a great deal of damage. Suddenly up came fires and foul fumes: the vents and shafts all over the plain began to spout and belch. Several of the Ents got scorched and blistered. One of them, Beech-bone I think he was called, a very tall handsome Ent, got caught in a spray of some liquid fire and burned like a torch: a horrible sight.

'That sent them mad. I thought that they had been really roused before; but I was wrong. I saw what it was like at last. It was staggering. They roared and boomed and trumpeted, until stones began to crack and fall at the mere noise of them. Merry and I lay on the ground and stuffed our cloaks into our ears. Round and round the rock of Orthanc the Ents went striding and storming like a howling gale, breaking pil-lars, hurling avalanches of boulders down the shafts, tossing up huge slabs of stone into the air like leaves. The tower was in the middle of a spinning whirlwind. I saw iron posts and blocks of masonry go rocketing up hundreds of feet, and smash against the windows of Orthanc. But Treebeard kept his head. He had not had any burns, luckily. He did not want his folk to hurt themselves in their fury, and he did not want Saruman to escape out of some hole in the confusion. Many of the Ents were hurling themselves against the Orthanc-rock; but that defeated them. It is very smooth and hard. Some wizardry is in it, perhaps, older and stronger than Saruman's. Anyway they could not get a grip on it, or make a crack in it; and they were bruising and wounding themselves against it.

'So Treebeard went out into the ring and shouted. His enormous voice rose above all the din. There was a dead silence, suddenly. In it we heard a shrill laugh from a high window in the tower. That had a queer effect on the Ents. They had been boiling over; now they became cold, grim as ice, and quiet. They left the plain and gathered round Treebeard, standing quite still. He spoke to them for a little in their own language; I think he was telling them of a plan he had made in his old head long before. Then they just faded silently away in the grey light. Day was dawning by that time.

'They set a watch on the tower, I believe, but the watchers were so well hidden in shadows and kept so still, that I could not see them. The others went away north. All that day they were busy, out of sight. Most of the time we were left alone. It was a dreary day; and we wandered about a bit, though we kept out of the view of the windows of Orthanc, as much as we could: they stared at us so threateningly. A good deal of the time we spent looking for something to eat. And also we sat and talked, wondering what was happening away south in Rohan, and what had become of all the rest of our Company. Every now and then we could hear in the distance the rattle and fall of stone, and thudding noises echoing in the hills.

'In the afternoon we walked round the circle, and went to have a look at what was going on. There was a great shadowy wood of Huorns at the head of the valley, and another round the northern wall. We did not dare to go in. But there was a rending, tearing noise of work going on inside. Ents and Huorns were digging great pits and trenches, and making great pools and dams, gathering all the waters of the Isen and every other spring and stream that they could find. We left them to it.

'At dusk Treebeard came back to the gate. He was humming and booming to himself, and seemed pleased. He stood and stretched his great arms and legs and breathed deep. I asked him if he was tired.

'"Tired?" he said, "tired? Well no, not tired, but stiff. I need a good draught of Entwash. We have worked hard; we have done more stone-cracking and earth-gnawing today than we have done in many a long year before. But it is nearly finished. When night falls do not linger near this gate or in the old tunnel! Water may come through – and it will be foul water for a while, until all the filth of Saruman is washed away. Then Isen can run clean again." He began to pull down a bit more of the walls, in a leisurely sort of way, just to amuse himself.

'We were just wondering where it would be safe to lie and get some sleep, when the most amazing thing of all happened. There was the sound of a rider coming swiftly up the road. Merry and I lay quiet, and Treebeard hid himself in the shadows under the arch. Suddenly a great horse came striding up, like a flash of silver. It was already dark, but I could see the rider's face clearly: it seemed to shine, and all his clothes were white. I just sat up, staring, with my mouth open. I tried to call out, and couldn't.

'There was no need. He halted just by us and looked down at us. "Gandalf!" I said at last, but my voice was only a whisper. Did he say: "Hullo, Pippin! This is a pleasant surprise!"? No, indeed! He said: "Get up, you tom-fool of a Took! Where, in the name of wonder, in all this ruin is Treebeard? I want him. Quick!"

'Treebeard heard his voice and came out of the shadows at once; and there was a strange meeting. I was surprised, because neither of them seemed surprised at all. Gandalf obviously expected to find Treebeard here; and Treebeard might almost have been loitering about near the gates on purpose to meet him. Yet we had told the old Ent all about Moria. But then I remembered a queer look he gave us at the time. I can only suppose that he had seen Gandalf or had some news of him, but would not say anything in a hurry. "Don't be hasty" is his motto; but nobody, not even Elves, will say much about Gandalf's movements when he is not there.

' "Hoom! Gandalf!" said Treebeard. "I am glad you have come. Wood and water, stock and stone, I can master; but there is a Wizard to manage here."

' "Treebeard," said Gandalf. "I need your help. You have done much, but I need more. I have about ten thousand Orcs to manage."

'Then those two went off and had a council together in some corner. It must have seemed very hasty to Treebeard, for Gandalf was in a tremendous hurry, and was already talking at a great pace, before they passed out of hearing. They were only away a matter of minutes, perhaps a quarter of an hour. Then Gandalf came back to us, and he seemed relieved, almost merry. He did say he was glad to see us, then.

' "But Gandalf," I cried, "where have you been? And have you seen the others?"

' "Wherever I have been, I am back," he answered in the genuine Gandalf manner. "Yes, I have seen some of the others. But news must wait. This is a perilous night, and I must ride fast. But the dawn may be brighter; and if so, we shall meet again. Take care of yourselves, and keep away from Orthanc! Good-bye!"

'Treebeard was very thoughtful after Gandalf had gone. He had evidently learnt a lot in a short time and was digesting it. He looked at us and said: "Hm, well, I find you are not such hasty folk as I thought. You said much less than you might, and no more than you should. Hm, this is a bundle of news and no mistake! Well, now Treebeard must get busy again."

'Before he went, we got a little news out of him; and it did not cheer us up at all. But for the moment we thought more about you three than about Frodo and Sam, or about poor Boromir. For we gathered that there was a great battle going on, or soon would be, and that you were in it, and might never come out of it.

' "Huorns will help," said Treebeard. Then he went away and we did not see him again until this morning.

'It was deep night. We lay on top of a pile of stone, and could see nothing beyond it. Mist or shadows blotted out everything like a great blanket all round us. The air seemed hot and heavy; and it was full of rustlings, creakings, and a murmur like voices passing. I think that hundreds more of the Huorns must have been passing by to help in the battle. Later there was a great rumble of thunder away south, and flashes of lightning far away across Rohan. Every now and then we could see mountain-peaks, miles and miles away, stab out suddenly, black and white, and then vanish. And behind us there were noises like thunder in hills, but different. At times the whole valley echoed.

'It must have been about midnight when the Ents broke the dams and poured all the gathered waters through a gap in the northern wall, down into Isengard. The Huorn-dark had passed, and the thunder had rolled away. The Moon was sinking behind the western mountains.

'Isengard began to fill up with black creeping streams and pools. They glittered in the last light of the Moon, as they spread over the plain. Every now and then the waters found their way down into some shaft or spouthole. Great white steams hissed up. Smoke rose in billows. There were explosions and gusts of fire. One great coil of vapour went whirling up, twisting round and round Orthanc, until it looked like a tall peak of cloud, fiery underneath and moonlit above. And still more water poured in, until at last Isengard looked like a huge flat saucepan, all steaming and bubbling.'

'We saw a cloud of smoke and steam from the south last night, when we came to the mouth of Nan Curunír,' said Aragorn. 'We feared that Saruman was brewing some new devilry for us.'

'Not he!' said Pippin. 'He was probably choking and not laughing any more. By the morning, yesterday morning, the water had sunk down into all the holes, and there was a dense fog. We took refuge in that guardroom over there; and we had rather a fright. The lake began to overflow and pour out through the old tunnel, and the water was rapidly rising up the steps. We thought we were going to get caught like Orcs in a hole; but we found a winding stair at the back of the store-room that brought us out on top of the arch. It was a squeeze to get out, as the passages had been cracked and half blocked with fallen stone near the top. There we sat high up above the floods and watched the drowning of Isengard. The Ents kept on pouring in more water, till all the fires were quenched and every cave filled. The fogs slowly gathered together and steamed up into a huge umbrella of cloud: it must have been a mile high. In the evening there was a great rainbow over the eastern hills; and then the sunset was blotted out by a thick drizzle on the mountain-sides. It all went very quiet. A few wolves howled mournfully, far away. The Ents stopped the inflow in the night, and sent the Isen back into its old course. And that was the end of it all.

'Since then the water has been sinking again. There must be outlets somewhere from the caves underneath, I think. If Saruman peeps out of any of his windows, it must look an untidy, dreary mess. We felt very lonely. Not even a visible Ent to talk to in all the ruin; and no news. We spent the night up on top there above the arch, and it was cold and damp and we did not sleep. We had a feeling that anything might happen at any minute. Saruman is still in his tower. There was a noise in the night like a wind coming up the valley. I think the Ents and Huorns that had been away came back then; but where they have all gone to now, I don't know. It was a misty, moisty morning when we climbed down and looked round again, and nobody was about. And that is about all there is to tell. It seems almost peaceful now after all the turmoil. And safer too, somehow, since Gandalf came back. I could sleep!'

They all fell silent for a while. Gimli re-filled his pipe. 'There is one thing I wonder about,' he said as he lit it with his flint and tinder: 'Wormtongue. You told Théoden he was with Saruman. How did he get there?'

'Oh yes, I forgot about him,' said Pippin. 'He did not get here till this morning. We had just lit the fire and had some breakfast when Treebeard appeared again. We heard him hooming and calling our names outside.

'"I have just come round to see how you are faring, my lads," he said; "and to give you some news. Huorns have come back. All's well; aye very well indeed!" he laughed, and slapped his thighs. "No more Orcs in Isengard, no more axes! And there will be folk coming up from the South before the day is old; some that you may be glad to see."

'He had hardly said that, when we heard the sound of hoofs on the road. We rushed out before the gates, and I stood and stared, half expecting to see Strider and Gandalf come riding up at the head of an army. But out of the mist there rode a man on an old tired horse; and he looked a queer twisted sort of creature himself. There was no one else. When he came out of the mist and suddenly saw all the ruin and wreckage in front of him, he sat and gaped, and his face went almost green. He was so bewildered that he did not seem to notice us at first. When he did, he gave a cry, and tried to turn his horse round and ride off. But Treebeard took three strides, put out a long arm, and lifted him out of the saddle. His horse bolted in terror, and he grovelled on the ground. He said he was Gríma, friend and counsellor of the king, and had been sent with important messages from Théoden to Saruman.

'"No one else would dare to ride through the open land, so full of foul Orcs," he said, "so I was sent. And I have had a perilous journey, and I am hungry and weary. I fled far north out of my way, pursued by wolves."

'I caught the sidelong looks he gave to Treebeard, and I said to myself "liar". Treebeard looked at him in his long slow way for several minutes, till the wretched man was squirming on the floor. Then at last he said: "Ha, hm, I was expecting you, Master Wormtongue." The man started at that name. "Gandalf got here first. So I know as much about you as I need, and I know what to do with you. Put all the rats in one trap, said Gandalf; and I will. I am the master of Isengard now, but Saruman is locked in his tower; and you can go there and give him all the messages that you can think of."

'"Let me go, let me go!" said Wormtongue. "I know the way."

'"You knew the way, I don't doubt," said Treebeard. "But things have changed here a little. Go and see!"

'He let Wormtongue go, and he limped off through the arch, with us close behind, until he came inside the ring and could see all the floods that lay between him and Orthanc. Then he turned to us.

'"Let me go away!" he whined. "Let me go away! My messages are useless now."

'"They are indeed," said Treebeard. "But you have only two choices: to stay with me until Gandalf and your master arrive; or to cross the water. Which will you have?"

'The man shivered at the mention of his master, and put a foot into the water; but he drew back. "I cannot swim," he said.

'"The water is not deep," said Treebeard. "It is dirty, but that will not harm you, Master Wormtongue. In you go now!"

'With that the wretch floundered off into the flood. It rose up nearly to his neck before he got too far away for me to see him. The last I saw of him was clinging to some old barrel or piece of wood. But Treebeard waded after him, and watched his progress.

'"Well, he has gone in," he said when he returned. "I saw him crawling up the steps like a draggled rat. There is some-one in the tower still: a hand came out and pulled him in. So there he is, and I hope the welcome is to his liking. Now I must go and wash myself clean of the slime. I'll be away up on the north side, if anyone wants to see me. There is no clean water down here fit for an Ent to drink, or to bathe in. So I will ask you two lads to keep a watch at the gate for the folk that are coming. There'll be the Lord of the Fields of Rohan, mark you! You must welcome him as well as you know how: his men have fought a great fight with the Orcs. Maybe, you know the right fashion of Men's words for such a lord, better than Ents. There have been many lords in the green fields in my time, and I have never learned their speech or their names. They will be wanting man-food, and you know all about that, I guess. So find what you think is fit for a king to eat, if you can." And that is the end of the story. Though I should like to know who this Wormtongue is. Was he really the king's counsellor?'

'He was,' said Aragorn; 'and also Saruman's spy and servant in Rohan. Fate has not been kinder to him than he deserves. The sight of the ruin of all that he thought so strong and magnificent must have been almost punishment enough. But I fear that worse awaits him.'

'Yes, I don't suppose Treebeard sent him to Orthanc out of kindness,' said Merry. 'He seemed rather grimly delighted with the business, and was laughing to himself when he went to get his bathe and drink. We spent a busy time after that, searching the flotsam, and rummaging about. We found two or three store-rooms in different places nearby, above the flood-level. But Treebeard sent some Ents down, and they carried off a great deal of the stuff.

' "We want man-food for twenty-five," the Ents said, so you can see that somebody had counted your company carefully before you arrived. You three were evidently meant to go with the great people. But you would not have fared any better. We kept as good as we sent, I promise you. Better, because we sent no drink.

' "What about drink?" I said to the Ents.

' "There is water of Isen," they said, "and that is good enough for Ents and Men." But I hope that the Ents may have found time to brew some of their draughts from the mountain-springs, and we shall see Gandalf's beard curling when he returns. After the Ents had gone, we felt tired, and hungry. But we did not grumble – our labours had been well rewarded. It was through our search for man-food that Pippin discovered the prize of all the flotsam, those Hornblower barrels. "Pipe-weed is better after food," said Pippin; that is how the situation arose.'

'We understand it all perfectly now,' said Gimli.

'All except one thing,' said Aragorn: 'leaf from the South-farthing in Isengard. The more I consider it, the more curious I find it. I have never been in Isengard, but I have journeyed in this land, and I know well the empty countries that lie between Rohan and the Shire. Neither goods nor folk have passed that way for many a long year, not openly. Saruman had secret dealings with someone in the Shire, I guess. Wormtongues may be found in other houses than King Théoden's. Was there a date on the barrels?'

'Yes,' said Pippin. 'It was the 1417 crop, that is last year's; no, the year before, of course, now: a good year.'

'Ah well, whatever evil was afoot is over now, I hope; or else it is beyond our reach at present,' said Aragorn. 'Yet I think I shall mention it to Gandalf, small matter though it may seem among his great affairs.'

'I wonder what he is doing,' said Merry. 'The afternoon is getting on. Let us go and look round! You can enter Isengard now at any rate, Strider, if you want to. But it is not a very cheerful sight.'

CHAPTER X

THE VOICE OF SARUMAN

They passed through the ruined tunnel and stood upon a heap of stones, gazing at the dark rock of Orthanc, and its many windows, a menace still in the desolation that lay all about it. The waters had now nearly all subsided. Here and there gloomy pools remained, covered with scum and wreckage; but most of the wide circle was bare again, a wilderness of slime and tumbled rock, pitted with blackened holes, and dotted with posts and pillars leaning drunkenly this way and that. At the rim of the shattered bowl there lay vast mounds and slopes, like the shingles cast up by a great storm; and beyond them the green and tangled valley ran up into the long ravine between the dark arms of the mountains. Across the waste they saw riders picking their way; they were coming from the north side, and already they were drawing near to Orthanc.

'There is Gandalf, and Théoden and his men!' said Legolas. 'Let us go and meet them!'

'Walk warily!' said Merry. 'There are loose slabs that may tilt up and throw you down into a pit, if you don't take care.'

They followed what was left of the road from the gates to Orthanc, going slowly, for the flag-stones were cracked and slimed. The riders, seeing them approach, halted under the shadow of the rock and waited for them. Gandalf rode forward to meet them.

'Well, Treebeard and I have had some interesting discussions, and made a few plans,' he said; 'and we have all had some much-needed rest. Now we must be going on again. I hope you companions have all rested, too, and refreshed yourselves?'

'We have,' said Merry. 'But our discussions began and ended in smoke. Still we feel less ill-disposed towards Saruman than we did.'

'Do you indeed?' said Gandalf. 'Well, I do not. I have now a last task to do before I go: I must pay Saruman a farewell visit. Dangerous, and probably useless; but it must be done. Those of you who wish may come with me – but beware! And do not jest! This is not the time for it.'

'I will come,' said Gimli. 'I wish to see him and learn if he really looks like you.'

'And how will you learn that, Master Dwarf?' said Gandalf. 'Saruman could look like me in your eyes, if it suited his purpose with you. And are you yet wise enough to detect all his counterfeits? Well, we shall see, perhaps. He may be shy of showing himself before many different eyes together. But I have ordered all the Ents to remove themselves from sight, so perhaps we shall persuade him to come out.'

'What's the danger?' asked Pippin. 'Will he shoot at us, and pour fire out of the windows; or can he put a spell on us from a distance?'

'The last is most likely, if you ride to his door with a light heart,' said Gandalf. 'But there is no knowing what he can do, or may choose to try. A wild beast cornered is not safe to approach. And Saruman has powers you do not guess. Beware of his voice!'

They came now to the foot of Orthanc. It was black, and the rock gleamed as if it were wet. The many faces of the stone had sharp edges as though they had been newly chiselled. A few scorings, and small flake-like splinters near the base, were all the marks that it bore of the fury of the Ents.

On the eastern side, in the angle of two piers, there was a great door, high above the ground; and over it was a shuttered window, opening upon a balcony hedged with iron bars. Up to the threshold of the door there mounted a flight of twenty-seven broad stairs, hewn by some unknown art of the same black stone. This was the only entrance to the tower;

but many tall windows were cut with deep embrasures in the climbing walls: far up they peered like little eyes in the sheer faces of the horns.

At the foot of the stairs Gandalf and the king dismounted. 'I will go up,' said Gandalf. 'I have been in Orthanc and I know my peril.'

'And I too will go up,' said the king. 'I am old, and fear no peril any more. I wish to speak with the enemy who has done me so much wrong. Éomer shall come with me, and see that my aged feet do not falter.'

'As you will,' said Gandalf. 'Aragorn shall come with me. Let the others await us at the foot of the stairs. They will hear and see enough, if there is anything to hear or see.'

'Nay!' said Gimli. 'Legolas and I wish for a closer view. We alone here represent our kindreds. We also will come behind.'

'Come then!' said Gandalf, and with that he climbed the steps, and Théoden went beside him.

The Riders of Rohan sat uneasily upon their horses, on either side of the stair, and looked up darkly at the great tower, fearing what might befall their lord. Merry and Pippin sat on the bottom step, feeling both unimportant and unsafe.

'Half a sticky mile from here to the gate!' muttered Pippin. 'I wish I could slip off back to the guardroom unnoticed! What did we come for? We are not wanted.'

Gandalf stood before the door of Orthanc and beat on it with his staff. It rang with a hollow sound. 'Saruman, Saruman!' he cried in a loud commanding voice. 'Saruman come forth!'

For some time there was no answer. At last the window above the door was unbarred, but no figure could be seen at its dark opening.

'Who is it?' said a voice. 'What do you wish?'

Théoden started. 'I know that voice,' he said, 'and I curse the day when I first listened to it.'

'Go and fetch Saruman, since you have become his

footman, Gríma Wormtongue!' said Gandalf. 'And do not waste our time!'

  The window closed. They waited. Suddenly another voice spoke, low and melodious, its very sound an enchantment. Those who listened unwarily to that voice could seldom report the words that they heard; and if they did, they wondered, for little power remained in them. Mostly they remembered only that it was a delight to hear the voice speaking, all that it said seemed wise and reasonable, and desire awoke in them by swift agreement to seem wise themselves. When others spoke they seemed harsh and uncouth by contrast; and if they gainsaid the voice, anger was kindled in the hearts of those under the spell. For some the spell lasted only while the voice spoke to them, and when it spoke to another they smiled, as men do who see through a juggler's trick while others gape at it. For many the sound of the voice alone was enough to hold them enthralled; but for those whom it conquered the spell endured when they were far away, and ever they heard that soft voice whispering and urging them. But none were unmoved; none rejected its pleas and its commands without an effort of mind and will, so long as its master had control of it.

  'Well?' it said now with gentle question. 'Why must you disturb my rest? Will you give me no peace at all by night or day?' Its tone was that of a kindly heart aggrieved by injuries undeserved.

  They looked up, astonished, for they had heard no sound of his coming; and they saw a figure standing at the rail, looking down upon them: an old man, swathed in a great cloak, the colour of which was not easy to tell, for it changed if they moved their eyes or if he stirred. His face was long, with a high forehead, he had deep darkling eyes, hard to fathom, though the look that they now bore was grave and benevolent, and a little weary. His hair and beard were white, but strands of black still showed about his lips and ears.

  'Like, and yet unlike,' muttered Gimli.

  'But come now,' said the soft voice. 'Two at least of you

I know by name. Gandalf I know too well to have much hope that he seeks help or counsel here. But you, Théoden Lord of the Mark of Rohan, are declared by your noble devices, and still more by the fair countenance of the House of Eorl. O worthy son of Thengel the Thrice-renowned! Why have you not come before, and as a friend? Much have I desired to see you, mightiest king of western lands, and especially in these latter years, to save you from the unwise and evil counsels that beset you! Is it yet too late? Despite the injuries that have been done to me, in which the men of Rohan, alas! have had some part, still I would save you, and deliver you from the ruin that draws nigh inevitably, if you ride upon this road which you have taken. Indeed I alone can aid you now.'

Théoden opened his mouth as if to speak, but he said nothing. He looked up at the face of Saruman with its dark solemn eyes bent down upon him, and then to Gandalf at his side; and he seemed to hesitate. Gandalf made no sign; but stood silent as stone, as one waiting patiently for some call that has not yet come. The Riders stirred at first, murmuring with approval of the words of Saruman; and then they too were silent, as men spell-bound. It seemed to them that Gandalf had never spoken so fair and fittingly to their lord. Rough and proud now seemed all his dealings with Théoden. And over their hearts crept a shadow, the fear of a great danger: the end of the Mark in a darkness to which Gandalf was driving them, while Saruman stood beside a door of escape, holding it half open so that a ray of light came through. There was a heavy silence.

It was Gimli the dwarf who broke in suddenly. 'The words of this wizard stand on their heads,' he growled, gripping the handle of his axe. 'In the language of Orthanc help means ruin, and saving means slaying, that is plain. But we do not come here to beg.'

'Peace!' said Saruman, and for a fleeting moment his voice was less suave, and a light flickered in his eyes and was gone. 'I do not speak to you yet, Gimli Glóin's son,' he said. 'Far

away is your home and small concern of yours are the
troubles of this land. But it was not by design of your own
that you became embroiled in them, and so I will not blame
such part as you have played – a valiant one, I doubt not.
But I pray you, allow me first to speak with the King of
Rohan, my neighbour, and once my friend.

'What have you to say, Théoden King? Will you have
peace with me, and all the aid that my knowledge, founded
in long years, can bring? Shall we make our counsels together
against evil days, and repair our injuries with such good will
that our estates shall both come to fairer flower than ever
before?'

Still Théoden did not answer. Whether he strove with
anger or doubt none could say. Éomer spoke.

'Lord, hear me!' he said. 'Now we feel the peril that we
were warned of. Have we ridden forth to victory, only to
stand at last amazed by an old liar with honey on his forked
tongue? So would the trapped wolf speak to the hounds, if
he could. What aid can he give to you, forsooth? All he
desires is to escape from his plight. But will you parley with
this dealer in treachery and murder? Remember Théodred
at the Fords, and the grave of Háma in Helm's Deep!'

'If we speak of poisoned tongues what shall we say of
yours, young serpent?' said Saruman, and the flash of his
anger was now plain to see. 'But come, Éomer, Éomund's
son!' he went on in his soft voice again. 'To every man his
part. Valour in arms is yours, and you win high honour
thereby. Slay whom your lord names as enemies, and be
content. Meddle not in policies which you do not understand.
But maybe, if you become a king, you will find that he must
choose his friends with care. The friendship of Saruman and
the power of Orthanc cannot be lightly thrown aside, whatever grievances, real or fancied, may lie behind. You have
won a battle but not a war – and that with help on which
you cannot count again. You may find the Shadow of the
Wood at your own door next: it is wayward, and senseless,
and has no love for Men.

'But my lord of Rohan, am I to be called a murderer, because valiant men have fallen in battle? If you go to war, needlessly, for I did not desire it, then men will be slain. But if I am a murderer on that account, then all the House of Eorl is stained with murder; for they have fought many wars, and assailed many who defied them. Yet with some they have afterwards made peace, none the worse for being politic. I say, Théoden King: shall we have peace and friendship, you and I? It is ours to command.'

'We will have peace,' said Théoden at last thickly and with an effort. Several of the Riders cried out gladly. Théoden held up his hand. 'Yes, we will have peace,' he said, now in a clear voice, 'we will have peace, when you and all your works have perished – and the works of your dark master to whom you would deliver us. You are a liar, Saruman, and a corrupter of men's hearts. You hold out your hand to me, and I perceive only a finger of the claw of Mordor. Cruel and cold! Even if your war on me was just – as it was not, for were you ten times as wise you would have no right to rule me and mine for your own profit as you desired – even so, what will you say of your torches in Westfold and the children that lie dead there? And they hewed Háma's body before the gates of the Hornburg, after he was dead. When you hang from a gibbet at your window for the sport of your own crows, I will have peace with you and Orthanc. So much for the House of Eorl. A lesser son of great sires am I, but I do not need to lick your fingers. Turn elsewhither. But I fear your voice has lost its charm.'

The Riders gazed up at Théoden like men startled out of a dream. Harsh as an old raven's their master's voice sounded in their ears after the music of Saruman. But Saruman for a while was beside himself with wrath. He leaned over the rail as if he would smite the King with his staff. To some suddenly it seemed that they saw a snake coiling itself to strike.

'Gibbets and crows!' he hissed, and they shuddered at the hideous change. 'Dotard! What is the house of Eorl but a thatched barn where brigands drink in the reek, and their brats roll on the floor among the dogs? Too long have they escaped the gibbet themselves. But the noose comes, slow in the drawing, tight and hard in the end. Hang if you will!' Now his voice changed, as he slowly mastered himself. 'I know not why I have had the patience to speak to you. For I need you not, nor your little band of gallopers, as swift to fly as to advance, Théoden Horsemaster. Long ago I offered you a state beyond your merit and your wit. I have offered it again, so that those whom you mislead may clearly see the choice of roads. You give me brag and abuse. So be it. Go back to your huts!

'But you, Gandalf! For you at least I am grieved, feeling for your shame. How comes it that you can endure such company? For you are proud, Gandalf – and not without reason, having a noble mind and eyes that look both deep and far. Even now will you not listen to my counsel?'

Gandalf stirred, and looked up. 'What have you to say that you did not say at our last meeting?' he asked. 'Or, perhaps, you have things to unsay?'

Saruman paused. 'Unsay?' he mused, as if puzzled. 'Unsay? I endeavoured to advise you for your own good, but you scarcely listened. You are proud and do not love advice, having indeed a store of your own wisdom. But on that occasion you erred, I think, misconstruing my intentions wilfully. I fear that in my eagerness to persuade you, I lost patience. And indeed I regret it. For I bore you no ill-will; and even now I bear none, though you return to me in the company of the violent and the ignorant. How should I? Are we not both members of a high and ancient order, most excellent in Middle-earth? Our friendship would profit us both alike. Much we could still accomplish together, to heal the disorders of the world. Let us understand one another, and dismiss from thought these lesser folk! Let them wait on our decisions! For the common good I am willing to redress the past, and to receive you. Will you not consult with me? Will you not come up?'

So great was the power that Saruman exerted in this last

effort that none that stood within hearing were unmoved. But now the spell was wholly different. They heard the gentle remonstrance of a kindly king with an erring but much-loved minister. But they were shut out, listening at a door to words not meant for them: ill-mannered children or stupid servants overhearing the elusive discourse of their elders, and wondering how it would affect their lot. Of loftier mould these two were made: reverend and wise. It was inevitable that they should make alliance. Gandalf would ascend into the tower, to discuss deep things beyond their comprehension in the high chambers of Orthanc. The door would be closed, and they would be left outside, dismissed to await allotted work or punishment. Even in the mind of Théoden the thought took shape, like a shadow of doubt: 'He will betray us; he will go – we shall be lost.'

Then Gandalf laughed. The fantasy vanished like a puff of smoke.

'Saruman, Saruman!' said Gandalf still laughing. 'Saruman, you missed your path in life. You should have been the king's jester and earned your bread, and stripes too, by mimicking his counsellors. Ah me!' he paused, getting the better of his mirth. 'Understand one another? I fear I am beyond your comprehension. But you, Saruman, I understand now too well. I keep a clearer memory of your arguments, and deeds, than you suppose. When last I visited you, you were the jailor of Mordor, and there I was to be sent. Nay, the guest who has escaped from the roof, will think twice before he comes back in by the door. Nay, I do not think I will come up. But listen, Saruman, for the last time! Will you not come down? Isengard has proved less strong than your hope and fancy made it. So may other things in which you still have trust. Would it not be well to leave it for a while? To turn to new things, perhaps? Think well, Saruman! Will you not come down?'

A shadow passed over Saruman's face; then it went deathly white. Before he could conceal it, they saw through the mask the anguish of a mind in doubt, loathing to stay and dreading to leave its refuge. For a second he hesitated, and no one breathed. Then he spoke, and his voice was shrill and cold. Pride and hate were conquering him.

'Will I come down?' he mocked. 'Does an unarmed man come down to speak with robbers out of doors? I can hear you well enough here. I am no fool, and I do not trust you, Gandalf. They do not stand openly on my stairs, but I know where the wild wood-demons are lurking, at your command.'

'The treacherous are ever distrustful,' answered Gandalf wearily. 'But you need not fear for your skin. I do not wish to kill you, or hurt you, as you would know, if you really understood me. And I have the power to protect you. I am giving you a last chance. You can leave Orthanc, free – if you choose.'

'That sounds well,' sneered Saruman. 'Very much in the manner of Gandalf the Grey: so condescending, and so very kind. I do not doubt that you would find Orthanc commodious, and my departure convenient. But why should I wish to leave? And what do you mean by "free"? There are conditions, I presume?'

'Reasons for leaving you can see from your windows,' answered Gandalf. 'Others will occur to your thought. Your servants are destroyed and scattered; your neighbours you have made your enemies; and you have cheated your new master, or tried to do so. When his eye turns hither, it will be the red eye of wrath. But when I say "free", I mean "free": free from bond, of chain or command: to go where you will, even, even to Mordor, Saruman, if you desire. But you will first surrender to me the Key of Orthanc, and your staff. They shall be pledges of your conduct, to be returned later, if you merit them.'

Saruman's face grew livid, twisted with rage, and a red light was kindled in his eyes. He laughed wildly. 'Later!' he cried, and his voice rose to a scream. 'Later! Yes, when you also have the Keys of Barad-dûr itself, I suppose; and the crowns of seven kings, and the rods of the Five Wizards, and have purchased yourself a pair of boots many sizes larger than those that you wear now. A modest plan. Hardly one in which my help is needed! I have other things to do. Do not be a fool. If you wish to treat with me, while you have a chance, go away, and come back when you are sober! And leave behind these cut-throats and small rag-tag that dangle at your tail! Good day!' He turned and left the balcony.

'Come back, Saruman!' said Gandalf in a commanding voice. To the amazement of the others, Saruman turned again, and as if dragged against his will, he came slowly back to the iron rail, leaning on it, breathing hard. His face was lined and shrunken. His hand clutched his heavy black staff like a claw.

'I did not give you leave to go,' said Gandalf sternly. 'I have not finished. You have become a fool, Saruman, and yet pitiable. You might still have turned away from folly and evil, and have been of service. But you choose to stay and gnaw the ends of your old plots. Stay then! But I warn you, you will not easily come out again. Not unless the dark hands of the East stretch out to take you. Saruman!' he cried, and his voice grew in power and authority. 'Behold, I am not Gandalf the Grey, whom you betrayed. I am Gandalf the White, who has returned from death. You have no colour now, and I cast you from the order and from the Council.'

He raised his hand, and spoke slowly in a clear cold voice. 'Saruman, your staff is broken.' There was a crack, and the staff split asunder in Saruman's hand, and the head of it fell down at Gandalf's feet. 'Go!' said Gandalf. With a cry Saruman fell back and crawled away. At that moment a heavy shining thing came hurtling down from above. It glanced off the iron rail, even as Saruman left it, and passing close to Gandalf's head, it smote the stair on which he stood. The rail rang and snapped. The stair cracked and splintered in glittering sparks. But the ball was unharmed: it rolled on down the steps, a globe of crystal, dark, but glowing with a heart of fire. As it bounded away towards a pool Pippin ran after it and picked it up.

'The murderous rogue!' cried Éomer. But Gandalf was

unmoved. 'No, that was not thrown by Saruman,' he said; 'nor even at his bidding, I think. It came from a window far above. A parting shot from Master Wormtongue, I fancy, but ill aimed.'

'The aim was poor, maybe, because he could not make up his mind which he hated more, you or Saruman,' said Aragorn.

'That may be so,' said Gandalf. 'Small comfort will those two have in their companionship: they will gnaw one another with words. But the punishment is just. If Wormtongue ever comes out of Orthanc alive, it will be more than he deserves.

'Here, my lad, I'll take that! I did not ask you to handle it,' he cried, turning sharply and seeing Pippin coming up the steps, slowly, as if he were bearing a great weight. He went down to meet him and hastily took the dark globe from the hobbit, wrapping it in the folds of his cloak. 'I will take care of this,' he said. 'It is not a thing, I guess, that Saruman would have chosen to cast away.'

'But he may have other things to cast,' said Gimli. 'If that is the end of the debate, let us go out of stone's throw, at least!'

'It is the end,' said Gandalf. 'Let us go.'

They turned their backs on the doors of Orthanc, and went down. The riders hailed the king with joy, and saluted Gandalf. The spell of Saruman was broken: they had seen him come at call, and crawl away, dismissed.

'Well, that is done,' said Gandalf. 'Now I must find Treebeard and tell him how things have gone.'

'He will have guessed, surely?' said Merry. 'Were they likely to end any other way?'

'Not likely,' answered Gandalf, 'though they came to the balance of a hair. But I had reasons for trying; some merciful and some less so. First Saruman was shown that the power of his voice was waning. He cannot be both tyrant and counsellor. When the plot is ripe it remains no longer secret.

Yet he fell into the trap, and tried to deal with his victims piece-meal, while others listened. Then I gave him a last choice and a fair one: to renounce both Mordor and his private schemes, and make amends by helping us in our need. He knows our need, none better. Great service he could have rendered. But he has chosen to withhold it, and keep the power of Orthanc. He will not serve, only command. He lives now in terror of the shadow of Mordor, and yet he still dreams of riding the storm. Unhappy fool! He will be devoured, if the power of the East stretches out its arms to Isengard. We cannot destroy Orthanc from without, but Sauron – who knows what he can do?'

'And what if Sauron does not conquer? What will you do to him?' asked Pippin.

'I? Nothing!' said Gandalf. 'I will do nothing to him. I do not wish for mastery. What will become of him? I cannot say. I grieve that so much that was good now festers in the tower. Still for us things have not gone badly. Strange are the turns of fortune! Often does hatred hurt itself! I guess that, even if we had entered in, we could have found few treasures in Orthanc more precious than the thing which Wormtongue threw down at us.'

A shrill shriek, suddenly cut off, came from an open window high above.

'It seems that Saruman thinks so too,' said Gandalf. 'Let us leave them!'

They returned now to the ruins of the gate. Hardly had they passed out under the arch, when, from among the shadows of the piled stones where they had stood, Treebeard and a dozen other Ents came striding up. Aragorn, Gimli and Legolas gazed at them in wonder.

'Here are three of my companions, Treebeard,' said Gandalf. 'I have spoken of them, but you have not yet seen them.' He named them one by one.

The Old Ent looked at them long and searchingly, and spoke to them in turn. Last he turned to Legolas. 'So you have come all the way from Mirkwood, my good Elf? A very great forest it used to be!'

'And still is,' said Legolas. 'But not so great that we who dwell there ever tire of seeing new trees. I should dearly love to journey in Fangorn's Wood. I scarcely passed beyond the eaves of it, and I did not wish to turn back.'

Treebeard's eyes gleamed with pleasure. 'I hope you may have your wish, ere the hills be much older,' he said.

'I will come, if I have the fortune,' said Legolas. 'I have made a bargain with my friend that, if all goes well, we will visit Fangorn together – by your leave.'

'Any Elf that comes with you will be welcome,' said Treebeard.

'The friend I speak of is not an Elf,' said Legolas; 'I mean Gimli, Glóin's son here.' Gimli bowed low, and the axe slipped from his belt and clattered on the ground.

'Hoom, hm! Ah now,' said Treebeard, looking dark-eyed at him. 'A dwarf and an axe-bearer! Hoom! I have good will to Elves; but you ask much. This is a strange friendship!'

'Strange it may seem,' said Legolas; 'but while Gimli lives I shall not come to Fangorn alone. His axe is not for trees, but for orc-necks, O Fangorn, Master of Fangorn's Wood. Forty-two he hewed in the battle.'

'Hoo! Come now!' said Treebeard. 'That is a better story! Well, well, things will go as they will; and there is no need to hurry to meet them. But now we must part for a while. Day is drawing to an end, yet Gandalf says you must go ere nightfall, and the Lord of the Mark is eager for his own house.'

'Yes, we must go, and go now,' said Gandalf. 'I fear that I must take your gatekeepers from you. But you will manage well enough without them.'

'Maybe I shall,' said Treebeard. 'But I shall miss them. We have become friends in so short a while that I think I must be getting hasty – growing backwards towards youth, perhaps. But there, they are the first new thing under Sun or Moon that I have seen for many a long, long day. I shall

not forget them. I have put their names into the Long List.
Ents will remember it.

> *Ents the earthborn, old as mountains,*
> *the wide-walkers, water drinking;*
> *and hungry as hunters, the Hobbit children,*
> *the laughing-folk, the little people,*

they shall remain friends as long as leaves are renewed. Fare
you well! But if you hear news up in your pleasant land, in
the Shire, send me word! You know what I mean: word or
sight of the Entwives. Come yourselves if you can!'

'We will!' said Merry and Pippin together, and they turned
away hastily. Treebeard looked at them, and was silent for
a while, shaking his head thoughtfully. Then he turned to
Gandalf.

'So Saruman would not leave?' he said. 'I did not think he
would. His heart is as rotten as a black Huorn's. Still, if I
were overcome and all my trees destroyed, I would not come
while I had one dark hole left to hide in.'

'No,' said Gandalf. 'But you have not plotted to cover all
the world with your trees and choke all other living things.
But there it is, Saruman remains to nurse his hatred and
weave again such webs as he can. He has the Key of Orthanc.
But he must not be allowed to escape.'

'Indeed no! Ents will see to that,' said Treebeard. 'Saruman
shall not set foot beyond the rock, without my leave. Ents
will watch over him.'

'Good!' said Gandalf. 'That is what I hoped. Now I can
go and turn to other matters with one care the less. But you
must be wary. The waters have gone down. It will not be
enough to put sentinels round the tower, I fear. I do not
doubt that there were deep ways delved under Orthanc, and
that Saruman hopes to go and come unmarked, before long.
If you will undertake the labour, I beg you to pour in the
waters again; and do so, until Isengard remains a standing
pool, or you discover the outlets. When all the underground

places are drowned, and the outlets blocked, then Saruman must stay upstairs and look out of the windows.'

'Leave it to the Ents!' said Treebeard. 'We shall search the valley from head to foot and peer under every pebble. Trees are coming back to live here, old trees, wild trees. The Watchwood we will call it. Not a squirrel will go here, but I shall know of it. Leave it to Ents! Until seven times the years in which he tormented us have passed, we shall not tire of watching him.'

CHAPTER XI

THE PALANTÍR

The sun was sinking behind the long western arm of the mountains when Gandalf and his companions, and the king with his Riders, set out again from Isengard. Gandalf took Merry behind him, and Aragorn took Pippin. Two of the king's men went on ahead, riding swiftly, and passed soon out of sight down into the valley. The others followed at an easy pace.

Ents in a solemn row stood like statues at the gate, with their long arms uplifted, but they made no sound. Merry and Pippin looked back, when they had passed some way down the winding road. Sunlight was still shining in the sky, but long shadows reached over Isengard: grey ruins falling into darkness. Treebeard stood alone there now, like the distant stump of an old tree: the hobbits thought of their first meeting, upon the sunny ledge far away on the borders of Fangorn.

They came to the pillar of the White Hand. The pillar was still standing, but the graven hand had been thrown down and broken into small pieces. Right in the middle of the road the long forefinger lay, white in the dusk, its red nail darkening to black.

'The Ents pay attention to every detail!' said Gandalf.

They rode on, and evening deepened in the valley.

'Are we riding far tonight, Gandalf?' asked Merry after a while. 'I don't know how you feel with small rag-tag dangling behind you; but the rag-tag is tired and will be glad to stop dangling and lie down.'

'So you heard that?' said Gandalf. 'Don't let it rankle! Be thankful no longer words were aimed at you. He had his eyes on you. If it is any comfort to your pride, I should say that, at the moment, you and Pippin are more in his thoughts than all the rest of us. Who you are; how you came there, and why; what you know; whether you were captured, and if so, how you escaped when all the Orcs perished – it is with those little riddles that the great mind of Saruman is troubled. A sneer from him, Meriadoc, is a compliment, if you feel honoured by his concern.'

'Thank you!' said Merry. 'But it is a greater honour to dangle at your tail, Gandalf. For one thing, in that position one has a chance of putting a question a second time. Are we riding far tonight?'

Gandalf laughed. 'A most unquenchable hobbit! All Wizards should have a hobbit or two in their care – to teach them the meaning of the word, and to correct them. I beg your pardon. But I have given thought even to these simple matters. We will ride for a few hours, gently, until we come to the end of the valley. Tomorrow we must ride faster.

'When we came, we meant to go straight from Isengard back to the king's house at Edoras over the plains, a ride of some days. But we have taken thought and changed the plan. Messengers have gone ahead to Helm's Deep, to warn them that the king is returning tomorrow. He will ride from there with many men to Dunharrow by paths among the hills. From now on no more than two or three together are to go openly over the land, by day or night, when it can be avoided.'

'Nothing or a double helping is your way!' said Merry. 'I am afraid I was not looking beyond tonight's bed. Where and what are Helm's Deep and all the rest of it? I don't know anything about this country.'

'Then you'd best learn something, if you wish to understand what is happening. But not just now, and not from me: I have too many pressing things to think about.'

'All right, I'll tackle Strider by the camp-fire: he's less testy. But why all this secrecy? I thought we'd won the battle!'

'Yes, we have won, but only the first victory, and that in

itself increases our danger. There was some link between Isengard and Mordor, which I have not yet fathomed. How they exchanged news I am not sure; but they did so. The Eye of Barad-dûr will be looking impatiently towards the Wizard's Vale, I think; and towards Rohan. The less it sees the better.'

The road passed slowly, winding down the valley. Now further, and now nearer Isen flowed in its stony bed. Night came down from the mountains. All the mists were gone. A chill wind blew. The moon, now waxing round, filled the eastern sky with a pale cold sheen. The shoulders of the mountain to their right sloped down to bare hills. The wide plains opened grey before them.

At last they halted. Then they turned aside, leaving the highway and taking to the sweet upland turf again. Going westward a mile or so they came to a dale. It opened southward, leaning back into the slope of round Dol Baran, the last hill of the northern ranges, greenfooted, crowned with heather. The sides of the glen were shaggy with last year's bracken, among which the tight-curled fronds of spring were just thrusting through the sweet-scented earth. Thornbushes grew thick upon the low banks, and under them they made their camp, two hours or so before the middle of the night. They lit a fire in a hollow, down among the roots of a spreading hawthorn, tall as a tree, writhen with age, but hale in every limb. Buds were swelling at each twig's tip.

Guards were set, two at a watch. The rest, after they had supped, wrapped themselves in a cloak and blanket and slept. The hobbits lay in a corner by themselves upon a pile of old bracken. Merry was sleepy, but Pippin now seemed curiously restless. The bracken cracked and rustled, as he twisted and turned.

'What's the matter?' asked Merry. 'Are you lying on an ant-hill?'

'No,' said Pippin, 'but I'm not comfortable. I wonder how long it is since I slept in a bed?'

Merry yawned. 'Work it out on your fingers!' he said. 'But you must know how long it is since we left Lórien.'

'Oh, that!' said Pippin. 'I mean a real bed in a bedroom.'

'Well, Rivendell then,' said Merry. 'But I could sleep any-where tonight.'

'You had the luck, Merry,' said Pippin softly, after a long pause. 'You were riding with Gandalf.'

'Well, what of it?'

'Did you get any news, any information out of him?'

'Yes, a good deal. More than usual. But you heard it all or most of it; you were close by, and we were talking no secrets. But you can go with him tomorrow, if you think you can get more out of him – and if he'll have you.'

'Can I? Good! But he's close, isn't he? Not changed at all.'

'Oh yes, he is!' said Merry, waking up a little, and begin-ning to wonder what was bothering his companion. 'He has grown, or something. He can be both kinder and more alarm-ing, merrier and more solemn than before, I think. He has changed; but we have not had a chance to see how much, yet. But think of the last part of that business with Saruman! Remember Saruman was once Gandalf's superior: head of the Council, whatever that may be exactly. He was Saruman the White. Gandalf is the White now. Saruman came when he was told, and his rod was taken; and then he was just told to go, and he went!'

'Well, if Gandalf has changed at all, then he's closer than ever that's all,' Pippin argued. 'That – glass ball, now. He seemed mighty pleased with it. He knows or guesses some-thing about it. But does he tell us what? No, not a word. Yet I picked it up, and I saved it from rolling into a pool. *Here, I'll take that, my lad* – that's all. I wonder what it is? It felt so very heavy.' Pippin's voice fell very low, as if he was talking to himself.

'Hullo!' said Merry. 'So that's what is bothering you? Now, Pippin my lad, don't forget Gildor's saying – the one Sam used to quote: *Do not meddle in the affairs of Wizards, for they are subtle and quick to anger.*

'But our whole life for months has been one long meddling in the affairs of Wizards,' said Pippin. 'I should like a bit of information as well as danger. I should like a look at that ball.'

'Go to sleep!' said Merry. 'You'll get information enough, sooner or later. My dear Pippin, no Took ever beat a Brandybuck for inquisitiveness; but is this the time, I ask you?'

'All right! What's the harm in my telling you what I should like: a look at that stone? I know I can't have it, with old Gandalf sitting on it, like a hen on an egg. But it doesn't help much to get no more from you than a *you-can't-have-it so-go-to-sleep!*'

'Well, what else could I say?' said Merry. 'I'm sorry, Pippin, but you really must wait till the morning. I'll be as curious as you like after breakfast, and I'll help in any way I can at wizard-wheedling. But I can't keep awake any longer. If I yawn any more, I shall split at the ears. Good night!'

Pippin said no more. He lay still now, but sleep remained far away; and it was not encouraged by the sound of Merry breathing softly, asleep in a few minutes after saying good night. The thought of the dark globe seemed to grow stronger as all grew quiet. Pippin felt again its weight in his hands, and saw again the mysterious red depths into which he had looked for a moment. He tossed and turned and tried to think of something else.

At last he could stand it no longer. He got up and looked round. It was chilly, and he wrapped his cloak about him. The moon was shining cold and white, down into the dell, and the shadows of the bushes were black. All about lay sleeping shapes. The two guards were not in view: they were up on the hill, perhaps, or hidden in the bracken. Driven by some impulse that he did not understand, Pippin walked softly to where Gandalf lay. He looked down at him. The wizard seemed asleep, but with lids not fully closed: there was a glitter of eyes under his long lashes. Pippin stepped back hastily. But Gandalf made no sign; and drawn forward once more, half against his will, the hobbit crept up again from behind the wizard's head. He was rolled in a blanket, with his cloak spread over the top; and close beside him, between his right side and his bent arm, there was a hummock, something round wrapped in a dark cloth; his hand seemed only just to have slipped off it to the ground.

Hardly breathing, Pippin crept nearer, foot by foot. At last he knelt down. Then he put his hands out stealthily, and slowly lifted the lump up: it did not seem quite so heavy as he had expected. 'Only some bundle of oddments, perhaps, after all,' he thought with a strange sense of relief; but he did not put the bundle down again. He stood for a moment clasping it. Then an idea came into his mind. He tiptoed away, found a large stone, and came back.

Quickly now he drew off the cloth, wrapped the stone in it and kneeling down, laid it back by the wizard's hand. Then at last he looked at the thing that he had uncovered. There it was: a smooth globe of crystal, now dark and dead, lying bare before his knees. Pippin lifted it, covered it hurriedly in his own cloak, and half turned to go back to his bed. At that moment Gandalf moved in his sleep, and muttered some words: they seemed to be in a strange tongue; his hand groped out and clasped the wrapped stone, then he sighed and did not move again.

'You idiotic fool!' Pippin muttered to himself. 'You're going to get yourself into frightful trouble. Put it back quick!' But he found now that his knees quaked, and he did not dare to go near enough to the wizard to reach the bundle. 'I'll never get it back now without waking him,' he thought, 'not till I'm a bit calmer. So I may as well have a look first. Not just here though!' He stole away, and sat down on a green hillock not far from his bed. The moon looked in over the edge of the dell.

Pippin sat with his knees drawn up and the ball between them. He bent low over it, looking like a greedy child stooping over a bowl of food, in a corner away from others. He drew his cloak aside and gazed at it. The air seemed still and tense about him. At first the globe was dark, black as jet, with the moonlight gleaming on its surface. Then there came a faint glow and stir in the heart of it, and it held his eyes, so that now he could not look away. Soon all the inside seemed on fire; the ball was spinning, or the lights within were revolving. Suddenly the lights went out. He gave a gasp and struggled; but he remained bent, clasping the ball with both hands. Closer and closer he bent, and then became rigid; his lips moved soundlessly for a while. Then with a strangled cry he fell back and lay still.

The cry was piercing. The guards leapt down from the banks. All the camp was soon astir.

'So this is the thief!' said Gandalf. Hastily he cast his cloak over the globe where it lay. 'But you, Pippin! This is a grievous turn to things!' He knelt by Pippin's body: the hobbit was lying on his back, rigid, with unseeing eyes staring up at the sky. 'The devilry! What mischief has he done – to himself, and to all of us?' The wizard's face was drawn and haggard.

He took Pippin's hand and bent over his face, listening for his breath; then he laid his hands on his brow. The hobbit shuddered. His eyes closed. He cried out; and sat up, staring in bewilderment at all the faces round him, pale in the moonlight.

'It is not for you, Saruman!' he cried in a shrill and toneless voice, shrinking away from Gandalf. 'I will send for it at once. Do you understand? Say just that!' Then he struggled to get up and escape, but Gandalf held him gently and firmly.

'Peregrin Took!' he said. 'Come back!'

The hobbit relaxed and fell back, clinging to the wizard's hand. 'Gandalf!' he cried. 'Gandalf! Forgive me!'

'Forgive you?' said the wizard. 'Tell me first what you have done!'

'I, I took the ball and looked at it,' stammered Pippin; 'and I saw things that frightened me. And I wanted to go away, but I couldn't. And then he came and questioned me; and he looked at me, and, and, that is all I remember.'

'That won't do,' said Gandalf sternly. 'What did you see, and what did you say?'

Pippin shut his eyes and shivered, but said nothing. They all stared at him in silence, except Merry who turned away. But Gandalf's face was still hard. 'Speak!' he said.

In a low hesitating voice Pippin began again, and slowly his words grew clearer and stronger. 'I saw a dark sky, and tall battlements,' he said. 'And tiny stars. It seemed very far away and long ago, yet hard and clear. Then the stars went in and out – they were cut off by things with wings. Very big, I think, really; but in the glass they looked like bats wheeling round the tower. I thought there were nine of them. One began to fly straight towards me, getting bigger and bigger. It had a horrible – no, no! I can't say.

'I tried to get away, because I thought it would fly out; but when it had covered all the globe, it disappeared. Then *he* came. He did not speak so that I could hear words. He just looked, and I understood.

' "So you have come back? Why have you neglected to report for so long?"

'I did not answer. He said: "Who are you?" I still did not answer, but it hurt me horribly; and he pressed me, so I said: "A hobbit."

'Then suddenly he seemed to see me, and he laughed at me. It was cruel. It was like being stabbed with knives. I struggled. But he said: "Wait a moment! We shall meet again soon. Tell Saruman that this dainty is not for him. I will send for it at once. Do you understand? Say just that!"

'Then he gloated over me. I felt I was falling to pieces. No, no! I can't say any more. I don't remember anything else.'

'Look at me!' said Gandalf.

Pippin looked up straight into his eyes. The wizard held his gaze for a moment in silence. Then his face grew gentler, and the shadow of a smile appeared. He laid his hand softly on Pippin's head.

'All right!' he said. 'Say no more! You have taken no harm.

There is no lie in your eyes, as I feared. But he did not speak long with you. A fool, but an honest fool, you remain, Peregrin Took. Wiser ones might have done worse in such a pass. But mark this! You have been saved, and all your friends too, mainly by good fortune, as it is called. You cannot count on it a second time. If he had questioned you, then and there, almost certainly you would have told all that you know, to the ruin of us all. But he was too eager. He did not want information only: he wanted *you*, quickly, so that he could deal with you in the Dark Tower, slowly. Don't shudder! If you will meddle in the affairs of Wizards, you must be prepared to think of such things. But come! I forgive you. Be comforted! Things have not turned out as evilly as they might.'

He lifted Pippin gently and carried him back to his bed. Merry followed, and sat down beside him. 'Lie there and rest, if you can, Pippin!' said Gandalf. 'Trust me. If you feel an itch in your palms again, tell me of it! Such things can be cured. But anyway, my dear hobbit, don't put a lump of rock under my elbow again! Now, I will leave you two together for a while.'

With that Gandalf returned to the others, who were still standing by the Orthanc-stone in troubled thought. 'Peril comes in the night when least expected,' he said. 'We have had a narrow escape!'

'How is the hobbit, Pippin?' asked Aragorn.

'I think all will be well now,' answered Gandalf. 'He was not held long, and hobbits have an amazing power of recovery. The memory, or the horror of it, will probably fade quickly. Too quickly, perhaps. Will you, Aragorn, take the Orthanc-stone and guard it? It is a dangerous charge.'

'Dangerous indeed, but not to all,' said Aragorn. 'There is one who may claim it by right. For this assuredly is the *palantír* of Orthanc from the treasury of Elendil, set here by the Kings of Gondor. Now my hour draws near. I will take it.'

Gandalf looked at Aragorn, and then, to the surprise of

the others, he lifted the covered Stone, and bowed as he presented it.

'Receive it, lord!' he said: 'in earnest of other things that shall be given back. But if I may counsel you in the use of your own, do not use it – yet! Be wary!'

'When have I been hasty or unwary, who have waited and prepared for so many long years?' said Aragorn.

'Never yet. Do not then stumble at the end of the road,' answered Gandalf. 'But at the least keep this thing secret. You, and all others that stand here! The hobbit, Peregrin, above all should not know where it is bestowed. The evil fit may come on him again. For alas! he has handled it and looked in it, as should never have happened. He ought never to have touched it in Isengard, and there I should have been quicker. But my mind was bent on Saruman, and I did not at once guess the nature of the Stone. Then I was weary, and as I lay pondering it, sleep overcame me. Now I know!'

'Yes, there can be no doubt,' said Aragorn. 'At last we know the link between Isengard and Mordor, and how it worked. Much is explained.'

'Strange powers have our enemies, and strange weaknesses!' said Théoden. 'But it has long been said: *oft evil will shall evil mar.*'

'That many times is seen,' said Gandalf. 'But at this time we have been strangely fortunate. Maybe, I have been saved by this hobbit from a grave blunder. I had considered whether or not to probe this Stone myself to find its uses. Had I done so, I should have been revealed to him myself. I am not ready for such a trial, if indeed I shall ever be so. But even if I found the power to withdraw myself, it would be disastrous for him to see me, yet – until the hour comes when secrecy will avail no longer.'

'That hour is now come, I think,' said Aragorn.

'Not yet,' said Gandalf. 'There remains a short while of doubt, which we must use. The Enemy, it is clear, thought that the Stone was in Orthanc – why should he not? And that therefore the hobbit was captive there, driven to look in the glass for his torment by Saruman. That dark mind will be filled now with the voice and face of the hobbit and with expectation: it may take some time before he learns his error. We must snatch that time. We have been too leisurely. We must move. The neighbourhood of Isengard is no place now to linger in. I will ride ahead at once with Peregrin Took. It will be better for him than lying in the dark while others sleep.'

'I will keep Éomer and ten Riders,' said the king. 'They shall ride with me at early day. The rest may go with Aragorn and ride as soon as they have a mind.'

'As you will,' said Gandalf. 'But make all the speed you may to the cover of the hills, to Helm's Deep!'

At that moment a shadow fell over them. The bright moon-light seemed to be suddenly cut off. Several of the Riders cried out, and crouched, holding their arms above their heads, as if to ward off a blow from above: a blind fear and a deadly cold fell on them. Cowering they looked up. A vast winged shape passed over the moon like a black cloud. It wheeled and went north, flying at a speed greater than any wind of Middle-earth. The stars fainted before it. It was gone.

They stood up, rigid as stones. Gandalf was gazing up, his arms out and downwards, stiff, his hands clenched.

'Nazgûl!' he cried. 'The messenger of Mordor. The storm is coming. The Nazgûl have crossed the River! Ride, ride! Wait not for the dawn! Let not the swift wait for the slow! Ride!'

He sprang away, calling Shadowfax as he ran. Aragorn followed him. Going to Pippin, Gandalf picked him up in his arms. 'You shall come with me this time,' he said. 'Shadowfax shall show you his paces.' Then he ran to the place where he had slept. Shadowfax stood there already. Slinging the small bag which was all his luggage across his shoulders, the wizard leapt upon the horse's back. Aragorn lifted Pippin and set him in Gandalf's arms, wrapped in cloak and blanket.

'Farewell! Follow fast!' cried Gandalf. 'Away, Shadowfax!'

The great horse tossed his head. His flowing tail flicked in the moonlight. Then he leapt forward, spurning the earth, and was gone like the north wind from the mountains.

'A beautiful, restful night!' said Merry to Aragorn. 'Some folk have wonderful luck. He did not want to sleep, and he wanted to ride with Gandalf – and there he goes! Instead of being turned into a stone himself to stand here for ever as a warning.'

'If you had been the first to lift the Orthanc-stone, and not he, how would it be now?' said Aragorn. 'You might have done worse. Who can say? But now it is your luck to come with me, I fear. At once. Go and get ready, and bring anything that Pippin left behind. Make haste!'

Over the plains Shadowfax was flying, needing no urging and no guidance. Less than an hour had passed, and they had reached the Fords of Isen and crossed them. The Mound of the Riders and its cold spears lay grey behind them.

Pippin was recovering. He was warm, but the wind in his face was keen and refreshing. He was with Gandalf. The horror of the stone and of the hideous shadow over the moon was fading, things left behind in the mists of the mountains or in a passing dream. He drew a deep breath.

'I did not know you rode bare-back, Gandalf,' he said. 'You haven't a saddle or a bridle!'

'I do not ride elf-fashion, except on Shadowfax,' said Gandalf. 'But Shadowfax will have no harness. You do not ride Shadowfax: he is willing to carry you – or not. If he is willing, that is enough. It is then his business to see that you remain on his back, unless you jump off into the air.'

'How fast is he going?' asked Pippin. 'Fast by the wind, but very smooth. And how light his footfalls are!'

'He is running now as fast as the swiftest horse could gallop,' answered Gandalf; 'but that is not fast for him. The land is rising a little here, and is more broken than it was beyond the river. But see how the White Mountains are drawing near under the stars! Yonder are the Thrihyrne peaks like black spears. It will not be long before we reach the branching roads and come to the Deeping-coomb, where the battle was fought two nights ago.'

Pippin was silent again for a while. He heard Gandalf singing softly to himself, murmuring brief snatches of rhyme in many tongues, as the miles ran under them. At last the wizard passed into a song of which the hobbit caught the words: a few lines came clear to his ears through the rushing of the wind:

> *Tall ships and tall kings*
> *Three times three,*
> *What brought they from the foundered land*
> *Over the flowing sea?*
> *Seven stars and seven stones*
> *And one white tree.*

'What are you saying, Gandalf?' asked Pippin.

'I was just running over some of the Rhymes of Lore in my mind,' answered the wizard. 'Hobbits, I suppose, have forgotten them, even those that they ever knew.'

'No, not all,' said Pippin. 'And we have many of our own, which wouldn't interest you, perhaps. But I have never heard this one. What is it about – the seven stars and seven stones?'

'About the *palantíri* of the Kings of Old,' said Gandalf.

'And what are they?'

'The name meant *that which looks far away*. The Orthanc-stone was one.'

'Then it was not made, not made' – Pippin hesitated – 'by the Enemy?'

'No,' said Gandalf. 'Nor by Saruman. It is beyond his art, and beyond Sauron's too. The *palantíri* came from beyond Westernesse, from Eldamar. The Noldor made them. Fëanor himself, maybe, wrought them, in days so long ago that the time cannot be measured in years. But there is nothing that

Sauron cannot turn to evil uses. Alas for Saruman! It was his downfall, as I now perceive. Perilous to us all are the devices of an art deeper than we possess ourselves. Yet he must bear the blame. Fool! to keep it secret, for his own profit. No word did he ever speak of it to any of the Council. We had not yet given thought to the fate of the *palantíri* of Gondor in its ruinous wars. By Men they were almost forgotten. Even in Gondor they were a secret known only to a few; in Arnor they were remembered only in a rhyme of lore among the Dúnedain.'

'What did the Men of old use them for?' asked Pippin, delighted and astonished at getting answers to so many questions, and wondering how long it would last.

'To see far off, and to converse in thought with one another,' said Gandalf. 'In that way they long guarded and united the realm of Gondor. They set up Stones at Minas Anor, and at Minas Ithil, and at Orthanc in the ring of Isengard. The chief and master of these was under the Dome of Stars at Osgiliath before its ruin. The three others were far away in the North. In the house of Elrond it is told that they were at Annúminas, and Amon Sûl, and Elendil's Stone was on the Tower Hills that look towards Mithlond in the Gulf of Lune where the grey ships lie.

'Each *palantír* replied to each, but all those in Gondor were ever open to the view of Osgiliath. Now it appears that, as the rock of Orthanc has withstood the storms of time, so there the *palantír* of that tower has remained. But alone it could do nothing but see small images of things far off and days remote. Very useful, no doubt, that was to Saruman; yet it seems that he was not content. Further and further abroad he gazed, until he cast his gaze upon Barad-dûr. Then he was caught!

'Who knows where the lost Stones of Arnor and Gondor now lie, buried, or drowned deep? But one at least Sauron must have obtained and mastered to his purposes. I guess that it was the Ithil-stone, for he took Minas Ithil long ago and turned it into an evil place: Minas Morgul, it has become.

'Easy it is now to guess how quickly the roving eye of Saruman was trapped and held; and how ever since he has been persuaded from afar, and daunted when persuasion would not serve. The biter bit, the hawk under the eagle's foot, the spider in a steel web! How long, I wonder, has he been constrained to come often to his glass for inspection and instruction, and the Orthanc-stone so bent towards Barad-dûr that, if any save a will of adamant now looks into it, it will bear his mind and sight swiftly thither? And how it draws one to itself! Have I not felt it? Even now my heart desires to test my will upon it, to see if I could not wrench it from him and turn it where I would – to look across the wide seas of water and of time to Tirion the Fair, and perceive the unimaginable hand and mind of Fëanor at their work, while both the White Tree and the Golden were in flower!' He sighed and fell silent.

'I wish I had known all this before,' said Pippin. 'I had no notion of what I was doing.'

'Oh yes, you had,' said Gandalf. 'You knew you were behaving wrongly and foolishly; and you told yourself so, though you did not listen. I did not tell you all this before, because it is only by musing on all that has happened that I have at last understood, even as we ride together. But if I had spoken sooner, it would not have lessened your desire, or made it easier to resist. On the contrary! No, the burned hand teaches best. After that advice about fire goes to the heart.'

'It does,' said Pippin. 'If all the seven stones were laid out before me now, I should shut my eyes and put my hands in my pockets.'

'Good!' said Gandalf. 'That is what I hoped.'

'But I should like to know———' Pippin began.

'Mercy!' cried Gandalf. 'If the giving of information is to be the cure of your inquisitiveness, I shall spend all the rest of my days in answering you. What more do you want to know?'

'The names of all the stars, and of all living things, and

the whole history of Middle-earth and Over-heaven and of the Sundering Seas,' laughed Pippin. 'Of course! What less? But I am not in a hurry tonight. At the moment I was just wondering about the black shadow. I heard you shout "messenger of Mordor". What was it? What could it do at Isengard?'

'It was a Black Rider on wings, a Nazgûl,' said Gandalf. 'It could have taken you away to the Dark Tower.'

'But it was not coming for me, was it?' faltered Pippin. 'I mean, it didn't know that I had . . .'

'Of course not,' said Gandalf. 'It is two hundred leagues or more in straight flight from Barad-dûr to Orthanc, and even a Nazgûl would take a few hours to fly between them. But Saruman certainly looked in the Stone since the orc-raid, and more of his secret thought, I do not doubt, has been read than he intended. A messenger has been sent to find out what he is doing. And after what has happened tonight another will come, I think, and swiftly. So Saruman will come to the last pinch of the vice that he has put his hand in. He has no captive to send. He has no Stone to see with, and cannot answer the summons. Sauron will only believe that he is withholding the captive and refusing to use the Stone. It will not help Saruman to tell the truth to the messenger. For Isengard may be ruined, yet he is still safe in Orthanc. So whether he will or no, he will appear a rebel. Yet he rejected us, so as to avoid that very thing! What he will do in such a plight, I cannot guess. He has power still, I think, while in Orthanc, to resist the Nine Riders. He may try to do so. He may try to trap the Nazgûl, or at least to slay the thing on which it now rides the air. In that case let Rohan look to its horses!

'But I cannot tell how it will fall out, well or ill for us. It may be that the counsels of the Enemy will be confused, or hindered by his wrath with Saruman. It may be that he will learn that I was there and stood upon the stairs of Orthanc – with hobbits at my tail. Or that an heir of Elendil lives and stood beside me. If Wormtongue was not deceived by the armour of Rohan, he would remember Aragorn and the title that he claimed. That is what I fear. And so we fly – not from danger but into greater danger. Every stride of Shadowfax bears you nearer to the Land of Shadow, Peregrin Took.'

Pippin made no answer, but clutched his cloak, as if a sudden chill had struck him. Grey land passed under them.

'See now!' said Gandalf. 'The Westfold dales are opening before us. Here we come back to the eastward road. The dark shadow yonder is the mouth of the Deeping-coomb. That way lies Aglarond and the Glittering Caves. Do not ask me about them. Ask Gimli, if you meet again, and for the first time you may get an answer longer than you wish. You will not see the caves yourself, not on this journey. Soon they will be far behind.'

'I thought you were going to stop at Helm's Deep!' said Pippin. 'Where are you going then?'

'To Minas Tirith, before the seas of war surround it.'

'Oh! And how far is that?'

'Leagues upon leagues,' answered Gandalf. 'Thrice as far as the dwellings of King Théoden, and they are more than a hundred miles east from here, as the messengers of Mordor fly. Shadowfax must run a longer road. Which will prove the swifter?

'We shall ride now till daybreak, and that is some hours away. Then even Shadowfax must rest, in some hollow of the hills: at Edoras, I hope. Sleep, if you can! You may see the first glimmer of dawn upon the golden roof of the house of Eorl. And in two days thence you shall see the purple shadow of Mount Mindolluin and the walls of the tower of Denethor white in the morning.

'Away now, Shadowfax! Run, greatheart, run as you have never run before! Now we are come to the lands where you were foaled, and every stone you know. Run now! Hope is in speed!'

Shadowfax tossed his head and cried aloud, as if a trumpet had summoned him to battle. Then he sprang forward. Fire flew from his feet; night rushed over him.

As he fell slowly into sleep, Pippin had a strange feeling: he and Gandalf were still as stone, seated upon the statue of a running horse, while the world rolled away beneath his feet with a great noise of wind.